MIMESIS INTERNATIONAL

KERSTIN BERGMAN

SWEDISH CRIME FICTION

The Making of Nordic Noir

MIMESIS
INTERNATIONAL

CONTENTS

For Daniel Elvin
– for a million reasons

INTRODUCTION

Despite a long and fascinating Swedish crime fiction tradition, it was not until Stieg Larsson's (1952–2004) *Millennium* trilogy (2005–07) that Swedish crime fiction truly became a worldwide phenomenon. While it is common to read about the success of Scandinavian crime fiction, of Nordic Noir, and of *le polar polaire*, the majority of the authors and books included in these more regional concepts actually originate from Sweden; indeed, the German term *Schwedenkrimi* is often used to designate crime fiction from all the Nordic countries. Additionally, the gathering of crime novels from Sweden, Denmark, Finland, Iceland and Norway under one common term tends to overlook the differences between the national traditions, instead stressing a homogeneity that is only partly there.[1] As Swedish crime fiction has turned into an international success story with authors such as Stieg Larsson, Henning Mankell (b. 1948), Liza Marklund (b. 1962), and Camilla Läckberg (b. 1974), among others, and with a growing number of Swedish crime stories reaching international audiences through film and television adaptations, there is now a significant demand all over the world – among readers and scholars alike – for knowledge about Swedish crime fiction. This book aims to provide a thorough survey of contemporary Swedish crime fiction, an account easily accessible to avid crime fiction readers, while simultaneously being useful to an academic audience of scholars, teachers, and students. It offers a comprehensive, research-based overview of contemporary Swedish crime fiction for an international audience.

The main focus of *Swedish Crime Fiction* is on the novels, authors, and trends from the most recent decades; these, however, will also be studied and explained in the context of Swedish crime fic-

---

1   The similarities and differences between the national crime fiction traditions are explored and explained in chapter 9.

tion history and tradition. In the nine chapters presented, the reader is first introduced to the history of Swedish crime fiction, spanning from the nineteenth century to the present day, followed by a chapter on the police procedural, the crime fiction sub-genre that has been predominant in Sweden since the late 1960s. Subsequent chapters are devoted to the portrayal of the Other in Swedish crime fiction, discussion of the numerous women authors entering the genre in the late 1990s and 2000s, examining the diverse use of the capital city of Stockholm as a setting, and exploring the neo-romantic tendencies, as represented by numerous recent novels set in the Swedish countryside. Additionally, the international success story represented by Stieg Larsson and the Europeanization of the genre taking place in recent years will be addressed. The final chapter turns to Sweden's Nordic neighbours and introduces the crime fiction traditions of Denmark, Finland, Iceland, and Norway.

Lund, Sweden, April 2013

Kerstin Bergman

I

A HISTORY OF SWEDISH CRIME FICTION:
FROM PRINS PIERRE TO STIEG LARSSON

A survey ranging from the first Swedish crime novel of 1893 to the present day; from the adventure crime stories of the early nineteenth century, through the Golden Age of the Whodunit after the Second World War, through the popularization of the police procedural in the 1960s and 1970s, and to the women writers and the new trends of the 2000s. The focus is on genre developments, important authors and popular themes.[1]

While the western crime fiction tradition is generally said to begin with Edgar Allan Poe's *The Murders in the Rue Morgue* (1841), Prins Pierre's (pen name for Fredrik Lindholm, 1861–1938) *Stockholms-detektiven* (1893, The Stockholm detective), appearing over half a century later, is often regarded as the first Swedish crime novel.[2] *Stockholms-detektiven* is the first Swedish novel where a coher-

---

1   This is a revised and updated version of my Swedish text 'Den svenska deckarhistorien'[The Swedish crime fiction history], in *Kriminallitteratur: Utveckling, genrer, perspektiv* [Crime fiction: Developments, genres, perspectives], by Kerstin Bergman and Sara Kärrholm (Lund: Studentlitteratur, 2011), pp. 33–51. Some of the observations concerning the last decades of Swedish crime fiction have previously appeared in Kerstin Bergman, 'Beyond Stieg Larsson: Contemporary Trends and Traditions in Swedish Crime Fiction', *Forum for World Literature Studies*, 2 (2012), 291–306.

2   However, Sweden – as well as Denmark and Norway – all have stories similar to Poe's (depicting the investigation of crimes while mixing gothic elements with rationalist logic) that predate the American author's. In Sweden's case, this is exemplified by Carl Jonas Love Almqvist's (1793–1866) short story 'Skällnora Qvarn' (1838, Skällnora mill) with its murderous intrigue; in Denmark by Steen Steensen Blicher's (1782–1848) novella *Præsten i Vejlbye* (1829; 'The Pastor of Vejlbye' 1996); and in Norway by Maurits Hansen's (1794–1892) novel *Mordet på maskinbygger Roolfsen:*

ent story about a crime and the investigation of that crime is at the centre of events. Prins Pierre based his novel on an authentic crime, where a factory in Eskilstuna, a small town west of Stockholm, had burned down under mysterious circumstances. Around the events of this fire, the author constructs a fictional story featuring Stockholm police detective Fridolf Hammar, who travels to Eskilstuna in order to investigate what happened. Hammar bears few similarities with those almost super-human detectives such as Poe's Auguste Dupin or Sir Arthur Conan Doyle's Sherlock Holmes. Instead, Hammar and his investigation are depicted relatively realistically. He is a Swedish policeman from the 1890s, using the methods and tools available to the police at the time: he conducts surveillance, examines the crime scene, interviews witnesses, and gathers and interprets evidence. *Stockholms-detektiven* also contains many ironic comments about the romantic super-detectives of European crime fiction from the nineteenth century. A similarly critical attitude is found in Sture Stig's (pen name for Frans Oscar Wågman, 1849–1913) two collections of short stories; *Sherlock Holmes i ny belysning* (1908, Sherlock Holmes in a new light), and *Nya Sherlock Holmes-historier* (1910, New Sherlock Holmes stories). Both can be regarded as parodies of the original Sherlock Holmes stories.

Crime fiction became consolidated as a genre in Sweden in the early decades of the twentieth century, and it is common to talk about a first generation of crime writers who were active up until the 1930s. Like Prins Pierre, most of these authors used foreign-sounding, preferably Anglo-American, pen-names, in order to be associated with the international genre and take advantage of its growing popularity.[3] Furthermore, the questionable status of the crime genre

---

Criminalanecdot fra Kongsberg (1839, The murder of engineer Roolfsen: Crime anecdote from Kongsberg). Although these stories are part of the Nordic crime fiction traditions' pre-history, none of them can be said to really initiate a vivid tradition, but should rather be regarded as precursors of what comes later – much like Poe's early stories in fact.

3   Bo Lundin, *The Swedish Crime Story*, trans. by Anna Lena Ringarp, Ralph A. Wilson, and Bo Lundin (Bromma: Jury, 1981), p. 15. Although pen names were mostly common among the early Swedish crime writers, it is a practice sometimes used even today, by for example Arne Dahl (pen name for Jan Arnald, b. 1963), Lars Kepler (pen name for Alexander Ahndoril, b. 1967, and Alexandra Coelho Ahndoril, b. 1966) and Erik Axl Sund (pen name for Jerker Eriksson, b. 1974, and Håkan Axlander-Sundquist, b. 1965). In the first two cases, the pen names were initially invented to hide

in Sweden at the time might have caused many authors to be wary
of losing their anonymity. Most of this first generation of authors
tended to mix the rational logic of writers such as Poe and Conan
Doyle with features found in classic adventure stories.[4] Their stories
were thus much less realistic than those found in later examples of
the genre, and showed an attempt by the authors to tap into the adventure genre, which had been popular in Sweden in the nineteenth
century.[5] Many of the authors also used elements from the whodunit. Furthermore, this first generation generally let their villains be of
foreign pedigree, commonly originating from the Mediterranean or
from some fictional South American republic.[6] This was an expression of the idea that evil was represented by individuals who did not
belong in the fundamentally good (mostly Swedish) society where
the novels were set. The villain then, once discovered, could easily
be removed, and peace and order could be restored.

Some of the most well-known authors from this first generation
are Robinson Wilkins (pen name for Harald Johnsson, 1886–1936),
SA Duse (1873–1933), Jul Regis (pen name for Julius Pettersson,
1889–1925), and Frank Heller (pen name for Gunnar Serner, 1886–
1947). All these writers took Sherlock Holmes as the model for their
heroes, who experience action-filled adventures while fighting
against foreign villains. Other authors who were mainly active in the
1930s, and who are sometimes considered as belonging to this generation – despite writing slightly more realistic novels – are Sture
Appelberg (1885–1947), Yngve Hedvall (1887–1946), August Jansson (1865–1942) and Torsten Sandberg (1900–1946).

---

the true identity of the authors who were already established writers of
mainstream fiction before entering the crime genre. Dahl actually succeeded to keep his identity secret until after his third novel was published, while
Kepler disclosed theirs around the time their first crime novel was published
– before that, however, the speculations about who was hiding behind the
pen name had resulted in plenty of extra publicity for the book. In the case
of Erik Axl Sund the use of a pen name (internationally and in Sweden starting from their fourth novel) was just a matter of convenience, the author duo
combining their names into something shorter and easier to remember.

4   Ibid., p. 15
5   On the popularity of the adventure story in the nineteenth century, see An-
    ders Öhman, *Äventyrets tid: Den sociala äventyrsromanen i Sverige
    1841–1859* [Time of adventure: The Swedish social-adventure novel
    1841–1859] (Umeå: Universitetet i Umeå 1990), p. 222 and passim.
6   Lundin, p. 15.

The Second Generation

When most of the authors associated with the first generation of Swedish crime writers eventually started to become outdated and less productive, a new and modern period in Swedish crime fiction began in the 1940s with the advent of the author Stieg Trenter (1914–1967). Swedish crime fiction expert Bo Lundin claims that 'there is hardly any modern Swedish crime writer who has not, in one way or another, been influenced by – or reacted to – his [Trenter's] style and the tradition he developed'.[7] By contrast, an author who ends up in-between the two generations is Kjerstin Göransson-Ljungman (1901–1971). Her debut novel, *Tjugosju sekundmeter, snö* (1939, 27 meters per second, snow), was a straightforward whodunit, where a group of people on a ski trip end up isolated in a remote mountain cabin after a snow storm, and one of them is murdered. Göransson-Ljungman was very much influenced by Agatha Christie and Dorothy L. Sayers, and it is primarily her qualities as a writer of whodunits – as displayed in a further seven novels up until 1960 – that qualify her as a forerunner to the more modern Swedish crime writers.

More common, however, is to regard Stieg Trenter as the first writer of the modern generation, beginning in 1943 with *Ingen kan hejda döden* (No one can hinder death). Trenter is also known for his excellent portrayals of Stockholm, and his descriptions of the Swedish capital are famous far beyond the circles of crime fiction readers.[8] The main detective in most of Trenter's novels is a Stockholm photographer, Harry Friberg. Friberg is introduced in *Farlig fåfänga* (1944, Dangerous vanity), and he functions as the first person narrator in many of the novels. Friberg has a friend in the Stockholm police, namely Inspector Vesper Johnson, and is often dragged into the cases being investigated by Johnson. Although Trenter's novels can primarily be regarded as whodunits, they also contain many elements from the American hard-boiled genre, for example, by employing dangerous *femmes fatales*, urban settings, and plenty of action. Some of Trenter's most well-known novels are *I dag röd...* (1945, Today

---

7   Ibid., p. 20.
8   Kerstin Bergman, 'From National Authority to Urban Underbelly: Negotiations of Power in Stockholm Crime Fiction', in *Crime Fiction in the City: Capital Crimes*, ed. by Lucy Andrew and Catherine Phelps (Cardiff: University of Wales Press, 2013), pp. 65–84 (p. 66-67). Also cf. chapter 5.

red), *Träff i helfigur* (1948, Full body hit), *Aldrig Näcken* (1953, Never Näcken) and *Narr på nocken* (1956, Jester on the ridge).[9] Stieg Trenter continued to write his popular Stockholm mysteries until the end of the 1960s, and after his death, Ulla Trenter (1936–), his wife, who had been very much involved in the writing of the earlier novels, continued to write about Friberg and Johnson.[10]

One of the most striking differences between the novels of the first generation of Swedish crime writers and those written by Trenter's generation is that the latter are generally much more realistic. The second generation tends to portray ordinary people, rather than superhuman master detectives and sensational international villains, and their stories bear a stronger resemblance to everyday Swedish life. How 'ordinary' the economically independent Friberg with his exclusive eating habits, or the extremely vain Inspector Johnson, in Trenter's novel really are is a matter for discussion, but compared with the heroes of Duse's and Regis' novels, Trenter's protagonists still seem relatively realistic. Despite their comparative realism, however, these so-called 'Golden Age' whodunits from the mid-twentieth century are nowhere near as realistic as Swedish crime fiction will become later on, beginning with Maj Sjöwall (b. 1935) and Per Wahlöö's (1926–1975) police procedurals in the mid-1960s.[11] At the time when Trenter and his contemporaries had their breakthrough, crime fiction was still regarded primarily as an entertainment genre, a genre that could not afford the risk of being so realistic as to become boring.

Even if Trenter is the first representative of his generation, he was soon followed by other Golden Age authors – writers who came to

---

9   Näcken is an evil water spirit of Swedish and Norwegian mythology, who lures his victims to drown in creeks and streams by playing the violin.

10   Ulla Trenter describes their cooperation in 'Hur var det att skriva deckare tillsammans med Stieg Trenter?' [What it was like to write crime novels with Stieg Trenter] in *En bok om Stieg Trenter* [A book about Stieg Trenter], ed. by Bertil R Widerberg (Bromma: Jury, 1982), pp. 58–63.

11   While the Golden Age for the whodunit genre internationally came in the 1920s and 1930s, it arrives later in Sweden, where the Golden Age normally refers to the period 1945–1965, with a strong focus on the 1950s. Sara Kärrholm outlines the Golden Age of Swedish crime fiction in *Konsten att lägga pussel: Deckaren och besvärjandet av ondskan i folkhemmet* [The art of doing a jig-saw puzzle: The detective novel and the conjuring up of evil in the Swedish Welfare State] (Stockholm/Stehag: Symposion, 2005), p. 41.

dominate the Swedish crime fiction scene for the next three decades: Maria Lang (pen name for Dagmar Lange, 1914–1991), H-K Rönblom (1901–1965), and Vic Suneson (pen name for Sune Lundquist, 1911–1975) – and who are regarded as the portal figures of modern Swedish crime fiction.[12] Lang was the first Swedish woman crime writer to reach a substantial audience. From her debut, *Mördaren ljuger inte ensam* (1949, The murderer does not lie alone), her novels constantly featured in the Swedish bestseller lists far into the 1970s. In particular, it was her combination of crime and romance that proved to be such a success. Lang was the first of the Swedish crime writers to let love and sexuality play an important part in her novels. Already in *Mördaren ljuger inte ensam*, Lang lets the motive for murder be the jealousy of a lesbian woman, and in subsequent stories, several of the main characters experience love. It is common in Lang's novels for passion to be the cause of the crime, or for the motive to be rooted either in family conflicts, or in incest or some other kind of sexual trauma. Lang's detective characters are Puck Ekstedt, who eventually marries Bure, a young woman equipped with a large amount of curiosity, and Inspector Christer Wijk (Wick in the English translations).[13] Lang and Trenter thus share the combination of the amateur investigator and the police officer in detective roles, but Lang's detectives do not work in tandem in all her novels as they typically do in Trenter's. Lang's mysteries always take place in an upper middle class setting, and mostly in the small fictitious town of Skoga (based on Nora in the Swedish region of Bergslagen). Lang wrote over forty novels up until 1990, and some of the most well-known are *En skugga blott* (1952, A shadow, only), *Tragedi på en lantkyrkogård* (1954, Tragedy in a countryside cemetery), *Se döden på dig väntar* (1955; *Death Awaits Thee, 1967*), and *Kung Liljekonvalje av dungen* (1957; *A Wreath for the Bride*, 1966). Lang writes in the spirit of Christie and Sayers, and she is often described as 'the Swedish queen of whodunits'.

A third Golden Age writer is H-K Rönblom. Today his name is not as well-known in Sweden as Trenter's and Lang's, but he is still often regarded as the most skilful of the three. Lundin describes him as a 'master of style and, more importantly from a crime- writing point

---

12   Cf. Johan Wopenka, 'Länge leve Lang!' [Long live Lang!], *Jury*, 18.2 (1989), 12–15 (p. 13).
13   The latter according to Lundin, p. 24.

of view, an artful weaver of elaborate plots, his speciality being original murders: he has killed with a pot [taken] off the stove and the dust from a horse'.[14] Rönblom's first novel, entitled *Död bland de döda* (Dead among the dead), was not published until 1954, and it introduced teacher and historian Paul Kennet, who was to become the detective-hero throughout Rönblom's whodunit series. Rönblom shares Lang's preference for the small town setting, but under a seemingly idyllic surface evil lurks in the shape of egocentrism, greed, peer pressure, and xenophobia. In Rönblom's novels, there are clear ambitions to portray contemporary society, and occasionally social critique is also evident. Some of the most well-known novels featuring Paul Kennet are *Höstvind och djupa vatten* (1955, Autumn wind and deep waters), *Tala om rep* (1958, Speaking of rope) och *Senatorn kommer tillbaka* (1959, The return of the Senator).

Another writer who made an important contribution to Swedish crime fiction history, but whose name is also somewhat forgotten today, is Vic Suneson. Like Trenter and Lang, Suneson started writing crime novels in the 1940s. His primary contribution to the development of Swedish crime fiction is that he was one of the first writers to use the police procedural genre, and he is commonly regarded the father of the Swedish police novel. It should be noted that Suneson, making his debut in 1948 with *Mord kring Maud* (Murder around Maud), is actually among the earliest of writers adopting the police procudural genre in an international context. The genesis of the genre is commonly associated with American novels like Lawrence Treat's *V as in Victim* (1945) or Hillary Waugh's *Last Seen Wearing ...* (1952; *È scomparsa una ragazza* 1954), and English examples such as Maurice Procter's *The Chief Inspector's Statement* (1951) and JJ Marrick's *Gideon's Day* (1955).

Most of the action in Suneson's novels takes place in Stockholm, and his main characters are inspectors, namely Kjell Myrman and OP Nilsson. Unlike Trenter, Suneson is not especially focused on providing a detailed depiction of the Swedish capital. He tends to portray the Stockholm of the lower social classes that was alien to Trenter: a Stockholm of the less fortunate, as when, for example, in *Uddagänget* (1974, The odd gang), he lets his story focus on a group of alcoholics. In terms of genre, Suneson's novels are a mix of the whodunit and the modern procedural of later decades. They contain

---

14   Ibid., p. 32.

a minimum of social critique and, apart from in his last few novels
from the early 1970s, Suneson's police officers have no private life
to speak of and are always confident about their profession and their
abilities, in fact two characteristic features of later Swedish police
procedurals.[15] Some of Suneson's novels, for example *I dimma dold*
(1951, In fog, hidden) also contain traces of the American hard-
boiled crime novel. In addition to introducing the police genre,
Suneson is also one of the first in Swedish crime fiction to use psychological perspectives in the depiction of characters and their developments, for example in *Fäll inga tårar* (1953, Shed no tears).
Suneson continued to write until the mid-1970s, and some of his
most well-known novels are *Är jag mördaren?* (1953, Am I the murderer?), *Så spelar döden* (1956, That's how death plays) and *Fallet
44:an* (1963, The 44 case).

In addition to these four most successful writers of the Golden
Age, one more author from this period ought to be mentioned, name-
ly Anders Jonason (1925–93). His detectives are journalists: first
Dick Mattsson who appears in, for example, *Mord med mera* (1953,
Murder, et cetera), and later Björn Andersson in *Fallet Grete* (1963,
The Grete case). Jonason is also somewhat forgotten today, but he is
interesting as he was the first Swedish crime writer to attempt to
write novels that could be placed primarily in the hard-boiled genre,
inspired by Dashiell Hammett and Raymond Chandler. Even if both
Trenter and Suneson used elements from the hard-boiled genre, they
never actually attempted to write in that genre the way Jonason did.
Despite Jonason's ambitions, his Stockholm novels were never to
turn out as hard-boiled as those produced by his American forerunners. Other important crime writers of this second generation were
Folke Mellvig (1913–1994), Helena Poloni (pen name for Ingegerd
Stadener, 1903–1968), and Arne Stigson (pen name for Arne Malm-
berg, 1918–2009).

The Golden Age period is also when crime novels written primarily for children achieved a breakthrough in Sweden. Towards the
end of the 1940s, several novels appeared that would set the bench-
mark by which later writers of children's literature were to be mea-
sured. Most important were Astrid Lindgren's (1907–2002) series
about the child detective Kalle Blomkvist, starting with *Mästerde-
tektiven Blomkvist* (1946; *Bill Bergson, Master Detective*, 1952;

---

15   Ibid., p. 27.

Kalle Blomkvist, il 'grande' detective, 2009), and Åke Holmberg's (1907–1991) Sherlock Holmes parodies featuring the eccentric detective Ture Sventon, the first being *Ture Sventon, privatdetektiv* (1948; *Tam Sventon, Private Detective* 1965). Furthermore, in the 1950s, radio also became a popular medium for the dissemination of crime fiction. In particular, the stories by Folke Mellvig (1913–94) featuring the amateur detectives John and Kajsa Hillman became immensely successful on Swedish radio.[16]

The Breakthrough of the Police Procedural

In 1960s Sweden, there was a general political 'awakening'– an increased awareness of social injustices and a politicization of the intellectual and public spheres, similar to what was happening in many other parts of Europe at the time –, and this was something that also affected Swedish crime fiction. This was the time when the hard-boiled genre and the inherent social critique within that genre became very influential and eventually evolved into a pattern that was to dominate the Swedish crime fiction scene for decades to come in the shape of the police procedural, characterized by social and political critique. During the 1960s there were also new and more varied social and geographical settings entering the genre. Furthermore, international crime syndicates, common in early Swedish crime fiction but hardly used after the 1930s, once again became credible actors in the Swedish literary (and social) context.

The most important authors to make their debuts during the 1960s were the writing duo Maj Sjöwall (b. 1935) and Per Wahlöö (1926–75), who will be only briefly introduced here and more extensively discussed in chapter 2. From 1965 to 1975, Sjöwall and Wahlöö published a series of police novels called *Roman om ett brott* (*The Story of a Crime* 1967–76; *Martin Beck indaga a Stoccolma* 1973–2011), starting with *Roseanna* (1965; *Roseanna* 1967; *Roseanna* 1973/2005), and ending with *Terroristerna* (1975; *The Terrorists* 1976; *Terroristi*

---

16 Cf. Kerstin Bergman, 'Deckare och andra medier' [Crime fiction and other media (than literature)], in *Kriminallitteratur: Utveckling, genrer, perspektiv* [Crime fiction: Developments, genres, perspectives], by Kerstin Bergman and Sara Kärrholm (Lund: Studentlitteratur, 2011), pp. 219–62 (pp. 232–33).

2011). These novels are similar in style to Ed McBain's police novels, and they portray a group of police officers with Martin Beck as the central character.[17] Sjöwall and Wahlöö's police officers always work as a team, but they all still have their individual talents, as well as their private lives. Psychological aspects are important, not least in the depiction of criminals and their motives, something that generates realistic and dynamic characters. The novels are set primarily in a modern, urban Stockholm, and the narrative is often built up around coincidences in a way otherwise characteristic of the whodunit, that is, for example by characters who happen to be in a certain place at a certain time and thus see or experience something that later turns out to be crucial for the solving of the case.

What made Sjöwall and Wahlöö's novels stand out from previous crime fiction – and what made it so influential in the following decades – was, above all, the conscious inclusion of a critical perspective on Swedish society. The authors themselves even claimed that this was the main reason why they chose to write in such a popular fiction genre: they wanted to reach as large an audience as possible with their social and political critique.[18] Internationally, they are also well known for having politicized the police procedural genre.[19] To what extent this is really true, and to what extent Sjöwall and Wahlöö succeeded in their ambition, is a matter for discussion. Nevertheless, there is no doubt that they did reach a wide readership and in doing so they managed to broaden the Swedish crime fiction audience, which had up until then mainly consisted of readers from the upper middle class. Bo Lundin even suggests that it is not until Sjöwall and Wahlöö that Swedish crime fiction finally takes the 'full step from entertainment toward serious fiction about people and crime'.[20] In recent years it has been suggested that the social critique that appears in the Sjöwall and Wahlöö series might not be as dominating or as sharp as had previously been claimed. Whether that is true or not, there is no question that their series has created a broad interest in crime fiction, and that, in the wake of Sjöwall and Wahlöö, the

---

17   Sjöwall and Wahlöö also translated McBain's police novels into Swedish.
18   Maj Sjöwall and Per Wahlöö, 'Kriminalromanens förnyelse' [The renewal of the crime novel], *Jury*, 1 (1972), 9–11 (passim).
19   Cf. George N Dove, *The Police Procedural* (Bowling Green: Bowling Green University Popular Press, 1982), pp. 19, 23, 217–24, 240, 242.
20   Lundin, p. 33.

police novel characterized by social critique continued to be the dominating crime fiction genre in Sweden for many decades. Also the Decalogue format, the ten novel series, has been immensely popular following *Roman om ett brott*, and is the one used by numerous Swedish crime writers.

Some of the Swedish authors who (in the 1970s, 1980s, and 1990s) wrote long series of police novels following the tradition of Sjöwall and Wahlöö, are: Leif GW Persson (b. 1945), who writes about officers Lars Martin Johansson and Bo Jarnebring in Stockholm; K Arne Blom (b. 1946), who in his extensive production includes a police series set in Lund; Olov Svedelid (1932–2008) with the Stockholm series about Roland Hassel; Hans Holmér (1930–2002) with the series about Arvid 'Loppan' Roos in Stockholm; Håkan Nesser (b. 1950) who set his series about Van Veeteren in a fictional city in north-west continental Europe called Maardam; Henning Mankell (b. 1948) with the Kurt Wallander series set in Ystad; and Åke Edwardson with Erik Winter in Gothenburg. Mankell is often regarded as the most important Swedish crime writer after Sjöwall and Wahlöö. As this list of authors hints at, with the exception of Maj Sjöwall, the Swedish police novel was for a very long period a genre primarily attracting male authors. In the 2000s, however, this situation has changed and now there are also many women writers of lengthy series of police novels, a matter which will be discussed later on.

Although the police novel, with both its implied and obvious social critique, has been the dominating crime fiction genre in Sweden since the 1970s, there are of course also authors who ignore all political dimensions and follow the whodunit tradition of Trenter and Lang. One such example is Jan Mårtenson (b. 1933), who has written a long, and very popular series with Stockholm antique dealer Johan Homan as the protagonist and amateur detective. Mårtenson's novels are filled with cultural references to art, design, and literature, as well as to food, wine, and cooking – many of his novels even contain recipes. It is obvious that he writes for a well-educated readership that are more likely to have bourgeois values, and his murders tend to take place at various parties or other social gatherings much frequented by artists and people from the cultural elite.[21]

---

21   So far only one of Mårtenson's Homan novels is available in English translation, *Häxhammaren* (1976, *Death Calls on the Witches* 1979).

Some Swedish authors also manage to mix the police and the whodunit genres in a way that is similar to what, for example, PD James and Ruth Rendell tend to do. In this way the actual mystery is focused on, as it is in traditional whodunits, whilst less attention is paid to the private lives of the police officers themselves – so often a common focus in today's police novels. These Swedish novels are, however, rarely set in the urban space of a big city like traditional police procedurals, but instead located in more rural settings or smaller towns. Good examples of such genre mixtures are Bertil Mårtensson's (b. 1945) novels set in Malmö, and Gösta Unefäldt's novels set in Strömstad, on the Swedish west coast.

A genre often seen to be balancing crime fiction and mainstream literature is the psychological thriller, where the most significant element is what happens inside and between the characters, and where the mystery often almost provides an excuse to depict the psychological development that unfolds. For example, Kerstin Ekman's (b. 1933) *Händelser vid vatten* (1993; *Blackwater* 1996; *Il buio scese sull'acqua* 1998) – which was awarded both best Nordic novel (Nordic Council's Literature Prize) and best Swedish novel (The August Prize), in addition to best Swedish crime novel (The Golden Crowbar, awarded by The Swedish Academy of Detection) – can be firmly placed in the psychological thriller genre, as can many of her early crime novels from the late 1950s and early 1960s, for example *Den brinnande ugnen* (1962, The burning oven), and *Dödsklockan* (1963, The death bell; *La caccia* 2002). Since the 1990s, the psychological thriller has become more widespread in Swedish crime fiction and, as a sub-genre, it has often been adopted by women authors. Worth mentioning here is, for example, Inger Frimansson (b. 1944), with novels such as *Godnatt min älskade* (1998; *Good Night, My Darling* 2007), and *Skuggan i vattnet* (2005; *The Shadow in the Water* 2008).

The political thriller, or spy thriller, is a sub-genre that has had its ups and downs in Sweden, perhaps suffering somewhat from the overarching popularity of the political police novel among both readers and writers. In the early 1960s, before he began collaborating with Maj Sjöwall, Per Wahlöö himself wrote a few thrillers. The most successful writer in the genre, however, is Jan Guillou (b. 1944) with his series of ten novels about the Swedish special agent Carl Hamilton, alias Coq Rouge; published 1986–1995. The first novel was *Coq Rouge* (1986; *The Scarlet Cockerel* 2005), and since the hero is portrayed as strong and quite glamorous, and the novels are filled with action, the whole series can almost be regarded as a Swedish version of Ian Fleming's James Bond novels. Carl Hamilton moves in international circles and settings – something that up until more recent years has been a relatively rare occurrence in Swedish crime fiction. Guillou also provides some very detailed descriptions of weapons, technology, and politics, though the character depiction as such is somewhat less elaborated. His novels also contain elements of strong (leftist) social and political critique, something that is a common feature of the spy thriller (though not of the Fleming archetype), and Guillou can thus still be said to follow in the footsteps of Sjöwall and Wahlöö, even though he is not using the police genre. During the first decade of the 2000s, Guillou returned to the thriller genre and to Hamilton in *Madame Terror* (2007, Madame Terror; *Madame terror* 2008), and *Men inte om det gäller din dotter* (2008, But not if it concerns your daughter).

Apart from Jan Guillou, the 1980s is generally considered to be a pretty weak decade in terms of Swedish crime fiction. By contrast, starting with the crime fiction debuts of Mankell with *Mördare utan ansikte* (1991; *Faceless Killers* 1997; *Assassino senza volto* 2001), and Nesser with *Det grovmaskiga nätet* (1993; *The Mind's Eye* 2008; *La rete a maglie larghe* 2001), however, the 1990s and early 2000s are often regarded as a new Golden Age of Swedish crime fiction.

Trends of the Early 2000s

The most obvious trend in Swedish crime fiction in the first decade of the 2000s is the large number of women writers represented. In the 1990s, a large proportion of Swedish crime fiction sales consisted of novels written by Norwegian and British women writers. These women writers were immensely popular and, particularly when compared with successful Norwegian women crime writers such as Karin Fossum (b. 1954) and Anne Holt (b. 1958), it seemed strange that Sweden had so few women writers in the genre. This began to change in the late 1990s, and most noticeably with Liza Marklund (b. 1962) being awarded the Poloni Prize in 1998 for her first crime novel, *Sprängaren* (1998; *The Bomber* 2000/2011; *Delitto a Stoccolma* 2001), which is often regarded as initiating a new wave of women writers in Swedish crime fiction, a wave that has continued right up till the present decade.[22] Although Marklund's novels invariably feature a woman journalist detective, and thus could perhaps be categorized as journalist procedurals, many of the new women writers not only use the police genre but also contribute to bringing more women characters into that genre, not least women police protagonists like Helene Tursten's (b. 1954) Irene Huss, Anna Jansson's (b. 1958) Maria Wern, and Åsa Nilsonne's (b. 1949) Monica Pedersen.

The women writers also contribute to the crime genre by their realistic portrayals of modern Swedish women's everyday life, such elements that had previously been almost absent from Swedish crime fiction. When Marklund's *Sprängaren* was first reviewed, a strong focus was placed on how her protagonist, the tabloid journalist Annika Bengtzon, was struggling to balance work and family life, a component that has since become almost a staple theme in the Swedish crime fiction of women writers in the early 2000s. Nevertheless, most of the recent crime novels by women writers appear far from being feminist, and it is evident that traditional female stereotypes are often used in the creation of women characters in these novels. Still, Swedish women writers have largely been very successful and popular with Swedish crime fiction readers. Additionally, many of them have received extensive attention by the media, in particular Marklund and Camilla Läckberg (b. 1974).[23] Some additional women writers who have been very successful in the wake of Marklund are Karin Alvtegen (b. 1965), Åsa Larsson (b. 1966), Mari Jungstedt (b. 1962), Aino Trosell (b. 1949), and Karin Wahlberg (b. 1959). Among those who have emerged in the last half decade but promise well for the future are Carin Gerhardsen (b. 1962), sister duo Camilla Grebe (b. 1968) and Åsa Träff (b. 1970), Ingrid Hedström (b. 1949), Kristina Ohlsson (b. 1979), and Katarina Wennstam (b. 1973).

In addition to the large number of women authors, a number of other clear trends and tendencies can also be identified in Swedish crime

---

22   More about the Poloni Prize and the women writers of the early 2000s is found in chapter 4.

23   Cf. Sara Kärrholm, 'Swedish Queens of Crime: The Art of Self-Promotion and the notion of Feminine Agency – Liza Marklund and Camilla Läckberg', in *Scandinavian Crime Fiction*, ed. by Andrew Nestingen and Paula Arvas (Cardiff: University of Wales Press, 2011), pp. 131–47 (passim).

fiction of the early 2000s. Although the bestselling crime writer on the national market is probably Camilla Läckberg, the most successful Swedish crime writer during this time in a wider context is unquestionably Stieg Larsson (1954–2004).[24] His posthumously published *Millennium* trilogy – *Män som hatar kvinnor* (2005; *The Girl with the Dragon Tattoo* 2008; *Uomini che odiano le donne* 2008), *Flickan som lekte med elden* (2006; *The Girl Who Played with Fire* 2009; *La ragazza che giocava con il fuoco* 2008), and *Luftslottet som sprängdes* (2007; *The Girl Who Kicked the Hornets' Nest* 2009; *La regina dei castelli di carta* 2009) – achieved an unprecedented national and international success and turned into a hyper-bestseller phenomenon, in the crime fiction genre comparable only to Dan Brown's *The Da Vinci Code* (2003; *Il codice da Vinci* 2003).[25] Following Larsson (and Mankell), Swedish crime writers have now successfully conquered the international crime fiction market. Larsson's triumphs in the English-speaking markets have been particularly important in paving the way for other authors, since trying to enter these markets had for a very long time constituted the biggest struggle for the Swedish writers (significantly, not only for Swedish writers, but for non-Anglophone writers in general).[26]

Following Larsson, the trilogy format itself has also had a revival among certain Swedish authors, and today it is a popular alternative to the Decalogue popularized by Sjöwall and Wahlöö. When, for example, Mons Kallentoft (b. 1968) made his debut as a crime writer in 2007, and Carin Gerhardsen and Viveca Sten (b. 1959) made theirs in 2008, their novels were all claimed to be the first instalment in forthcoming trilogies. These particular authors did not, however, manage to restrict themselves to the trilogy format, and all have continued their series beyond the third novels, so in their case the concept of a trilogy was obviously a marketing gimmick designed to ride on the success of Larsson's novels. In general, the cur-

---

24   Cf. Karl Berglund, *Deckarboomen under lupp: Statistiska perspektiv på svensk kriminallitteratur 1977–2010* [The crime fiction boom under the magnifying glass: Statistical perspectives on Swedish crime fiction 1977–2010] (Uppsala: Avd. för litteratursociologi Uppsala universitet, 2012), pp. 79–84.

25   Cf. Kerstin Bergman, 'Genre-Hybridization – A Key to Hyper-Bestsellers? The Use and Function of Different Fiction Genres in *The Da Vinci Code* and *The Millennium Trilogy*,' *Academic Quarter*, 7 (2013).

26   This will be discussed more at length in chapter 7.

rent tendency among Swedish crime writers appears to be to pro-
duce a longer series, with no previously set limitation to the number
of novels.

Stieg Larsson has also become immensely influential in Swedish
crime fiction in terms of genre. The *Millennium* trilogy broke with
the concept that to be truly successful, a Swedish crime writer had
to write police procedurals, preferably in the manner of Sjöwall and
Wahlöö. Larsson's novels are complex and playful genre hybrids,
incorporating elements from many different crime fiction sub-
genres as well as from other (primarily popular) fiction genres, and
following their success, diversity in genres has increased substantially among Swedish crime writers.[27] Some writers have even attempted to create their own genres, thus aiming to brand themselves
more clearly. Denise Rudberg (b. 1971), a former chick-lit author,
now writes what she calls 'Elegant Crime', where she mixes elements of crime and romance in novels set in present-day Swedish
high society. Jens Lapidus (b. 1974) has written a very successful
series of novels set in the criminal underbelly of Stockholm, and his
concept, which is heavily influenced by James Ellroy, he calls
'Stockholm Noir'. By contrast, Christoffer Carlsson writes so-called
'Countryside Noir', in thrillers set in the Swedish countryside. With
the exception of Lapidus' novels, most of these attempts have not,
however, brought anything really new to the genre.[28]

Yet there are still many successful mixes of genres on offer today.
There was already in the early 2000s, even before Larsson, an increase in the use of romance and sex in Swedish crime fiction, a tendency that has been turned into a staple theme in current Swedish
crime fiction. Also, elements from the action genre have, primarily
after Larsson, found their way into Swedish crime novels. Among
the more successful attempts are the novels by Lars Kepler (pen
name for Alexander Ahndoril, b. 1967, and Alexandra Coelho Ahndoril, b. 1966). Especially in their *Paganini-kontraktet* (2010; *The*

---

27   Concerning Larsson's play with different genres, see Kerstin Bergman,
      'From "The Case of the Pressed Flowers" to the Serial Killer's Torture
      Chamber: The Use and Function of Crime Fiction Sub-genres in Stieg
      Larsson's *The Girl with the Dragon Tattoo*', in *Critical Insights: Crime
      and Detective Fiction*, ed. by Rebecca Martin (Ipswich, MA: Salem Press,
      2013), pp. 38–53 (passim).
28   Lapidus' novels are further discussed in chapter 5.

Nightmare 2012; *L'Esecutore* 2010) there are several scenes which would be fit for inclusion in any Hollywood action movie.

A genre that has also been making inroads into Swedish crime fiction recently is the horror genre. This is a trend that also coincides with the international success of Swedish vampire films, for example *Frostbiten* (2006; *Frostbite*, directed by Anders Banke) and *Låt den rätte komma in* (2008; *Let the Right One In*, directed by Tomas Alfredson, based on John Ajvide Lindqvist's (b. 1968) novel of the same title from 2004; *Lasciami entrare* 2006). The most successful crime writer in terms of integrating elements from the horror genre into his novels is Johan Theorin (b. 1963), who portrays mysterious events taking place on the island of Öland, off Sweden's south-east coast. In *Skumtimmen* (2007; *Echoes from the Dead* 2008; *L'ora delle tenebre* 2008), *Nattfåk* (2008; *The Darkest Room* 2009; *La stanza più buia* 2011), and *Blodläge* (2009; *The Quarry* 2011), he employs dark gothic moods and strange events bordering on the supernatural, thus bringing the horror genre to mind. Theorin never lets his stories actually cross over into the sphere of the supernatural, but there are other Swedish crime writers who have. For instance, Amanda Hellberg (b. 1973) lets her protagonist in *Döden på en blek häst* (2011, Death on a pale horse) experience supernatural events while attempting to solve the murder of her mother, and Åsa Larsson and Mons Kallentoft both let their dead speak in long monologues while being stuck in limbo, from where they can observe what is going on in the world of the living. These monologues could be interpreted simply as narrative strategies, although sometimes the dead can almost be sensed by the living, particularly in Kallentoft's series about Linköping police officer Malin Fors.

Although there has been much development of the genre in the past decade, there are still authors who continue writing in the tradition of Sjöwall and Wahlöö.[29] Some successful examples are Åke Edwardsson, and, not least, Arne Dahl (pen name for Jan Arnald b. 1963), who is currently on his second series of police novels, once again filled with social and political critique. In his first series, from *Ont blod* (1998; *Bad blood* 2013; *La linea del male* 2006) to *Elva* (2008, Eleven), Dahl portrays a Stockholm police team called *A-gruppen*, the A-

---

29   When it comes to political critique, Stieg Larsson can be said to belong to this category, despite having left the police genre behind. But there are a number of authors who still combine critique with the police genre.

group (in English translations the Intercrime Group, The A-unit and the A-team are alternately used), who investigate crimes with international connections, while his new series is centered around an experimental, operative unit within Europol and thus is set primarily outside Sweden, integrating both European and global perspectives. Dahl pays equal attention to all members of his investigative teams and, despite including many literary themes, allusions, and intertextual connections, he essentially depicts a realistic present and pays great attention to current social and political issues.[30]

Even though there are thus still authors who follow the pattern created by Sjöwall and Wahlöö, an increasing number of writers of police novels simultaneously step away from the critical and leftist perspectives, and instead promote conservative bourgeoisie values. Following Mankell's example, many of the new writers choose to set their novels in small towns in the Swedish countryside, but unlike Mankell, they tend to avoid discussing current events and societal problems, and instead they focus on more personal motives for murder. Representative of these are the police series of, for example, Camilla Läckberg and Mari Jungstedt.[31]

Other general current trends in Swedish crime fiction are to use children to an increasing extent as murder victims, and to trace the motive for murder back to traumatic events in the murderer's childhood – similar tendencies are also seen in current crime fiction from many parts of the world. To some extent the increased presence of child victims can be regarded a "natural" step in the often stressed movement of crime fiction towards rawer, scarier and more violent scenarios. Additionally, Sweden – like many other countries – has in recent decades seen a gradual development where more relevance has been ascribed to children's perspectives and opinions, and where it has become more important to pay attention to children in general and to their needs in all aspects of society. Today violence against children is one of the greatest fears and taboos of present society,

---

30   Dahl is more extensively discussed in chapter 8.
31   This neo-romantic tendency, inspired by the British police procedural tradition, will be further discussed in chapter 6. Additionally, I have previously discussed this tendency in Swedish crime fiction in Kerstin Bergman, 'The Well-Adjusted Cops of the New Millennium: Neo-Romantic Tendencies in the Swedish Police Procedural', in *Scandinavian Crime Fiction*, ed. by Andrew Nestingen and Paula Arvas, (Cardiff: University of Wales Press), pp. 34–45.

and it is far from surprising that this is reflected also in crime fiction. There is also a tendency to demonize Eastern Europe, and as far as organized crime is involved, the villains of Swedish crime fiction are often brought in from some former Soviet republic or from former Yugoslavia. Human-trafficking and prostitution are common themes, the Internet enables everything from paedophilia to the abuse of women, and gang-related violence has now reached Swedish cities also in the form of crime fiction. When it comes to detectives, the police detective format is still very widely used, but it has become increasingly common to focus more on one protagonist than on a team as such, and also to combine one particular police hero with an amateur detective. The latter can be exemplified by how Läckberg lets her police protagonist cooperate with his wife, who is an author, or how Jungstedt places a police officer and a journalist in the leading roles. Additionally, since the 1990s, a common theme has been to examine Sweden's relationship with Germany during World War II, and numerous crime novels trace the motive for murder back to occurrences involving Swedish Nazis during the war. This is a feature evident in all variations of the crime genre, from Dahl's *Europa Blues* (2001, Europe blues; *Europa blues* 2012) to Läckberg's *Tyskungen* (2007; *The Hidden Child* 2011; *Il bambino segreto* 2013).[32]

Despite the success of Sjöwall and Wahlöö, collaborative crime writing projects have until very recently been quite rare in Swedish crime fiction, but now they seem increasingly common. In addition to Kepler, and Grebe and Träff (the previously mentioned sister duo), some of the most well-known writer 'double acts' today are Anders Roslund (b. 1961) and Börge Hällström (b. 1957); Dan Buthler (b. 1965) and Dag Öhrlund (b. 1957); Cilla Börjlind (b. 1961) and Rolf Börjlind (b. 1943); Michael Hjorth (b. 1963) and Hans Rosenfeldt (b. 1964); and Jerker Eriksson (b. 1974) and Håkan Axlander-Sundquist (b. 1965), sometimes using the pen name Erik Axl Sund. It is worth mentioning that Hjorth and Rosenfeldt also

---

32 The theme of Sweden's relationship with Germany during the war, as portrayed in Swedish crime novels during the first decade of the 2000s, is surveyed in Kerstin Bergman, 'The Good, The Bad, and the Collaborators: Swedish World War II Guilt Redefined in 21st Century Crime Fiction', in *Imagining Mass Dictatorships: The Individual and the Masses in Literature and Cinema*, ed. by Michael Schoenhals and Karin Sarsenov (New York: Palgrave, 2013), pp. 183–210 (passim).

present one of the least sympathetic heroes in Swedish crime fiction, Sebastian Bergman: a narcissistic psychologist with a sex-addiction and an attitude problem.

In the past decade, the crime novel for children and young adults has also undergone a revival in Sweden. Authors such as Mårten Sandén (b. 1962), Laura Trenter (b. 1961), Veronika von Schenck (b. 1971), amongst others, have revitalized the genre with modern and intricate mystery stories.

II

THE POLICE PROCEDURAL – SWEDEN'S FAVOURITE KIND OF CRIME: *MAJ SJÖWALL AND PER WAHLÖÖ*

This chapter is focused on 'the founders of the modern Swedish crime novel', Maj Sjöwall and Per Wahlöö, and how, with their groundbreaking Martin Beck series, The Story of a Crime *(1965–1975) they succeeded in making the police procedural, characterized by social critique, the paradigm for the genre in Sweden in the decades to follow.*

The 1960s was in many ways a turbulent time worldwide, politically, economically and socially, and it impacted life in Sweden, too. In retrospect, it is clear that Swedish culture in general went through considerable politicization during this decade, and this is often described in terms of a 'political awakening', an increased political and social awareness, affecting not least the intelligentsia and the cultural elite. Swedish literature became more political, realist ideals pertained, and much of the fiction produced in the 1960s contained documentary elements. This transformation of Swedish culture and literature did not go unmarked in the crime fiction genre either. In 1965, journalists Maj Sjöwall (b. 1935) and Per Wahlöö (1926–75) published their first co-written crime novel *Roseanna* (1965; *Roseanna* 1967; *Roseanna* 1973/2005). It is a novel that already at that time intended to be the first in a series of ten, all with the clear purpose of exposing the shortcomings of the Swedish welfare state.[1] In retrospect, Sjöwall has explained:

> We realized that people read crime, and through the stories we could show the reader that under the official image of welfare-state Sweden there was another layer of poverty, criminality and brutality. We want-

---

1 Cf. Maj Sjöwall and Per Wahlöö, 'Kriminalromanens förnyelse' [The renewal of the crime novel], *Jury*, 1 (1972), 9–11 (passim).

ed to show where Sweden was heading: towards a capitalistic, cold and
inhuman society, where the rich got richer, the poor got poorer.[2]

And as George N. Dove was to stress: Sweden 'itself may be considered a major character, as both victim and villain' in Sjöwall and
Wahlöö's novels.[3]

The Swedish welfare state was firmly established after the end of
the Second World War, based on the premise all citizens were regarded as equals, 'every person deserves a good, decent life, and
[...] everybody should be cared for' in the best way possible.[4] This
had resulted in the state providing education, healthcare, infrastructure, et cetera, accessible for all and financed by tax money. What
Sjöwall and Wahlöö saw in the mid-1960s was that the foundation
of the Swedish welfare system had started to crack. Behind the fine
words about welfare and equality, economic concerns were being
prioritized over the welfare state ideals, and Sweden was turning
into an increasingly capitalistic, harsh and brutal society where the
class divides were growing. Sjöwall and Wahlöö wanted to call attention to the ongoing deterioration by pointing to the inequalities
stemming from these developments, and how the writer duo went
about this task will be further explored afterwards. With their critique, Sjöwall and Wahlöö set a strong trend for generations of
crime writers to come, and Katarina Gregersdotter has pointed to
how many Swedish crime novels still today express nostalgia for the
well-functioning Swedish welfare state of the past.[5]

Sjöwall and Wahlöö's series was called *Roman om ett brott*
(1965–75; *The Story of a Crime* 1967–76; *Martin Beck indaga a*

---

2   Quoted from interview in Louise Frances, 'Queen of Crime', *The Observ-
     er*, 22 November 2009, http://www.guardian.co.uk/books/2009/nov/22/
     crime-thriller-maj-sjowall-sweden [accessed 30 August 2013].
3   George N Dove, *The Police Procedural* (Bowling Green OH: Bowling
     Green University Popular Press, 1982), p. 218.
4   The quote is from Katarina Gregersdotter, 'The Body, Hopelessness, and
     Nostalgia: Representations of Rape and the Welfare State in Swedish
     Crime Fiction', in *Rape in Stieg Larsson's Millennium Trilogy and Be-
     yond: Contemporary Scandinavian and Anglophone Crime Fiction*, ed.
     by Berit Åström, Katarina Gregersdotter and Tanya Horeck (Basingstoke:
     Palgrave Macmillan, 2013), pp. 81–96 (p. 82).
5   Gregersdotter also identifies Stieg Larsson (1954–2004) as a notable ex-
     ception, as there is no nostalgia found in his *Millennium Trilogy* (2005–
     2007) (Gregersdotter, p. 82).

Stoccolma 1973–2011), and continued after *Roseanna* according to plan with *Mannen som gick upp i rök* (1966; *The Man Who Went Up in Smoke* 1969; *L'uomo che andò in fumo* 1974/2009), *Mannen på balkongen* (1967; *The Man on the Balcony* 1968; *L'uomo al balcone* 1973/2006), *Den skrattande polisen* (1968; *The Laughing Policeman* 1970; *Il poliziotto che ride* 1973/2007), *Brandbilen som försvann* (1969; *The Fire Engine That Disappeared* 1970; *L'autopompa fantasma* 1974/2008), *Polis, polis, potatismos!* (1970; *Murder at the Savoy* 1971; *Omicidio al Savoy* 1974/2008), *Den vedervärdige mannen från Säffle* (1971; *The Abominable Man* 1972; *L'uomo sul tetto* 2010), *Det slutna rummet* (1972; *The Locked Room* 1973; *La camera chiusa* 2010), *Polismördaren* (1974; *Cop Killer* 1975; *Un assassino di troppo* 1976/2005), up until the last instalment, *Terroristerna* (1975; *The Terrorists* 1976; *Terroristi* 2011), was published shortly before the death of Per Wahlöö.[6]

Sjöwall and Wahlöö's series belongs to the police procedural genre, and as such clearly broke with the Golden Age whodunits that had previously dominated the Swedish crime fiction scene. In 1960s Sweden, the police were seen as more realistic in the detective role than the amateur detectives who had been so popular in the earlier fiction. Although Swedish attempts were made in the police procedural genre even before the advent of Sjöwall and Wahlöö, these were largely lacking in any socio-political agenda. Social critique was previously often excluded altogether, since crime fiction used to be chiefly regarded as an entertainment genre, and including politics in such a genre was considered to pose a risk for the entertainment value. Gösta Pettersson's (1905–79?) *Vådaskottet* (1938, The accidental discharge) is often mentioned as the first Swedish police novel, but it is not until the 1950s, when Vic Suneson (pen name for Sune Lundquist 1911–75) established himself as 'the father of the Swedish police novel', that the genre became an integral part of the Swedish crime fiction tradition.[7] In his early novels, Suneson combined the classical adventure story with elements from the British whodunit and the American hard-boiled detective novel.[8] Inspired by the earlier crime fiction tra-

---

6   *Den skrattande polisen* won a 'Best Novel' Edgar Award in 1971, and was turned into a Hollywood film in 1973, starring Walter Matthau.
7   Suneson wrote thirty police novels between 1948 and 1975.
8   Kerstin Bergman, 'Polisromanen' [The police novel], in *Kriminallitteratur: Utveckling, genrer, perspektiv* [Crime fiction: Developments, genres,

dition, rather than by the international police procedural of his time, it was not until the 1970s that Suneson introduced any kind of social critique in his novels.[9] By that stage, however, Sjöwall and Wahlöö had already made politics and social critique an integral part of the Swedish police novel.

The use of the police genre allowed Sjöwall and Wahlöö to create a number of heroes with different skills, characteristics, and opinions – something that enabled the portrayal of a more diverse and realistic cross section of Swedish society. Although the authors certainly paid attention to all members of the police team, it was still its central character, Martin Beck, who was the main protagonist and whose perspective the authors followed closely in order to reveal what was wrong with the Swedish welfare state. Beck starts out as a melancholic man in a sad marriage with two teenage children, but during the series he gets divorced and eventually enters a new and more passionate relationship. Despite this, Beck remains a quite gloomy and disillusioned character filled with self-doubt, and his team is portrayed as the last outpost of sanity and honesty in a police organization described by Sjöwall and Wahlöö as both mad and corrupt. The Beck character was to become almost emblematic for Swedish crime fiction heroes during the decades to follow, as Beck acted as a model for many famous crime fiction detectives, most notably Henning Mankell's (b. 1948) Kurt Wallander, but also for example Håkan Nesser's (b. 1958) Van Veeteren, and Mari Jungstedt's (b. 1962) Anders Knutas. Swedish crime fiction expert Bo Lundin coined the term 'The Ulcer School' to describe novels portraying such an archetypal figure in Swedish crime fiction, and he has gone on to claim that in addition to a strong focus on setting, the personal predicaments of 'The Ulcer School' constitute the most distinguishing feature of Swedish crime fiction.[10]

---

perspectives], Kerstin Bergman and Sara Kärrholm (Lund: Studentlitteratur, 2011), pp. 105–21 (p. 115).

9   Most explicitly in *Uddagänget* (1974, The odd gang), cf. Kerstin Bergman, 'Deckare och samhällskritik' [Crime fiction and social criticism], in *Kriminallitteratur: Utveckling, genrer, perspektiv* [Crime fiction: Developments, genres, perspectives], Kerstin Bergman and Sara Kärrholm (Lund: Studentlitteratur, 2011), pp. 165–83 (p. 175).

10   Bo Lundin, *The Swedish Crime Story*, trans. by Anna Lena Ringarp, Ralph A Wilson, and Bo Lundin (Bromma: Jury, 1981), pp. 8–10.

Scrutinizing the Swedish Welfare State:
From Roseanna *to* The Terrorists

During the late 1960s and early 1970s, the Swedish economy was flourishing, and both social and material welfare increased. It was during this time that the international image of Sweden as a successful welfare society was established. The progress continued until the oil crisis struck in 1973, and there was an economic downturn. The period when Sjöwall and Wahlöö wrote their novels was also characterized by a general increase in political awareness in Sweden, and their novels were an expression of this.

Even on the first page of *Roseanna* (1965), Sjöwall and Wahlöö comment on the Swedish state by describing its heavy bureaucracy.[11] They may do it rather tongue-in-cheek, but it still has a critical edge, and the message reads loud and clear: the processes of Swedish administration are ridiculously complicated and time-consuming, resulting in nothing being done without serious delays. The initial passage forebodes the prolonged murder investigation to come: the six months it will take before the killer is finally caught. Nevertheless, after this initial critical passage, what is found in *Roseanna* in terms of social and political critique is rather implicit. Something is not quite right about the Swedish welfare state and increasing criminality is presented as a sign of this. Martin Beck, who in his professional capacity represents the police and, in his private capacity, the average Swede, also illustrates Sweden's problems: he displays the symptoms of a society that is 'unwell'. Throughout *Roseanna*, Beck is constantly prone to sickness: he endures stomach problems and headaches, he suffers from a lack of sleep, and he seems to be continuously infected by colds and bouts of flu. In fact, the maladies form a major part of the descriptions of Beck and his daily work routine.

Beck is depicted as average looking; he dresses plainly, is in a dull marriage, and yet his career seems to move on effortlessly,

---

11   Maj Sjöwall and Per Wahlöö, *Roseanna*, transl. by Lois Roth (London: Fourth Estate, 2011), p. 1. Some of my observations concerning Sjöwall and Wahlöö have previously been presented in Kerstin Bergman, 'From National Authority to Urban Underbelly: Negotiations of Power in Stockholm Crime Fiction', in *Crime Fiction in the City: Capital Crimes*, ed. by Lucy Andrew and Catherine Phelps (Cardiff: University of Wales Press, 2013), pp. 65–84 (pp. 67–71).

whether he wants it to or not. He is simply part of the machinery of the well-functioning, but slow-moving and not very exciting, welfare state. This is all summarized in the description of how Beck collects his gun as he prepares to travel to the small town of Motala by Lake Vättern, where the murder victim has been found: 'The pistol was an ordinary 7.6 millimetre Walther, licensed in Sweden. It was useless in most situations and he was a pretty poor shot anyway'.[12] The description of Beck's gun and his relationship with it simultaneously contributes to the establishment of an image of the Swedish police as being somewhat old-fashioned, with outdated equipment, not really fit for purpose, and with officers that do not really have the skills required for the job. To underscore this further, the police are soon stuck without clues and have to resort to asking the public for help at a press conference. The attitude of the media representatives present is said to 'show compassion and understanding. The photographers yawned. The room was already thick with cigarette smoke'.[13] The journalists do not expect the police to have come up with anything, and they do not really blame them for failing either. Police representatives and journalists are all enclosed in the same grey cigarette smoke, a haze that seems to permeate everything in the novel, symbolizing that it is impossible for anyone to have a clear view of what actually happened.[14] This can also be interpreted as an image of the ever present bureaucracy of the welfare state.

In addition to this relatively vague criticism of Swedish bureaucracy and police, Sweden is also indirectly compared to the US. The murder victim, Roseanna McGraw, happens to be American and is presented as a modern girl, different from most Swedish women appearing in the novel. Furthermore, it is an American police detective, with whom Beck corresponds and cooperates, who actually identifies the murder victim. The American's work is swift and thorough and proves essential to the Swedish investigation. In *Roseanna*, the US is thus presented in a favourable light, expressing the idea commonly held in Sweden in the 1950s and early 1960s about

---

12   Sjöwall and Wahlöö, *Roseanna*, p. 11.
13   Ibid., p. 29.
14   Andrew Nestingen discusses the similar use of fog in Henning Mankell's novels, and Mankell can be regarded as further developing Sjöwall and Wahlöö's concept (Andrew Nestingen, *Crime and Fantasy in Scandinavia: Fiction, Film, and Social Change* (Seattle/London: University of Washington Press, 2008), pp. 237–38.)

the US being a country of progress and modernity. But this is before the Swedish protests against the war in Vietnam started to grow in intensity, and thus before a much more negative and critical image of the US developed in the late 1960s and in the 1970s.

According to Beck, the ideal policeman is of the opinion that: 'A murderer is just a regular human being, only more unfortunate and maladjusted'.[15] With no signs of sarcasm or irony, this stance towards criminals is well in line with Swedish society of the Social Democracy era and with the fundamental idea that everyone should be treated the same. Beck's characterization of the general criminal is also repeated in the description of the novel's specific murderer and his background, as he has a quite ordinary but sad existence. Nevertheless, after their first meeting, Beck is certain the man is the murderer, even though nothing incriminating has surfaced during their conversation.[16] When Beck and his team finally interrupt the murderer in the process of killing a police woman decoy, the murderer is described as a frightened animal.[17] Soon thereafter, when he is caught, Beck hears a 'short, wild scream of pain', and the murderer lies there with 'tears streaming down his cheeks'.[18] The crying is then repeated during the interrogation that follows.[19] The crying scenes and the fact that the murderer is described in terms that explicitly and implicitly evoke the image of a trapped animal, actually serve to make him appear more human. He comes across as a tragic and miserable man who has 'just lost it', and for whom the reader is encouraged to feel slightly sorry – despite the atrocious murder and the attempted murder he has committed. The murderer can thus be regarded as another symptom of a society where things are not right, and in the light of Beck's ideas about murderers, quoted above, perhaps anyone could have ended up in the murderer's shoes.

Despite the general ideas about equality presented in the novel, the women in *Roseanna* are excluded from all attempts at equality – only men are concerned when equality is considered. Nevertheless, gender politics is an important ingredient in the novel, as the male murderer's motive is to punish women who are independent, who

---

15   Sjöwall and Wahlöö, *Roseanna*, p. 44.
16   Ibid., p. 186.
17   Ibid., p. 231.
18   Ibid., p. 232.
19   Ibid., p. 243.

enjoy their sexuality, and take sexual initiatives. The 1960s was a time when Swedish women were becoming more independent, and when sexuality began to be recognized as a normal and healthy activity of relevance to both men and women. By making the murderer overwhelmingly conservative in such matters and the murder victim a modern and open-minded woman, Sjöwall and Wahlöö criticize the idea that only men are entitled to their sexuality. Still, the general attitude toward gender equality in the novel is not especially progressive. Women police officers are mentioned, but they are described in slightly patronizing terms, and have no part in the investigative team.[20] The only woman police officer given a somewhat active role in *Roseanna* is used as a decoy in order to trap the murderer, and Beck's team selects her for the job based mainly on her looks and marital status (she is single). She is described in a rather stereotypical way, and among other things she is portrayed as quite emotional. The other most significant woman character in the novel is Beck's wife, who plays a very minor role. She is a homemaker, a fact that is somewhat criticized by Beck's irritation over her reluctance to take a job, even though their children are no longer infants. Simultaneously, Beck never questions that she takes care of him – she cooks, cleans, cares for the children, does the laundry, and even packs his suitcase when he goes on his work-related trips. This presents an image of the Swedish welfare society in the mid-1960s in which traditional gender roles were still fundamental. In contrast to these Swedish women is Roseanna, the American murder victim, who is presented as an open-minded and sexually-liberated woman, someone who would have been considered very modern in the mid-1960s. Roseanna, however, does not represent the women of the Swedish Welfare state, and, in general, the image of women in *Roseanna* must be considered quite conservative.

In 1975, ten years after the publication of *Roseanna*, it is time for the tenth and last instalment in Sjöwall and Wahlöö's police procedural series. Much has happened in the series and in Swedish soci-

---

20   1957 was the first year women were accepted into the Swedish Police Academy, and the first women officers joined the force in 1958. Today about every fourth Swedish police officer is a woman. Cf. 'Polisen i Sverige växer fram' [The emergence of the police in Sweden], in *Polismuseet* [The police museum] http://www.polismuseet.se/Samlingar/Polishistoria/Framvaxten-av-ett-polisvasende/ [accessed 13 February 2013].

ety in the meantime and *Terroristerna* is quite different from *Roseanna*. The final novel is over four hundred pages long, more than twice the length of the first novel, it covers three separate cases instead of just one, and not only is the tone of the writing much more humorous than at the beginning of the series, but the social and political critique has become much more explicit. David Geherin concludes that as the series progresses, Sjöwall and Wahlöö's 'criticisms about Sweden's political state become more and more overt', and he also claims that 'their tone turns increasingly bitter and sarcastic'.[21] However, I would not describe the tone in *Terroristerna* as bitter, but rather as humorous and disillusioned, even somewhat bantering, and ironic. Even on the cover of the first edition of *Terroristerna*, it is stated that the novel constitutes 'a critical analysis of today's Swedish society'.[22]

In *Terroristerna*, Beck has been promoted to chief of the National Homicide Squad, but he still has mostly the same people in his team as in *Roseanna*. Moreover, he is divorced and has started dating a new woman, Rhea Nielsen, an outspoken socialist with a strong voice of reason and, in this novel, an exponent of social and political critique. Beck himself is no outspoken socialist, but when Rhea puts a poster of Mao over their bed, he leaves it there, musing over what his colleagues would say if they knew about it.[23]

In addition to the title case of the novel – in which international terrorists are attempting to kill a controversial US senator visiting Sweden – Beck's team investigates the death of a Swedish porn film producer and the case of a naïve young woman who first 'accidentally' robs a bank and then eventually goes on to kill the Swedish Prime Minister.[24] The latter cases are clearly distinguished by a capitalism-against-socialism rhetoric, where capitalism is considered to

---

21   David Geherin, *Scene of the Crime: The Importance of Place in Crime and Mystery Fiction* (Jefferson, NC: McFarland, 2008), p. 166.

22   Maj Sjöwall and Per Wahlöö, *Terroristerna* (Stockholm: Norstedts, 1975), my translation.

23   Maj Sjöwall and Per Wahlöö, *The Terrorists*, transl. by Joan Tate (New York: Vintage Books, 2010), p. 49.

24   Although the Prime Minister is never named in the novel, the descriptions (cf. Sjöwall and Wahlöö, *Terrorists*, p. 188–89) make it clear that he is Olof Palme, Prime Minister of Sweden 1969–1976 and 1982–1986. By letting the Prime Minister be shot, Sjöwall and Wahlöö presage the actual murder of Palme in 1986.

be evil and socialism good. The terrorist story cannot clearly be categorized in these terms, as the members of the terrorist organization
in question have no political agenda, but rather attempt to perfect
their methods by trying them out on all kinds of targets. It is reasonable, however, to believe that since they lack a political agenda, they
will ultimately work to serve the highest bidders, i.e. capitalism.

The political stance taken by Sjöwall and Wahlöö in *Terroristerna*
is also clearly visible in how the different criminals are judged. The
police team, and Beck in particular, are very understanding and show
compassion for both the young woman – even after she shoots the
prime minister – and the gardener who killed the porn film producer
by crushing his skull with an iron rod. The woman evidently did not
understand how society worked and did not get the help she needed
from the authorities, whereas the gardener was clearly taking revenge after the porn film producer had ruined his young daughter's
life. Both these murderers are made to represent the ordinary Swede
from the lower classes, people who, for moral and ethical reasons,
challenge 'big bad capitalism', whilst being in a no-win-situation.
David Geherin concludes that the case of the woman who murders
the Prime Minister is an 'example of a crime being attributed to the
failures of the welfare state rather than to the individual'.[25] The woman is made to appear more human as she is trying to take care of her
baby in difficult circumstances, namely after the father, an American
Vietnam deserter, has been lured back to the US and is locked up in
prison, where he eventually kills himself. The gardener is similarly
given a more human face, as it is stressed that he is a single father
who raised his daughter on his own. Additionally, he is portrayed as
an intellectual soul who makes other peoples' gardens flourish and
reads poetry in his spare time.[26] In contrast, the murdered porn producer is presented as a dirty old man with a dubious reputation. The
reader is thus clearly encouraged to sympathize with the murderers
rather than with the victims, not least since Beck, the main object of
reader identification in *Terroristerna*, does so. Nevertheless, the
young woman and the gardener are both arrested for their crimes.
She is confined to a psychiatric ward where she soon commits sui-

---

25   Geherin, pp. 165–166.
26   Cf. Sjöwall/Wahlöö, *Terrorists*, pp. 108–09. To an attentive reader it is ac-
       tually the poetry preferences of the gardener that first point to him as the
       murderer.

cide, something Robert P. Winston and Nancy C. Mellerski regard as 'the logical conclusion of a series that includes numerous examples of crimes against their fellow Swedes by the nation's captains of industry'.[27] The reader is never actually told what the final sentence of the gardener is likely to be, but Beck assumes he will serve twelve years in prison. Rhea Nielsen, the voice of reason in the novel, is not happy about this potential sentence, but assumes the gardener might still consider his deed worth the punishment.[28]

When it comes to the terrorists, however, the situation is very different: the main terrorist, Reinhard Heydt, is portrayed as the primary villain of the novel. He is a South African mercenary who in the past worked for many different regimes. Heydt is contrasted with Gunvald Larsson, a member of the police team. They both happen to be tall, strong, intelligent, and violent when needed, but where Heydt lacks any moral guidelines, Larsson is very opinionated about what is right and wrong. Heydt functions as the evil arch-enemy of traditional detective fiction: the villain never bothered by scruples or conscience. The narrator shows no compassion for him and he is thus contrasted with the novel's two Swedish murderers, as well. While they are portrayed as victims of an evil, capitalist society, Heydt is never afforded any such sympathy, but is rather described as being evil by nature. Therefore, there is no chance of rehabilitation for him and, like so many villains of the thriller genre, he is eliminated at the end of the novel.[29] In *Terroristerna*, the terrorists themselves and their seemingly aimless organization represent the spectre of increased violence in western society, circumstances that are repeatedly referred to in the novel. The organization's lack of specific political affiliation makes their excessive violence particularly pointless.[30] The terrorists thus become representatives, or perhaps rather a symptom, of capitalism, violence, and all that is wrong with society.

---

27 Ibid., p. 232; Robert P Winston and Nancy C Mellerski, *The Public Eye: Ideology and the Police Procedural* (Houndsmills/London: Macmillan, 1992), p. 39.

28 Sjöwall and Wahlöö, *Terrorists*, p. 145.

29 Ibid., p. 277. Sjöwall and Wahlöö's novels are otherwise straight-forward police procedurals, but here the influences from the political thriller are obvious.

30 The work of the terrorist organization (ULAG) is described in ibid., pp. 94–96, and 124–26.

The police force is also the subject of criticism in the novel. With the exception of Beck and his team – an exception repeatedly stressed – the police are described as a group of violent and unintelligent brutes, incapable of doing their jobs properly. This is partly attributed to their deficient training, which has taught them nothing about psychology and ethics.[31] The police are further said generally to take advantage of their position by 'cheating or bribery and corruption'.[32] Particular police divisions, such as the immigration and customs police, are also pointed to specifically as being incompetent.[33] Additionally, the security police are the target of scorn in the novel, and it is said to be common knowledge that their only task was to 'register, persecute and in general make life a misery for people with left-wing views'.[34] A member of the security police even sells classified information to the terrorists.[35]

The police are further said to serve and protect only 'the regime and certain privileged social classes and groups'.[36] In consequence, the Swedish police are described as an organization that terrorizes 'socialists and people who couldn't make it in our class society'.[37] Additionally, it is noted that the police force is turning more and more into a 'paramilitary force with frightening technical resources' of unknown purposes.[38] It is thus described as an altogether inhuman, militarized, and unfair organization. While the police in *Roseanna* are primarily presented as overworked, somewhat old fash-

---

31   Sjöwall and Wahlöö, *Terroristerna*, pp. 241–242 (this has been excluded from the English translation).
32   Sjöwall and Wahlöö, *Terrorists*, p. 44.
33   Cf. ibid., p. 124.
34   Without naming it, the Swedish so called 'IB affair' is also described (ibid., p. 90). The IB affair was a big scandal, where in 1973 the existence of a secret faction within the Swedish security police was revealed to the public. This faction, IB, had initially had the purpose of mapping communists in Sweden, but had taken upon themselves to gather information on a much larger portion of Swedes. The journalists who made the revelation were imprisoned for espionage (cf. Wilhelm Agrell, 'IB-affären' [The IB affair], in *Nationalencyclopedin* [The national encyclopedia] http://www.ne.se/lang/ib-affären [accessed 3 April 2013]).
35   Sjöwall and Wahlöö, *Terroristerna*, p. 190–191, this information has been excluded from the English translation.
36   Ibid., p. 77, my translation. This passage has been excluded from the English translation.
37   Sjöwall and Wahlöö, *Terrorists*, p. 144.
38   Ibid., p. 153.

ioned, and inefficient, it is clear they have completely fallen from grace in *Terroristerna* in 1975. Geherin concludes that during the series, Sjöwall and Wahlöö depict 'a serious decline in the quality of the police as a result of the nationalization of the force in 1965'.[39] Apart from Beck's own team, the Swedish police is treated with contempt in *Terroristerna*, and had Sjöwall and Wahlöö written a second series of crime fiction in the years to follow, it seems very unlikely that their heroes would have been police officers. From the socialist perspective characterizing the novel, the Swedish police are described as the lackeys of the capitalist enemy, incapable of, and generally uninterested in improving in any way a society that is on such a self-destructive path.

In *Terroristerna*, Sweden is described as a terrible place to live, where 'even the weather seemed to be part of the conspiracy against the poor inhabitants'.[40] Not only is meaningless violence escalating in Swedish society, Stockholm is also described as filled with girls in their lower teens involved in prostitution and drugs, something that is said to make even the cold terrorist depressed.[41] The economy and greed are pointed to as the driving forces of Swedish politics.[42] The Swedish Social Democratic Party went through a popularity crisis in the late 1960s and early 1970s, with the strongest criticism coming from the radical left (to which Sjöwall and Wahlöö can be said to

---

39   Geherin, p. 163. The "nationalization" in 1965 meant a centralization of power and resources within the Swedish police. Additionally, the number of police districts was cut radically, by almost 80 percent, making each unit larger and increasing the central bureaucracy of the organization. Cf. 'Polisen i Sverige växer fram' [The emergence of the police in Sweden], in *Polismuseet* [The police museum] http://www.polismuseet.se/Samlingar/Polishistoria/Framvaxten-av-ett-polisvasende/ [accessed 13 February 2013].

40   Sjöwall and Wahlöö, *Terroristerna*, p. 57, my translation. This passage has been excluded from the English translation.

41   Sjöwall and Wahlöö, *Terrorists*, p. 128.

42   Sjöwall and Wahlöö, *Terroristerna*, p. 45, this part has been excluded from the English translation. David Geherin points out that while in most crime fiction the 'crime and depravation' of a city is portrayed as being caused by economic conditions, Sjöwall and Wahlöö's attributes the decay of Stockholm to political mismanagement (Geherin, p. 163–164). This claim is, however, somewhat misleading, as Sjöwall and Wahlöö – not least in *Terroristerna* and other novels late in the series – associate Swedish politics and politicians with capitalism and greed, features closely related to the Swedish economy.

have belonged). In the election of 1976, the right wing parties defeated Swedish Prime Minister Olof Palme and the Social Democratic Party, and between 1976 and 1980 Sweden had its first conservative government since the 1930s. In *Terroristerna*, the Swedish social democratic government is accused of being socialist by name only, and of lying to the people.[43] The ruling Social Democratic Party is also referred to as 'the big bogus party'.[44] It had eventually become 'neither socialist, nor democratic, if it had ever even been so, and its name constituted an increasingly frail screen casing a purely capitalist state power'.[45] The Swedish Parliament is said to be completely powerless, and controlled by people with money and personal power.[46] That the Swedish Government invited the American senator is criticized throughout the novel, and Swedish 'neutrality' politics is questioned.[47] Furthermore, the Swedish authorities are described as unreliable and inadequate. The woman who killed the Prime Minister says that the authorities cannot be trusted to help 'ordinary people who aren't famous or rich', and Beck does not try to argue with her as he believes that she 'was largely right'.[48] She further explains that she shot the prime minister as a leading representative of a mendacious society that does not care about people in need.[49]

There is also a general criticism of capitalism in *Terroristerna*, as for instance when the business methods of Swedish property-owners are described.[50] Property owners and construction companies in Sweden are described as multinational giants, habitually suing each other as badly constructed buildings are falling apart.[51] The dealings of the rich are also said to result in destruction of the Swedish countryside, where old farms, farmland, and the most beautiful natural landscapes – the ultimate symbols of traditional Sweden – are turned

---

43   Sjöwall and Wahlöö, *Terrorists*, p. 90, and Sjöwall and Wahlöö, *Terroristerna*, p. 218 (this part has been excluded from the English translation).
44   Ibid., p. 367, my translation. This part has been excluded from the English translation.
45   Ibid., p. 242, my translation. This passage has been excluded from the Engliah translation.
46   Sjöwall and Wahlöö, *Terrorists*, p. 122.
47   Ibid., p. 145, this discussion has been substantially shortened in the English translation.
48   Ibid., p. 213.
49   Ibid., p. 217.
50   Ibid., p. 118.
51   Ibid., p. 242.

into fancy summer houses, golf courses, highways, airports, and nuclear power plants. This is further stressed as it is seen through the eyes of the 'innocent' young woman, whose dream is to 'live a healthy and simple life, close to nature', but who cannot afford it.[52] Sweden as a capitalist society is also criticized in a humorous description of a Christmas shopping frenzy, and in doing so, Sjöwall and Wahlöö also throw punches at the Swedish book market and the state-owned Railway Company.[53]

By portraying the visiting US senator in a critical light, Sjöwall and Wahlöö also question the USA and its brand of politics. The senator in question is regarded as particularly despicable as he 'has tens of thousands of lives on his conscience. He was one of the most active forces behind the strategic bombing in North Vietnam. And he was right in there even during the Korean War. He supported MacArthur when he wanted to drop atomic bombs on China'.[54] Since 1965, US foreign policy and in particular the war in Vietnam, was the main cause of criticism of the US among Swedes. 1965 was the year in which the often fierce debates about the US involvement in Vietnam started in Sweden, and even by 1975 there were still a large number of active local protest groups (FNL groups, supporting the resistance movement in South Vietnam, *Front national de libération du Viêt-nam du Sud*) in Sweden.[55] This contributed to a much more negative image of the US in 1975 than in 1965 when *Roseanna* was published.

Another object of criticism in the novel is the media, and here Sjöwall and Wahlöö present ironic comments about media celebrity.[56] The media is also criticized for broadcasting very explicit footage from a South American terrorist attack. In particular, the US news media is implicated, specifically when an American commentator's voice is described as being filled with lust and excitement

---

52 Sjöwall and Wahlöö, *Terroristerna*, p. 176, my translation, these passages have been excluded from the English translation.

53 Sjöwall and Wahlöö, *Terrorists*, p. 269, the passage about the book market has been excluded from the English translation.

54 Ibid., p. 146.

55 Kim Salomonson, 'FNL-rörelsen' [The FNL movement], in *Nationalencyclopedin* [The national encyclopedia] http://www.ne.se/lang/fnl-r%C3%B6relsen [accessed 13 February 2013].

56 Sjöwall and Wahlöö, *Terrorists*, p. 41.

while describing the horrific images.[57] Additionally, the Swedish media is ridiculed through the description of press photographers grovelling in front of the politicians, as they literally roll about on the floor trying to take pictures of the visiting US senator and the Swedish Prime Minister.[58] The willingness of the media to promote the official political stance of the Swedish state is shown by descriptions of how the US senator is presented by Swedish radio and television. Everything from his pet dogs to his favorite sports is brought up, but there is no mention of him being in any way controversial. The reader is distanced from the content of the media coverage by the ironic comments made by the police protagonists listening to and watching the broadcasts.[59]

Not everything is getting worse, though. While women police officers were described as a questionable novelty in *Roseanna*, *Terroristerna* shows them as an integral part of the force. Åsa Torell, a woman officer on Beck's team, is consequently described as a well-established and highly competent officer, who also shows feminist tendencies.[60] Furthermore, it is her work that leads the investigative team to a possible motive for the murder of the porn producer and makes them take a closer look at the gardener.[61] Beck's health has also improved dramatically since *Roseanna*, and he no longer suffers from headaches and stomach problems. The only thing bothering him health-wise is that he sometimes gets depressed, and the reason for this is said to be that 'he was a relatively highly positioned civil servant in a society where nothing ever seemed to change for the better'.[62] Beck's health is thus still an indication of the state of society and, instead of affecting only his body, it is now getting to his mind in the shape of depressive tendencies. Society is thus still not well, and it even appears to be caught up in a negative spiral.

Terroristerna ends with Beck and his former colleague Kollberg reminiscing and recalling the case from *Roseanna*, ten years earlier. They return to the increasing violence, and as Kollberg tells

---

57   Ibid., p. 53.
58   Ibid., p. 189.
59   Ibid., p. 190.
60   Cf. ibid., pp. 102–03.
61   Ibid., pp. 106–07.
62   Sjöwall and Wahlöö, *Terroristerna*, pp. 243–244, my translation, the reason for Beck's bouts of depression is left out in the English translation.

Beck: 'Violence has rushed like an avalanche throughout the whole Western world over the last ten years. You can't stop or steer that avalanche on your own. It just increases. That is not your fault'.[63] The conversation resembles a talk they had in *Roseanna*, where Kollberg reassured Beck that he did not have to save the world all by himself. The conclusion of Sjöwall and Wahlöö's series is thus that no matter what Beck and his colleagues do, the welfare state is going downhill, and fast. There is no way of stopping this negative process. Sjöwall and Wahlöö criticize Sweden from a socialist perspective and expose a society where capitalism has conquered every authority, making these abandon the key ideas of the welfare system. The social and political critique in *Terroristerna* thus strike right at the heart of the Swedish welfare state; against those authorities expected to create a safety-net and provide welfare for all Swedish citizens through 'social engineering'. As a final statement, the novel ends with a crossword-puzzle game, similar to Scrabble, where Beck's former colleague Kollberg picks the letter X, 'X as in Marx'.[64]

The Swedish Police Novel Beyond Sjöwall and Wahlöö

When Sjöwall and Wahlöö completed their ten novel series, it took quite a while before Swedish crime fiction writing regained momentum. Although some authors, such as Olov Svedelid (1932–2008) continued with the tradition of police novels, partly inspired by Sjöwall and Wahlöö, realism in general was not in vogue in Swedish literature in the 1980s, and this tended to have a diminishing effect on the popularity of writing in the genre. Consequently, the 1980s is considered a particularly weak decade in Swedish crime fiction, with the exception of Jan Guillou (b. 1944), who wrote a series of political thrillers about the Swedish special Agent Carl Hamilton, alias Coq Rouge, a series filled with adventure and drama.[65]

---

63 Sjöwall and Wahlöö, *Terrorists*, p. 279.
64 Ibid., p. 280.
65 The most extensive study of Guillou's series to date is to be found in Lars Wendelius, *Rationalitet och kaos: Nedslag i svensk kriminalfiktion efter 1965* [Rationality and chaos: Case studies of Swedish crime fiction after 1965] (Hedemora: Gidlunds, 1999), pp. 107–68.

Guillou was inspired by Sjöwall and Wahlöö's political spirit, but employed a crime fiction genre that better suited the decade's preference for escapism.

In the 1990s and early 2000s, however, many Swedish crime writers took up the torch from Sjöwall and Wahlöö, and set about presenting social critique in police procedurals, often even using the ten instalment format. One of them, Henning Mankell, initiated his series about Kurt Wallander in the early 1990s, closely following the pattern set out by Sjöwall and Wahlöö. In Mankell's novels, however, it is the disintegration of the welfare state that is portrayed, rather than just its shortcomings. In 2009, in the last Wallander novel, Mankell even lets Wallander leave the police profession, and he is seen acting rather like a private investigator as he examines the last remnants of the welfare state.[66] Other authors who have followed a similar path are Håkan Nesser, Helene Tursten (b. 1954), Åke Edwardson (b. 1953), and Arne Dahl (pen name for Jan Arnald, b. 1963), just to mention a few. Nevertheless, in the first decade of the 2000s, the traditional Swedish police procedural characterized by social critique, also encountered competition from a rather different source. Many writers – Camilla Läckberg (b. 1974) and Mari Jungstedt among them – developed neo-romantic, apolitical police novels set in an almost timeless countryside characterized by a small-town bourgeoisie mentality. Even if some writers still follow the path of Sjöwall and Wahlöö and Mankell, it is clear that a majority of the Swedish crime writers today are leaving the political strand behind, while still pursuing the police procedural genre.[67] Despite this division of the genre in the 2000s, the police procedural is still to date *the* dominant crime fiction genre among Swedish authors, although this has begun to change as greater genre variation and hybrid forms have followed on from the success of Stieg Larsson's (1954–2004) *Millennium* trilogy (2005–2007).

---

66   Mankell will be further discussed in chapter 3.
67   Cf. Kerstin Bergman, 'The Well-Adjusted Cops of the New Millennium: Neo-Romantic Tendencies in the Swedish Police Procedural', in *Scandinavian Crime Fiction*, ed. by Andrew Nestingen and Paula Arvas (Cardiff: University of Wales Press, 2011), pp. 34–45 (passim). It is notable that many authors of neo-romantic police procedurals are women, although there are also male writers using this version of the genre. The neo-romantic tendency and the authors representing it will be further examined in chapter 6.

III

THE SWEDES AND 'THE OTHER':
HENNING MANKELL

A central theme throughout the history of Swedish crime fiction has been the problematic relationship to 'the Other'. This chapter will primarily address how Henning Mankell in his Kurt Wallander series and in his other crime novels deals with issues of immigration, multiculturalism, and the ethnic Other.[1]

In the late nineteenth and early twentieth centuries, it was common practice in Swedish crime fiction to bring in villains from the Mediterranean or from some made-up Latin American republic. However, from the 1930s until the early 1960s, the foreign villains and crime syndicates were no longer regarded as credible and almost disappeared from the genre.[2] Then, in the 1960s, international criminality started reappearing, even though home-grown criminals still dominated. In the 1990s and early 2000s, however, it has been increasingly common to let organized crime originate from the former Soviet republics or have ties to the republics of former Yugoslavia.[3] However, villains are not the only representatives of the Other

---

1   This article builds to a great extent on my previous articles on Henning Mankell: 'Paradoxes of Understanding the Other: Mankell Explores the "African Darkness"', *Scandinavian Studies* 82.3 (2010), 337–354; 'Initiating a European Turn in Swedish Crime Fiction: Negotiation of European and National Identities in Mankell's *The Troubled Man* (2009)', *Scandinavica* 51.1 (2012), 56–78; and 'The Good, the Bad and the Collaborators: Swedish World War II Guilt Redefined in Twenty-First Century Crime Fiction?', in *Imagining Mass Dictatorships: The Individual and the Masses in Literature and Cinema*, ed. Michael Schoenhals and Karin Sarsenov (New York: Palgrave, 2013), pp. 183-210.

2   Cf. Bo Lundin, *The Swedish Crime Story*, trans. by Anna Lena Ringarp, Ralph A Wilson, and Bo Lundin (Bromma: Jury, 1981), p. 15.

3   Cf. Bergman, 'European Turn', p. 58.

in crime fiction, and, furthermore, any discussions of the relationship to the Other have become increasingly more complex in Swedish crime fiction in recent decades.

Sweden is located in the far north of Europe and is a country with vast open spaces, large natural resources, and few inhabitants. While the northern part of the nation is home to the indigenous Sami people, among others, most of the (by now) nine and a half million Swedes live in the southern regions of the country. Sweden has not been actively involved in a war since 1809, when the last war with Russia ended. Throughout history, there has always been immigration to Sweden; for centuries people have moved there to take advantage of work opportunities, in order to escape political oppression or ethnic cleansing in other parts of the world, and for numerous other reasons. Swedes have also always been keen travellers, from the escapades of the Vikings during the Middle Ages, the world explorations of the disciples of Swedish botanist Carl von Linné (1707–78) in the second half of the eighteenth century, and the mass emigration to the United States in the late nineteenth and early twentieth century, to modern-day educational and recreational travels. Nevertheless, throughout the twentieth century, the Swedish population in many respects remained relatively homogenous and, it was only towards the turn of the Millennium, that large numbers of foreign migrants began to enter the country and that xenophobia became an increasing problem in Sweden – as in many other parts of Europe and the world.

Crime fiction is a genre prone to address and discuss contemporary issues. Despite crime novels often being read primarily for entertainment purposes, Jeanne E Glesener argues that 'in the age of multiculturalism they have become a platform where multicultural issues and realities are being explored,' and where 'the vexed and complicated relationship between different cultures does not only get [sic.] illustrated but investigated'.[4] Since the 1990s, Swedish crime fiction has devoted much attention to the clash between traditional national identities and the processes of Europeanization and

---

4   Jeanne E Glesener, 'The Crime Novel: Multiculturalism and its Impact on the Genre's Conventions', in *Crime and Nation: Political and Cultural Mappings of Criminality in New and Traditional Media*, ed. by Immacolata Amodeo and Eva Erdmann (Trier: Wissenschaftlicher Verlag Trier, 2009), pp. 15–26 (p. 15).

globalization, and an author who more than anyone else has dedicated his life's work to exploring the Swede's relationship to the Other is Henning Mankell (b. 1948). Mankell started out in the early 1970s as an author in the genre of proletarian realism, another important genre in twentieth-century Swedish literature.[5] In his debut novel, *Bergsprängaren* (1973, The rock blaster), the working conditions among Swedish miners are discussed. From the start, Mankell was a staunch socialist, and throughout his oeuvre he has repeatedly returned to investigating the role of the individual in relation to the system of the Swedish welfare state. In many ways he can be regarded as one of the primary heirs of Maj Sjöwall (b. 1935) and Per Wahlöö (1926–75).[6] After writing several novels in the proletarian genre, Mankell decided in the early 1990s that crime fiction was a better genre if one's aim was to discuss important issues in society while simultaneously reaching a large audience.[7] This explicit political ambition is shared by Mankell with several other Swedish crime writers, amongst them Maj Sjöwall and Per Wahlöö, and Liza Marklund (b. 1962).

Mankell's first crime novel, *Mördare utan ansikte* (1991; *Faceless Killers* 1997; *Assassino senza volto* 2001) became an immediate success, and was awarded the prize for best Swedish crime novel of the year, The Golden Crowbar, by The Swedish Academy of Detection.[8] This was Mankell's first novel about Inspector Kurt Wallander with the Ystad police, and it was to be followed by another nine novels – *Hundarna i Riga* (1992; *The Dogs of Riga* 2001; *I cani di Riga* 2002), *Den vita lejoninnan* (1993; *The White Lioness* 1998; *La leonessa Bianca* 2003), *Mannen som log* (1994; *The Man Who Smiled* 2005; *L'uomo che sorrideva* 2004), *Villospår* (1995; *Sidetracked* 1999; *La falsa pista* 1998), *Den femte kvinnan* (1996; *The Fifth Woman* 2000; *La quinta donna* 1999), *Steget efter* (1997;

---

5   For an exploration of the proletarian realist literature in Sweden, see Philippe Bouquet, *La bêche et la plume: L'aventure du roman prolétarien suédois* [The spade and the pen: The Adventure of the Swedish proletarian novel] (Bassac: Plein chant, 1986).

6   Sjöwall and Wahlöö are further discussed in chapter 2.

7   Cf. Ian Thomson, 'True Crime', *The Guardian*, 1 November 2003.

8   'Bästa svenska kriminalroman' [The best Swedish crime novel of the year], in *Svenska Deckarakademin* [The Swedish Academy of Detection], http://deckarakademin.org/hem/priser/basta-svenska-kriminalroman_[accessed 15 August 2013].

One Step Behind 2002; Delitto di mezza estate 2000), *Brandvägg*
(1998; *Firewall* 2002; *Muro di fuoco* 2005), *Innan Frosten* (2002;
Before the Frost 2005; *Prima del gelo* 2007), and *Den orolige mannen* (2009; *The Troubled Man* 2011; *L'uomo inquieto* 2010) – and a
collection of short stories, *Pyramiden* (1999; *The Pyramid* 2008; *Pi-
ramide* 2006), about Wallander.[9] Additionally, Mankell has to date
written three crime novels independent of the Wallander series:
Danslärarens återkomst (2000; *The Return of the Dancing Master*
2004; *Il ritorno del maestro di danza* 2007), *Kennedys hjärna* (2005;
Kennedy's Brain 2007; *Il cervello di Kennedy* 2007), and *Kinesen*
(2007; *The Man from Bejing* 2010; *Il cinese* 2009). Mankell's large
oeuvre also includes numerous mainstream novels – many of them
for children and young adults – and more than forty plays. Before
and parallel to his career as an author, Mankell has always worked
with theatre, and today he is an artistic director at Teatro Avenida in
Maputo, Mozambique, where he lives part of the year.

As noted by Shane McCorristine, 'Mankell's major concern at
the outset of the [Wallander] project was to highlight the alarming
rise in racism, xenophobia and anti-immigration feeling in
Sweden'.[10] Throughout his extensive repertoire, Mankell has shown
a growing concern for xenophobia and an increasing interest in exploring the relation to the Other.[11] Many of his projects have been di-

---

9   Supposedly, *Mördare utan ansikte* was planned to be a stand-alone novel,
     but the success of the novel and the character made Mankell rethink his
     original intention. An additional short novel about Wallander was pub-
     lished in the Netherlands in 2004 under the title *Het graf* (*An Event in Au-
     tumn* 2014). The events of this novel takes place between *Innan frosten*
     and *Den orolige mannen*, and it was later released in Swedish as *Handen*
     (2013, The hand).

10   Shane McCorristine, 'Pessimism in Henning Mankell's Kurt Wallander
     Series', in *Scandinavian Crime Fiction*, ed. by Andrew Nestingen and
     Paula Arvas (Cardiff: University of Wales Press, 2011), pp. 77–88 (p. 78).

11   Andrew Nestingen's Mankell chapter in *Crime and Fantasy in Scandina-
     via: Fiction, Film, and Social Change* (Seattle/London: University of
     Washington Press, 2008), pp. 223–54 really shows the consistency be-
     tween Mankell's crime fiction and the rest of his oeuvre, something that
     often tends to be ignored when Mankell is discussed primarily as the au-
     thor of the Wallander novels. Additionally, the role of the Other in Man-
     kell's fiction is addressed by Anna Westerståhl Stenport, 'Bodies Under
     Assault: Nation and Immigration in Henning Mankell's Faceless Killers',
     Scandinavian Studies 79.1 (2007), 1–24 (p. 6); Bergman, 'Paradoxes',
     passim; and McCorristine (passim), among others.

rectly related to Africa, and he has tried to raise global awareness of the problematic situation in Africa, particularly of the AIDS crisis.[12] Andrew Nestingen stresses that 'Mankell's novels are a discourse on solidarity and they attempt to force readers to think through solidarity's ethical and political dimensions'.[13] Africa, or more specifically Mozambique, is also the main setting of Mankell's crime novel *Kennedys hjärna*, and parts of the Wallander novel *Den vita lejoninnan* are set in South Africa. Throughout all Mankell's crime novels, however, the problematic relationship to the Other is a recurring theme, mirroring the increasing problems with xenophobia in Sweden in the last decades – a continuous threat to all notions of true solidarity.

When the European Union expanded and its influence grew in the 1990s, this brought with it an increase in intra-European migration. This, in combination with the economic crises in the early years of the decade, caused people in many parts of Europe to feel that their independence was threatened by the growing power of the EU, and that the increased number of immigrants might put their established sense of national identity in jeopardy. The political scientists Leslie Holmes and Philomena Murray note that this gave rise to more explicit expressions of racism and nationalism in many countries, as well as to an increased focus on identity formation.[14] Discussions of racism, nationalism, and identity formation are central to Mankell's crime novels and, as he has been one of the most influential writers in Swedish crime fiction in the last decades, examining how he handles these topics will shed light on recent tendencies in Swedish crime fiction more generally. By taking a closer look at three of Mankell's crime novels, namely *Danslärarens återkomst*, *Kennedys hjärna*, and *Den oroligen mannen*, I will scrutinize how Mankell investigates the relationship to the Other. The

---

12   Cf. Bergman, 'Paradoxes', passim. Although Mankell is primarily known as a crime writer, he is also an intellectual who is often invited to comment on current social issues, and his social engagement is strong, especially when it comes to issues concerning the injustices in the world (cf. Nestingen, pp. 223–32).

13   Nestingen, p. 232.

14   Leslie Holmes and Philomena Murray, 'Introduction: Citizenship and Identity in Europe', in *Citizenship and Identity in Europe*, ed. by Leslie Holmes and Philomena Murray (Aldershot: Ashgate, 1999), pp. 1–23 (pp. 1–8).

first novel is a police procedural, discussing how to deal today with Sweden's past relationship with the German Nazis during World War II. The second is a thriller, centered on the exploitation of impoverished Africans in search for a cure for AIDS, and the third, the last novel in the Wallander series, is a novel in which Wallander acts primarily as a private detective rather than in his official capacity as a police officer. This novel focuses on Sweden's position during the Cold War, and on Swedes today being Europeans, rather than primarily Swedes.

Mankell's crime fiction career began in 1991 with the police novel *Mördare utan ansikte*, and throughout the Wallander series, there is a recurring discussion of how Wallander feels lost and alienated in a Sweden he perceives as changing. He repeatedly claims to feel like a stranger, or perhaps rather obsolete: like a dinosaur in the present version of his own home country. Anna Westerståhl Stenport notes that already in the first novel of the series, Wallander 'perceives the demise of the [Swedish] Welfare State as related not only to immigration, but also to the very fabric of a national ideology that draws on the cultural implications of landscape, like those of his home province Skåne, to sustain itself'.[15] In examining the first seven Wallander novels, Shane McCorristine further suggests that Mankell in these novels 'offer[s] a veritable taxonomy of threats to notions of a secure Swedish identity, sometimes the evil to be combated originates outside the community, sometimes it comes from within, but it is always linked to spectres of the Other'.[16] The sense of estrangement experienced by Wallander could be discussed in terms of an identity crisis, where Mankell's protagonists – not only Wallander, but also for example police officer Stefan Lindman in *Danslärarens återkomst* and archeologist Louise Cantor in *Kennedys hjärna* – are struggling with their perceived cultural identities.[17] Central to the idea of cultural identity is the relationship to 'the Other', towards those who are not part of the group at

---

15   Westerståhl Stenport, p. 6.
16   McCorristine, p. 78.
17   With the term cultural identity, I mean a collective identity that can be ascribed to a group of people rather than primarily to an individual; a sense of belonging to a group that could be expressed through concepts such as Swedishness or Europeanness. That is, the type of cultural identity that Martin Kohli defines as combining a 'territorial reference with ethnic, cultural, economic, and legal-political components' that can be explicitly

hand, but against whom the group positions and defines itself, as being different from. *Danslärarens återkomst, Kennedys hjärna,* and *Den orolige mannen* all address Swedishness and Swedish cultural identity from different perspectives. This identity is first destabilized in *Danslärarens återkomst* by the revelations of past events that are difficult to incorporate into the contemporary concept of Swedishness; then, in *Kennedys hjärna,* Swedish identity is confronted with the desire to overcome the distance to the African Other; and, finally, in *Den orolige mannen,* there is the question of contrasting a perhaps obsolete Swedishness with a more current notion of being European.

The Evil Other of the Past in Danslärarens återkomst

Since the 1990s, it has become public knowledge that Sweden was not as neutral during World War II as had previously been claimed in the Swedish public arena. There was actually extensive support for the Nazis in Sweden during the war: from individuals, groups, and political parties. In the 1990s and early 2000s, these revelations were addressed by numerous Swedish crime writers, among them Henning Mankell in *Danslärarens återkomst* (2000); Arne Dahl (pen name for Jan Arnald, b. 1962) in *Europa blues* (1999, Europe blues; *Europa blues* 2012); Aino Trosell (b. 1949) in *Om hjärtat ännu slår* (2000, If the heart still beats); Stieg Larsson in *Män som hatar kvinnor* (2005; *The Girl with the Dragon Tattoo* 2008; *Uomini che odiano le donne* 2008); and Camilla Läckberg (b. 1974) in *Tyskungen* (2007; *The Hidden Child* 2011; *Il bambino segreto* 2013), just to mention a few.[18]

The central murder victim of Mankell's novel is an elderly Swede, Herbert Molin, who during World War II joined the German Waffen-SS, and who until his death remained a confirmed Nazi. Molin returned to Sweden and changed his name after the war, and until his

---

or implicitly 'experienced by the individual' ('The Battlegrounds of European Identity', *European Societies* 2.2 (2000), 113–37 (pp. 117 and 122)).

18   An extensive discussion of thirty Swedish crime novels from the first decade of the twenty-first century is found in Bergman, 'The Good, the Bad', passim. The general conclusions, presented in the present chapter concerning Swedish crime novels from that decade dealing with Sweden's wartime past, are based on the analysis presented in that article.

retirement a few years before, he worked as a police officer. The last years of his life, Molin spent hiding in a desolate house in the Swedish mountains, as he feared his past might eventually catch up with him. During the war, Molin had murdered a Jewish dance teacher in Berlin, and in 1999, the son of the dance teacher tracks Molin down and flogs him to death in order to avenge his father's murder.[19] This is a very typical scenario from the novels dealing with Swedish World War II Nazism. In general an old Nazi or former Nazi is murdered by one of his wartime victims or by a descendant of one of those victims, and the novels are then dedicated to finding this out. Such novels, including Mankell's, can be regarded as an attempt to incorporate the newly discovered knowledge about Sweden's wartime history into the concept of Swedish cultural identity as we know it today. The novels thus take part in a public negotiation about the wartime past: a negotiation that aims to create an image of the past that would be acceptable and possible to incorporate into the common notion of Swedish identity.

Many Swedish crime writers have made it their mission to educate the public about the wartime situation. A common strategy has been to let the characters of their novels ponder the lack of awareness in Sweden about Swedish wartime Nazi-affiliation: a lack reflected both in the Swedish educational system and in the public arena. By letting his protagonist, Stefan Lindman, represent the majority of Swedish readers, who learned about World War II as it impinged on Sweden only in retrospect, Mankell tells his readers about how widely pro-Nazi sentiments affected Swedish society in the 1930s and 1940s.[20]

> He [Lindman] wondered what had happened to all that history when he was a schoolboy. What he vaguely remembered from his history classes was a very different picture: a Sweden that had succeeded – by means of extremely clever policies and by skillfully walking the tightrope – in staying out of the war. The Swedish government had remained strictly neutral and thus saved the country from being crushed by the German military machine. He'd heard nothing about quantities of homegrown Nazis.[21]

---

19   Henning Mankell, *The Return of the Dancing Master*, trans. by Laurie Thompson (London: Vintage, 2003), pp. 465–66.
20   Ibid., pp. 256–57.
21   Ibid., pp. 256–57.

Mankell brings the knowledge about the Swedish past closer to the reader by letting Lindman – the primary object of reader identification in *Danslärarens återkomst* – discover that his own father had been a Nazi.[22] By showing how shocking this revelation is to Lindman, Mankell tells his reader that anyone might have been, or might even still be, a closet Nazi. This is further emphasized as Molin's seemingly innocent daughter, turns out to be an active member of a present day global neo-Nazi network.[23]

Although not without notable exceptions, in most crime fiction blame is primarily ascribed to the murderer. The crime novels addressing Sweden's World War II past diverge from this pattern, however, as the blame is almost always attributed to the victim, the murdered Nazi, whereas the killer is considered justified in his or her actions, having been the sufferer of past atrocities. It is actually quite rare in these novels for the murderer to be brought to justice. In *Danslärarens återkomst*, the murderer eludes the police and disappears, never to be heard of again. Additionally, Mankell even encourages the reader to feel empathy for the murderer, and towards the end of the novel Stefan Lindman explicitly wishes that the murderer will never be caught. The real criminals of the novel are the murdered Molin and the other Nazi sympathizers; they are the ones singled out as the Other in the most adverse sense. They and other Nazi criminals in recent Swedish crime novels are presented as monsters and represent a return to the purely evil criminals of the late nineteenth-century and early twentieth-century crime fiction, where unrepentant criminals had to be removed from society – often by being literally eliminated. Throughout *Danslärarens återkomst*, Mankell also repeats that Nazism is an ideology still potent today, in Sweden and worldwide. Nevertheless, the Nazis in Swedish crime fiction always remain the Other, and as this distance is kept up, the Nazi characters are never incorporated as part of Swedish cultural identity, neither in the past nor the present.

In contrast with this intention to disclose issues of secret past allegiances in recent crime novels, many Swedish crime writers let the truth about their fictional murdered wartime Nazis (unlike that of their latter-day neo-Nazis) remain concealed from the public in their novels, even after the police have found out the truth about them.

---

22   Ibid., pp. 265, 269–73, 311, 360, and 501.
23   Cf. ibid., p. 485–86.

The reader might have learnt about the past while reading, but the message in most of these novels thereby still appears to be that it serves no purpose to discuss this in public. Furthermore, in *Danslärarens återkomst* – as in most of the other novels addressing World War II Nazism – there is a strong reluctance to associate in any way the detective heroes, or any other object of reader identification, with the Nazis. This creates a distance to any Swedish guilt regarding World War II events, rather than a coming-to-terms with the past. Distancing elements thus dominate, despite some occasional attempts to draw readers in close, as for example the Nazi involvement of Lindman's long-dead father in Mankell's novel.

By associating the Swedish collaborators solely with the Germans and German guilt, they are simultaneously excluded from any Swedish community. The Swedish crime writers thus appear to choose the easy way out when it comes to ascribing Swedish responsibility, as they merely assign guilt to single individuals and create a distance between those individuals and Swedish society, rather than implicate the Swedish government or Swedish society as a whole. A joint Swedish 'we', whom crime fiction readers and protagonists could possibly identify with, is thus never blamed. When these crime writers in their novels occasionally address Nazi history not associated with specific individuals, they bring up for example facts about the German concentration camps, the camps in Norway and Denmark, or other matters not commonly associated with Sweden. Indeed, there is a strong focus on events in Norway and Denmark in many of these novels, something that further contributes to divert attention from what happened in Sweden during the war.

Although eager to address the dangers of Nazism, past as well as present, Mankell and his fellow Swedish crime writers still keep a very safe distance from Nazism, as they avoid associating it with anyone or anything readers might identify with. In this way the crime writers contribute to reshaping the Swedish collective World War II memory into an inoffensive version of history, which lets Swedes feel better about themselves and their past. Readers might learn about history, but hardly learn from history. In this way the war past has been acknowledged, but is never ever incorporated into Swedish cultural identity. The Other is thus even further established as *Other*, and the image of what it means to be Swedish is allowed to remain pretty much intact.

Attempts to Approach the African Other in Kennedys hjärna

Kennedys hjärna is a very different novel from *Dansläraren återkomst*. It is a thriller where Mankell depicts how black, under-privileged 'Africans' are exploited and used as guinea pigs by powerful Western pharmaceutical companies aiming to develop a cure for AIDS.[24] Readers of Mankell's novel are clearly expected to side against the economic and scientific tactics of the corporations, but does that automatically cause one to identify with the novel's 'African' AIDS victims?

Swedish archeologist Louise Cantor, protagonist of Mankell's novel, finds Henrik, her son, dead in his apartment in Stockholm. Cantor suspects murder, as she is unable to believe that Henrik would have killed himself. Tracing her son's recent past, she travels from Stockholm to Australia, to Spain, until she eventually ends up in Mozambique. Cantor is a well-educated, middle-aged Swede, an experienced international traveller who has lived and worked abroad (in Greece) for many years. Nevertheless, 'Africa' is completely different from everything she has previously encountered. Mankell makes Cantor the object of reader identification and the representative of Swedish identity in *Kennedys hjärna*, and it is through her eyes that the reader encounters Mozambique and 'Africa'.

Many of Louise Cantor's experiences in Mozambique alienate and frighten her, but nevertheless, Mankell obviously aims to spread knowledge and understanding of the situation in 'Africa' and also to evoke empathy for 'the African people'. Living in villages financed by a mysterious American philanthropist are people infected with AIDS who receive medical treatment, but in these villages experiments are being conducted where medicines under development are being tested on humans. Both sick and previously healthy 'Africans' are ruthlessly exploited, and anyone who knows about what is taking place is killed before they can draw attention to what is going

---

24 This part about *Kennedys hjärna* builds primarily on Bergman, 'Paradox-es'. The term 'Africans' is of course generalizing and using it is problematic in many ways. I am using it here and below following Mankell, who throughout the novel emphazises a divide between black Africans and white Westerners in order to make his point and who – in line with that – generally talks about the continent of 'Africa' rather than about specific nations or regions.

on.[25] Cantor's first visit to one of these villages resembles a journey into Dante's hell. Additionally, Mankell evokes Joseph Conrad's *Heart of Darkness* (1899/1902; *Cuore di tenebra* 1924), and the pregnant symbolism of light and darkness in Conrad's novel spills over into Cantor's experiences in Mozambique. In *Kennedys hjärna*, the darkness simultaneously symbolizes the foreignness of 'Africa' and the lies and evil that Cantor finds – a combination that is quite problematic. Mankell thus depicts 'Africa' and 'the Africans' as Other according to colonial patterns, and shows that these patterns are still very much alive today, but the double symbolism of the darkness also links 'the African' with evil. Despite the polarization between the victimized 'Africans' and the evil medical companies, both exist hidden in a common darkness.

It is hardly possible for Mankell's Western readers to identify with the AIDS victims that Cantor meets. Mankell shows how they live in horrific circumstances in the AIDS villages, and in these depictions, the sick are dehumanized, as they almost become one with their abysmal environment. Occasionally, someone talks or makes an attempt to talk to Cantor, but then their primary function is always to convey information important to the story or to Mankell's message, and their presence is only momentarily strengthened. Henrik's 'African' girlfriend Lucinda constitutes the only exception, as she is given a bigger role and more room to evolve. In her meetings with Lucinda, Cantor's prejudices and fears are made explicit and confronted. During one of their first encounters Lucinda addresses Cantor: 'You despise black people. Maybe not consciously, but it's there even so. You think it's our own weaknesses that have made the agonies of Africa so devastating'.[26] While Lucinda is explicitly addressing Cantor, Mankell simultaneously lets her address all his non-African readers, who are likely to identify with Cantor's uncertainties. Cantor, in turn, tries to explain to Lucinda that she is constantly afraid of being there. 'Im frightened of everything that happens here, of the darkness, of being mugged by people I can neither see nor hear. Im frightened because I don't understand'.[27] There is clearly a distance between the two women that not even their devel-

25   Cf. Henning Mankell, *Kennedy's Brain*, transl. by Laurie Thompson (London: Vintage Books, 2008), pp. 428–29.
26   Ibid., pp. 212–13.
27   Ibid., p. 195.

oping friendship can bridge. Additionally, all the Europeans and Americans that Cantor meets in Mozambique, talk about the native inhabitants of Mozambique as 'them', thereby showing lack of identification with and stressing the Otherness of all black 'Africans'. The only – and very feeble – hope of actually reaching the Other found in the novel, can be sensed in the open discussions between Lucinda and Cantor. Still, that hope dies as Lucinda dies before she is able to reveal to the world the truth about the AIDS villages.

Nevertheless, with *Kennedys hjärna* Mankell makes a serious attempt to tell the world about the plight of Africa, and by using the crime genre he manages to reach a larger number of readers. Perhaps that is as good as anyone can hope to do, and optimistically some readers after reading Mankell's novel might actually understand the severity of the AIDS crisis. Even with the best of intentions, however, there is no way for Mankell to avoid presenting the Africans as Other. He thereby illustrates the unfeasibility of identification with, and of really understanding, the Other. Unfortunately, the western world perceiving Africans as Other remains a major obstacle preventing the engagement that would actually make it possible to get something done about the AIDS situation in Africa.

In both *Danslärarens återkomst* and *Kennedys hjärna*, Swedish cultural identity is thus confronted with alterities that are examined and considered for inclusion in what constitutes Swedishness, but that in the end are not. In the first novel, the morally reasonable thing would have been somehow to incorporate the history of Swedish Nazism into Swedish cultural identity, but instead it is made out to be further alien and something against which to define Swedishness. In the second novel, it would have been morally impossible actually to overcome the distance from the African Other, but the novel still expresses a strong desire to create sympathy for the suffering Africans, and it seems possible to incorporate that sympathy into Swedish cultural identity. Perhaps it is reasonable to assume that this can be attributed to the idea of that sympathy for the less fortunate and opposition to multinational corporate interests being in line with a traditionally accepted notion of Swedishness, while the breaching of the image of neutrality and acceptance of association with the German Nazis during the war proves more alien. Read together, *Kennedys hjärna* also shows that the racism associated with Nazism in *Danslärarens återkomst* could not be shaken off that easily. *Kennedys hjärna* shows that even a humanist and compassionate

Swede like Louise Cantor can have preconceptions about the African Other (Mankell enables the reader to identify with Cantor and her biases, while simultaneously realizing that the biases are nothing but just prejudices that ought to be fought and suppressed) that are obviously rooted in ideas about race differences and that, in turn, shows that even if Nazism is excluded as being un-Swedish, a certain amount of racism is still part of Swedish cultural identity.

From National to European Identity in Den orolige mannen

In this final example, the whole concept of Swedish identity is brought more seriously into question.[28] The focus in the last decades of Swedish crime fiction on the clash between, on the one hand, traditional national identities and, on the other, processes of Europeanization and globalization reveals a considerable shift in the perception of how cultural identities seem to be constructed. Traditionally, these identities have been seen as primarily rooted in folk culture, language, and national history, but today they increasingly come across as a result of the emergence of a common, transnational cultural and medial environment. Henning Mankell's latest – and last – novel about Kurt Wallander, *Den orolige mannen*, can be considered a recapitulation of these recent negations of cultural identities and, additionally, a concluding comment on the time of the Wallander series and the image of Swedish identity the series presents, and perhaps even represents. Furthermore, the novel shows what the earlier Wallander novels were heading towards: what the new times, so often feared by Wallander in these novels, could really be like.

Den orolige mannen is Wallander's final farewell as he is developing Alzheimer's disease, and this is Mankell's way of telling his readers that society has fundamentally changed during the twenty years that have passed since he initiated the Wallander series in 1991. Wallander's generation, the generation born in the 1940s, which for so long has occupied all the positions of power and influence in Swedish society, is now ageing and retiring, something that coincides with the new society's need for new and different sorts of people. The

---

28   The observations concerning *Den orolige mannen* have previously been
       presented, and much more extensively discussed, in Bergman, 'European
       Turn', *passim*.

main mystery in *Den orolige mannen* is not even a case that Wallander handles in his official capacity as a police officer. Instead, in his
spare time he investigates what happened to his daughter Linda's in-
laws, the former military and submarine captain Håkan von Enke and
his wife, who have gone missing. Wallander suffering from Alzheimer's disease becomes an image not just for the end of the Wallander
series, but also for the end of the Swedish traditional police detective
and, in combination with the promotion of a more European cultural
identity, this clearly illustrates that it is time for a new and more European generation of crime fiction detectives.

Just like the main mystery of *Den orolige mannen*, the genera-
tional shift is mainly presented in terms of Wallander's private life,
in which Linda's having a baby, Wallander's first grandchild, is central. The fact that Linda tells him about the baby on the very beach
where Wallander once truly realized that there was another world
out there – a realization that was a big turning point in his life, and
the point in time where his previously nationally-confined perspectives were shown no longer to be sufficient – marks the shift of the
generations also as a shift in world views.[29] Linda and her baby represent the new generations that are part of and at home in the new
Europe, in a way Wallander could never be. Wallander's daughter
and grand-daughter thus represent a new and less nationally-confined cultural identity. This new identity is presented as developed
from within and below (rather than being the result of some kind of
cultural or political imposition), and implicitly it is assumed to be a
result of Swedes travelling more, of working environments becoming more international in all senses, and of culture being produced
and consumed without regard for national borders.[30]

National identity is generally outlined in contrast to 'the Other,
the unknown, and the foreign'.[31] The Other has been a common figure throughout the Wallander series, but in *Den orolige mannen*, the
Other is rather transformed into a character of the past. The only

---

29 Cf. Henning Mankell, *The Troubled Man*, transl. by Laurie Thompson
(London: Harvill Secker, 2011), p. 283.

30 The development of European identities and of general Europeanizing
tendencies in recent Swedish crime fiction will be further addressed in
chapter 8.

31 Cf. Wendy Everett, 'Introduction: European Film and the Quest for Identity,' in *European Identity in the Cinema*, Second Edition, ed. by Wendy
Everett (Bristol/Portland, OR: Intellect, 2005), pp. 7–14 (p. 10).

non-native Swedes in the novel's present time are a family of assimilated immigrants who live in the building where Wallander lived as a child. They are now typical 'Swedes', the 'replacement Wallanders', who appreciate the safeness of a neighbourhood and share Wallander's middle-class values.[32] They can therefore no longer be regarded as Other in the traditional sense. Interestingly, Wallander himself could be considered the Other of the equation, now that he appears as obsolete in relation to younger generations of Europeans.

In *Danslärarens återkomst*, the history of World War II was part of creating the Other against which a Swedish national identity could be defined. In *Den orolige mannen* it is the history of the Cold War – the conflict between the capitalist Western Bloc dominated by the United States and the communist Eastern Bloc dominated by the Soviet Union, that lasted from the end of the Second World War in 1945 up until 1989–90 when the communist system in Eastern Europe fell apart – that is central. Mankell repeatedly points out how Sweden during the Cold War period was just a playground for the representatives of the superpowers, something that is also true for other major parts of Europe.[33] History is thus used to create an identification rather than a divergence between Swedes and other Europeans. The Cold War thereby contributes to showing today's Europe as a unified cultural space delineated by its expanding Eastern and Western borders rather than one divided by specific national borders. National historical differences become small in relation to the master narrative of the Cold War, and this creates a framework for seeing similarities within Europe, rather than national differences. If *Danslärarens återkomst* and *Kennedys hjärna* explored the boundaries of Swedish identity while leaving it reasonably intact, *Den orolige mannen* moves one step further by portraying national identity as obsolete, as an element of the past. In the twenty-first century of Europeanization, globalization, and social media, the concept of national identity is no longer useful. It limits people rather than enabling them to take part successfully in the new communities that spread far beyond national and cultural borders.

---

32   Mankell, *The Troubled Man*, p. 449.
33   For a discussion of Sweden's role during the Cold War and Swedish political agendas during the period, see Aryo Makko, 'Sweden, Europe, and the Cold War: A Reappraisal,' *Journal of Cold War Studies*, 2 (2012), 68–97.

Further Attempts to Portray a Heterogeneous Sweden
at the Turn of the Millennium

The three Mankell novels examined here are just a small sample, both of Mankell's oeuvre, and of recent Swedish crime fiction. As previously stated, the relationship to the Other has often been examined as a topic in the genre in recent decades. Throughout most of the Wallander series, Mankell lets Wallander represent the 'average Swede' in relation to the Other. Mankell then portrays the Other – generally in shape of immigrants, Swedes with foreign roots, or foreigners – from outside, through the eyes of Wallander. Wallander also displays the prejudices and fears (sometimes even racist tendencies) that many Swedes share, although he consciously tries to hide these from people around him. In this way, Mankell enables the reader to identify with Wallander and his biases, while simultaneously realizing that the biases are nothing but just prejudices that ought to be fought and suppressed. A completely different approach was taken by, for example, Åke Edwardson (b. 1953) in *Vänaste land* (2006, Most beautiful land), the eighth novel of the series about Inspector Erik Winter in Gothenburg. Edwardson attempts to portray immigrants from the 'inside' in almost poetic passages that stand out sharply against the mode of narration found in the rest of his novel and thus dares to move in closer to the Other than Mankell does. Despite the ambitious attempt at depicting a heterogeneous Swedish society, however, the effect is that the immigrants of *Vänaste land* are exoticized in a manner that leaves a somewhat sour aftertaste.

An author who turns the tables, who does not attempt to portray immigrants as Other, is Jens Lapidus (b. 1974). Most of Lapidus' protagonists are criminals who have some kind of non-Swedish ancestry. As he portrays the criminal underbelly of Stockholm, these protagonists become the norm, while the 'average Swedes' – who constitute the norm in almost all other Swedish crime fiction – become the Other against whom the protagonists (with whom the reader engages) identify themselves. Unlike Edwardson, however, Lapidus convincingly uses language to portray his protagonists from the 'inside', and thereby he makes his readers view Sweden and Swedes from a different perspective, something that feels fresh and new.[34] Showing Sweden from the outside is difficult for most Swedish

---

34   This is further explored in chapter 5.

writers, but one crime writer who has sometimes attempted to do this, is Arne Dahl (pen name for Jan Arnald, b. 1963). In his second crime series in particular, centered on a secret and experimental operative unit within Europol, Dahl strives to show Sweden from new perspectives. One of the best examples is found in *Viskleken* (2011, Chinese whispers), where during a sequence of the novel set in Latvia, it is demonstrated that Latvians view Swedish banks as just as bad as the mafia and blame these banks for completely ruining the Latvian economy. Although capitalism, as well as those institutions associated with capitalism, are often the target of criticism in crime novels set in Sweden, too, Dahl's depiction, by showing them from a completely different perspective, makes the reader see the Swedish banks in a whole new light – as Other.

The concepts of Otherness and identity formation are closely intertwined. Zygmunt Bauman, for instance, proposes identification as 'a never-ending, always incomplete, unfinished and open-ended activity in which we all, by necessity or by choice, are engaged'.[35] Identification constitutes an important component in the construction of cultural identities. Stewart Hall has even suggested that identities are 'constructed within, not outside representation', and assuming this is true, crime fiction – a genre probably reaching more people than any other literary genre today – should be a good place to start looking for new cultural identities.[36]

---

35   Zygmunt Bauman, 'Identity in the Globalizing World', in *Identity, Culture and Globalization*, ed. by Eliezer Ben-Rafael and Yitzak Sternberg (Leiden: Brill, 2001), pp. 471–82 (p. 482).

36   Stewart Hall, 'Introduction: Who Needs Identity?', in *Questions of Cultural Identity*, ed. by Stewart Hall and Paul du Gay (London/Thousand Oaks/New Delhi: Sage Publications, 1996), pp. 1–17 (p. 4). As I finish writing this chapter in the early spring of 2013, racism and xenophobia are frequently discussed in the Swedish media. Sverigedemokraterna, a Swedish nationalistic political party with racist tendencies and a strong aversion towards immigration, who by receiving 5,7% of the votes got seats in the Swedish parliament in the 2010 elections, currently (March 2013) hold about 9% of the votes in the official polls leading up to the Swedish elections in September 2014 (cf. 'Väljarbarometern mars 2013' [Voter survey March 2013], in *TNS Sifo* [The Swedish Institute for Opinion Surveys, a subsidiary of TNS Global] http://www.tns-sifo.se/media/453564/vb_mar_2013_svd.pdf [accessed 3 April 2013].

IV

WOMEN AUTHORS AND DETECTIVES: *FROM LIZA MARKLUND TO KRISTINA OHLSSON*

From the end of the 1990s, Swedish crime fiction has been characterized by a strong wave of women crime writers and an increasing number of women detectives. Liza Marklund is often regarded as a most influential figure in these developments. The chapter also addresses the role of feminism in Swedish crime fiction.[1]

Internationally, Sweden is often perceived as a country of gender equality, and it is true that the situation for women is better in Sweden than in many other countries. The Swedish legislation concerning parental leave (maternity as well as paternity leave) is allegedly one of the most generous in the world, and the free education and free healthcare provided by the Swedish Welfare State in modern times have enabled Swedish women to choose their own paths and live healthy lives. Swedish universities began accepting women students in 1870, women were given the right to vote in public elections start-

---

1   Parts of this chapter draws on observations previously presented in Kerstin Bergman, 'Beyond Stieg Larsson: Contemporary Trends and Traditions in Swedish Crime Fiction', *Forum for World Literature Studies*, 4.2 (2012), 291–306 (pp. 296–99); and in Kerstin Bergman, 'Lisbeth Salander and her Swedish Crime Fiction "Sisters": Stieg Larsson's Hero in a Genre Context', in *Men Who Hate Women and Women Who Kick Their Asses: Stieg Larsson's Millennium Trilogy in Feminist Perspective*, ed. by Donna King and Carrie Lee Smith (Nashville: Vanderbilt University Press, 2012), pp. 135–144. Additionally, a Swedish version of this chapter is published as 'Inför lagen och den patriarkala genren: Kvinnliga deckarförfattare i 2000-talets Sverige' [In presence of the law and the patriarchal genre: Women crime writers in 21st century Sweden], in *'Det universella och det individuella': Festskrift till Eva Hættner Aurelius* ['The universal and the individual': Festschrift in honour of Eva Hættner Aurelius], ed. by Kerstin Bergman et.al. (Göteborg/Stockholm: Makadam, 2013), pp. 39–46.

ing in 1921, and the strong feminist movement of the 1960s and 1970s contributed to an increased equality in many areas.[2] Today most Swedish women work outside of the home, participating in all lines of work and holding positions in most areas of society. At the time of writing (2013), 43% of the seats in the Swedish Parliament are occupied by women, and in the current Government of Sweden, 13 out of the 24 ministers are women.[3] Nevertheless, Sweden is still a patriarchal society where men are often paid more than women for doing the same job, where most positions of real power – in both the private and the public sector – tend to be occupied by men, and where violence against and discrimination of women still constitute a sometimes hidden but grave problem. Furthermore, Sweden is currently experiencing an anti-feminist backlash, and post-feminist ideas have become increasingly dominant. The last decades have also witnessed intensifying privatization of the public sector (education, health care, child care, care of the elderly, infrastructure), a development that brings with it not only growing class differences, but also increased gender inequalities.

Crime fiction is traditionally a very male genre, no matter how important authors like Agatha Christie and Dorothy L Sayers were for the formation of the canon in the 1920s and 1930s, and irrespective of how many women and feminist practitioners there are today. This gender perspective holds true also for Swedish crime fiction, and

---

2   Initially women students were accepted only in the Faculty of Medicine (Tore Frängsmyr, 'Universitet' [Universities], *Nationalencyklopedin* [The National Encyclopedia], http://www.ne.se/lang/universitet, [accessed 23 August 2013]). On women's right to vote, cf. Ulla Manns, 'Kvinnlig rösträtt' [Women's right to vote], *Nationalencyklopedin* [The National Encyclopedia], http://www.ne.se/lang/kvinnlig-r%C3%B6str%C3%A4tt, [accessed 23 August 2013]. On the Swedish feminist movement of the 1960s and 1970s, see for example Ingela K. Naumann, 'Child Care and Feminism in West Germany and Sweden in the 1960s and 1970s,' *Journal of European Social Policy*, 1 (2005), 47–63 (pp. 54–58). A comparison of the developments in gender equality in the Nordic countries is found in Diane Sainsbury, 'Gender and Social-Democratic Welfare States,' in *Gender and Welfare State Regimes*, ed. Diane Sainsbury (Oxford/New York: Oxford UP, 1999), pp. 75–115.

3   'Members and Parties,' *Sveriges Riksdag* [The Swedish Parliament], http://www.riksdagen.se/en/Members-and-parties/, [accessed 23 August 2013]; 'The Swedish Government,' *Regeringskansliet* [The Swedish Government office], http://www.regeringen.se/content/1/c6/20/76/70/349be510.pdf, [accessed 23 August 2013].

with a few notable exceptions – such as Maria Lang (pen name for Dagmar Lange, 1914-91), Kerstin Ekman (b. 1933), Ulla Trenter (b. 1936), and Maj Sjöwall (b. 1935) – the genre was for a very long time male-dominated also in Sweden.[4] However, during the 1990s something happened: suddenly Swedish bookstores and libraries were being flooded with novels by British and Norwegian women crime writers, among the latter for example Anne Holt (b. 1958), Karin Fossum (b. 1954), and Kim Småge (pen name for Anne Karin Thorshus, b. 1945). These writers became immensely popular among Swedish crime fiction readers, and suddenly people started to wonder why there were no Swedish women crime writers.[5] Then the crime fiction journal *Jury* (1972–2008) decided to try to do something about this, and simultaneously set up crime-writing classes for women and instituted a new crime fiction prize, The Poloni Prize, named after a then relatively unknown Swedish woman crime writer, Helena Poloni (pen-name for Ingegerd Stadener 1903–1968), who had written a few crime novels in the 1950s and 1960s.[6]

The Poloni prize was to be given to a promising woman crime writer, and in the first year, 1998, it was awarded to Liza Marklund (b. 1962), a journalist who herself had taken a writing class and just published her first crime novel, *Sprängaren* (1998; *The Bomber* 2000/2011; *Delitto a Stoccolma* 2001). Three years later – after the prize had been given to Aino Trosell (b. 1949), Åsa Nilsonne (b. 1949), and Eva-Marie Liffner (b. 1957) – it was decided the prize had fulfilled its duty to promote women's authorship in the genre and was no longer needed. By then this new wave of women crime writers in Sweden had been initiated. In 1998–2007 more than

---

4   Although it can actually be claimed that the first Swedish crime writer was a woman, Claude Gérard (male pen name for Aurora Ljungstedt, 1821–1908), who wrote the long short story 'Hastfordska vapnet' (1870; *The Hastfordian Escutcheon* 2005), where also the first woman investigator of Swedish crime fiction appears, and two novels, *Psykologiska gåtor* (1868, Psychological riddles) and *Inom natt och år* (1876, Within night and year) bordering on the genre (Johan Wopenka, 'Kvinnlig Deckarhistoria: Från 1800-talets mitt till 1900-talets slut' [Women's crime fiction history: From the mid-1800s to the end of the 1900s], in *Tretton svenska deckardamer* [Thirteen Swedish crime ladies] (Lund: BTJ, 2009), pp. 7–30 (p. 9)).

5   It has been claimed that more than half of the Swedish crime fiction readers are women (Wopenka, p. 29).

6   Cf. ibid., pp. 28–29.

eighty women made their debut as crime writers in Sweden.[7] In 2010, forty-one out of a total of 112 new Swedish crime novels published were written by women.[8] Although the number of women writers thus increased substantially during the early 2000s, this also coincided with a large increase in Swedish crime fiction publication in general, and the ratio of women versus men crime writers remained almost identical in 2010 as it was in 2001, with around 35–40% being women writers. Nevertheless, there is a tendency for women writers to be somewhat more successful than men in terms of sales, and in fact in 2010, ten of the twenty-two Swedish crime novels reaching the top ten places on the Swedish bestseller list, that is 45%, were written by women.[9]

Liza Marklund is often regarded a leading light in this wave of women crime writers, and for several reasons. First, her winning the Poloni Prize received extensive media attention, and since then she has continued to be one of the women crime writers most acknowledged by the media. The media have thus been an important factor in the creation of Marklund's career as a crime writer and a public figure in Sweden.[10] Second, Marklund's more feminist agenda and her strong woman protagonist have placed her close to the tradition of Swedish crime fiction promoting social and political critique, following in the footsteps of, for example, Maj Sjöwall and Per Wahlöö (1926-75), and of Henning Mankell (b. 1948), thus firmly placing her novels in the very centre of the Swedish crime fiction tradition. Even though Marklund does not use the police procedural genre, it could easily be said that she has transferred the procedural genre into the tabloid newspaper environment, thus reviving this most popular

---

7   Ibid., p. 7.
8   'Deckarkatalogen' [The crime fiction catalogue], in *Svenska deckarakademin* [The Swedish Academy of Detection], http://deckarakademin.org/hem/deckarkatalogen-3 [accessed 15 August 2013]. In this count, two short story collections and one novel written in Swedish but published in Finland, were left out.
9   'Topplistor' [Bestseller lists], in *Svensk bokhandel* [Swedish book trade magazine], http://www.svb.se/bokfakta/svenskatopplistor, [accessed 11 January 2012]. Also cf. Bergman, 'Beyond Stieg Larsson', p. 297.
10   Cf. Sara Kärrholm, 'Swedish Queens of Crime: The Art of Self-Promotion and the Notion of Feminine Agency – Liza Marklund and Camilla Läckberg', in *Scandinavian Crime Fiction*, ed. by Andrew Nestingen and Paula Arvas (Cardiff: University of Wales Press, 2011), pp. 131–47 (pp. 133–38).

Swedish crime genre. Although there are several other women who began writing crime fiction at the same time as Marklund, and who have probably in many cases been equally successful in terms of sales, they have generally either written traditional police-focused novels but been less concerned with social critique, or written novels that could not as easily be inscribed in the principal tradition in Swedish crime fiction.[11] Due to either a lack of social and political critique or to writing in a less recognized genre, it has not been possible to classify them in terms of being the new heirs of Sjöwall and Wahlöö or Mankell, and this has probably made them somewhat less interesting in the eyes of the Swedish media and literary critics.

Marklund's Generation of Women Crime Writers

The most prominent of the women authors who are generally said to belong to Marklund's 'generation' are Inger Frimansson (b. 1944) and Åsa Nilsonne, who actually made their debuts as crime writers in the early 1990s, but had their big breakthroughs at the end of the 1990s; Helene Tursten (b. 1954), Karin Alvtegen (b. 1965), Anna Jansson (b. 1958), and Aino Trosell, all of whom published their first crime novels around the same time as Marklund, at the end of the 1990s; and, finally, Åsa Larsson (b. 1966), Mari Jungstedt (b. 1962), and Camilla Läckberg (b. 1974), who all entered the scene a few years later, in 2003.[12] These women writers have all written long series of novels, all feature on the Swedish bestseller lists, and have all been widely translated outside of the Scandinavian context.

If Marklund can be said to use the procedural genre in a tabloid newspaper environment, portraying a team of investigative journal-

---

11   A brilliant example of the latter is Aino Trosell's novels, taking place in different low status workplaces in the countryside, with an uneducated, working-class, middle-aged woman in the investigative role.

12   In this context, 'generation' has nothing to do with age or year of birth, but is rather a way to describe a group of writers who came forward and became successful in the genre during the same time period. Another woman author who also belongs to Marklund's generation and who would have been presented in a more extensive survey is Karin Wahlberg (b. 1950), who has a woman medical doctor, Veronika Lundborg, as one of her protagonists in police novels set in and around Oskarshamn on the east coast of Sweden.

ists working at the crime desk, Nilsonne, Tursten, Jansson, Jungstedt, and Läckberg all write relatively traditional police novels.
Nilsonne and Tursten use the urban setting so commonly found in
the genre, locating their stories in Stockholm and Gothenburg, respectively. Nilsonne portrays Stockholm police officer Monika Pedersen, who in the first novel, *Tunnare än blod* (1991, Thinner than
blood), is young and new to the profession. During the series she
displays a growing frustration with her work situation, criticizing in
particular the lack of resources in, and the downsizing of, Swedish
law enforcement, as well as the patriarchal structures dominating
her workplace. In her third novel, *Kyskhetsbältet* (2000, The chasti-
ty belt), Nilsonne also extends her social and feminist critique to the
health care environment, as she draws parallels between Pedersen's
situation and the impossible work situation of a woman medical
doctor. Nilsonne's novels are characterized by psychological perspectives and by a sense of righteousness, focusing on inequalities
related to gender, race, and professional status.[13] Nilsonne's background is in medical psychology, and many of her novels involve
hospitals and the scientific research environment, something that is
relatively rare in Swedish crime fiction. In particular, the scientific
perspectives are prominent in Nilsonne's early novels, and there 'the
most prominent function of the use of elements from the scientific
world is to criticize that world from a moral and social standpoint'.[14]

Helene Tursten primarily uses urban Gothenburg settings for her
novels about Detective Inspector Irene Huss and her colleagues, although there are sometimes also excursions away from the city, as in
Tatuerad torso (2000; *The Torso* 2006; *Senza nessuna colpa* 2013)
where Huss works part of her case in the rougher parts of Copenhagen. From the start, with *Den krossade tanghästen* (1998; *Detective
Inspector Huss* 2003; *Sezione crimini violenti: Il primo caso
dell'ispettrice Huss* 2011), Tursten's novels are characterized by the

---

13   Cf. Sara Kärrholm, 'Kvinna på gränsen till nervsammanbrott: Åsa
     Nilsonne (1949–)' [Woman on the verge of a nervous breakdown: Åsa
     Nilsonne (b. 1949)], in *Tretton svenska deckardamer* [Thirteen Swedish
     crime ladies] (Lund BTJ Förlag, 2009), pp 184–98 (p. 195).
14   Kerstin Bergman, 'Crime Fiction as Popular Science: The Case of Åsa
     Nilsonne', in *Codex and Code: Aesthetics, Language and Politics in an
     Age of Digital Media*, ed. by Kerstin Bergman et.al. (Linköping: Linköping
     University Electronic Press, 2009), pp. 193–207 (p. 197) http://www.
     ep.liu.se/ecp/042/017/ecp0942017.pdf [accessed 20 September 2012].

contrast between Huss's often raw and violent working environment and extensive depiction of her cosy family life. Like Marklund, Tursten often highlights the struggle of balancing work and family responsibilities, but compared to Marklund's Annika Bengtzon, Huss's situation is much less conflict-ridden. Her family tends to be loving and very supportive, and even though in some of the novels they also get involved in the crime cases, the reader can rest assured that in the end they are there for each other. Huss also resembles Bengtzon in that she is very much of a hard-boiled hero type, who always stands up for herself and her cases against figures of authority and tough criminals alike, and at times she also projects a feminist outlook. Both women detectives also tend to end up in grave danger, but as a former European jujitsu champion, Huss is well able to defend herself whenever necessary. While belonging primarily to the police procedural genre, the early Huss novels are often inspired by the British whodunit tradition and the psychological thriller, while some of the later novels show greater ambitions to depict contemporary society and current issues, for example human-trafficking in *En man med litet ansikte* (2007, A man with a small face) and net-grooming in *Det lömska nätet* (2008, The insidious net).[15] Many of the novels about Irene Huss have also been adapted for film and television, and what is striking about the film versions is that they are much more violent than most other visualizations of Swedish police series.

While Nilsonne and Tursten use the big city and take inspiration primarily from the American police procedural tradition, Jansson, Jungstedt, and Läckberg all use a small town setting and as such display a stronger affinity with the British small-town police novels, and with the stories of the first major 'Queen' of Swedish crime fiction, Maria Lang, writing from 1949–1990. In the wake of Henning Mankell's Wallander novels from the 1990s, the small-town setting has once again been immensely popular among Swedish crime writers, women and men alike. Almost every corner of Sweden now has its 'local' crime writer. Anna Jansson and Mari Jungstedt both set their novels primarily on the island of Gotland, in the Baltic Sea on

---

15   Cf. Gunilla Wedding, 'När tonårsmamman blev deckarhjälte: Helene Tursten (1954–)' [When the mother of teenagers became a crime hero], in *Tretton svenska deckardamer* [Thirteen Swedish crime ladies] (Lund BTJ Förlag, 2009), pp. 219–237 (pp. 224–226, 232).

the east coast of Sweden.[16] Jansson's protagonist is Detective Inspector Maria Wern, who has a troubled private life and eventually gets a divorce. In many of the Wern novels Jansson draws on her background in the health care sector. Also, psychological explanations are commonly found in all her novels, and some of them display strong influences from the whodunit. Both these elements are particularly noticeable in *Inte ens det förflutna* (2008, Not even the past), where Maria Wern together with a group of women partake in a kind of survival course in ecological living, located on the isolated, uninhabited island of Gotska Sandön, close to Gotland. With no means of communication with the outside world the women are left stranded on the island, and it soon transpires that there must be a murderer among them.

The isolated island is also an important image in Jungstedt's novels, where Gotland is portrayed almost as a self-enclosed universe, where the outside world hardly exists.[17] Jungstedt's two protagonists are both male: Johan Berg, who like Jungstedt herself is a journalist, and Anders Knutas, Detective Superintendent of the Gotland Police, and they first meet in Jungstedt's *Den du inte ser* (2003; *Unseen* 2005). The use of the police procedural genre, but focusing more on one protagonist than on the team, has become increasingly common in Swedish crime fiction, sometimes in combination with adding an external, non-police hero who, often somewhat reluctantly, works together and/or in parallel with the police protagonist.[18] The Gotland of Jungstedt's novels is very much a tourist paradise and numerous pages are dedicated to descriptions of the island's attractive setting, and in particular of its popular tourist spots. There is, however, no reason for any potential Gotland tourists to be frightened, as the motives behind the crimes in Jungstedt's novels can always be traced

---

16   Jansson's first novels are set on the mainland, but use the same police protagonist who eventually moves to Gotland, where the rest of the series takes place.

17   I have previously presented Jungstedt's authorship more extensively in Swedish in 'Isolerad idyll och svart barndom: Marie Jungstedt (1962–)' [Isolated idyll and dark childhood: Mari Jungstedt (b. 1962)], in *Tretton svenska deckardamer* [Thirteen Swedish crime ladies] (Lund: BTJ förlag, 2009), pp. 96–111; and in 'The Well-Adjusted Cops of the New Millennium: Neo-Romantic Tendencies in the Swedish Police Procedural', in *Scandinavian Crime Fiction*, ed. Andrew Nestingen och Paula Arvas (Cardiff: University of Wales Press, 2011), pp. 34–45.

18   Bergman, 'Beyond Stieg Larsson', p. 294.

back to the criminals' personal past, and no 'strangers' are ever in danger.[19] While it is not uncommon for male Swedish crime writers to use women protagonists, it is rarer among women writers like Jungstedt to use mainly male investigators in the central roles. The female stereotypes – all women in Jungstedt's novels are heavily associated with motherhood, small children, sensuality, and caring qualities – and the lack of feminist viewpoints in her novels is, however, quite typical for the women writers of this generation, where primarily Marklund and Trosell stand out for their feminist perspectives.[20]

Camilla Läckberg has been one of the very best-selling Swedish crime writers of the early 2000s, and she has also given Marklund a match in that she is the woman writer getting most attention by the Swedish media. To an even greater extent than Marklund, Läckberg, with her background in accounting, has also taken advantage of the possibilities provided by the media, making sure of getting herself and her books maximum exposure.[21] Sara Kärrholm concludes that Läckberg 'wants to earn a good living for herself and she does not want to apologize for being a woman, for writing in a lowbrow genre or for being successful', and continues: 'This can be seen as a feminist agenda, although not as explicitly political as Marklund's'.[22] Although one might agree with Kärrholm up to a point, it is difficult to categorize all of Läckberg's media presence as being feminist-inspired, and her novels, which tend to promote traditional family values and gender stereotypes, certainly resist such categorization. Like Jungstedt, Läckberg works with two protagonists, in her case one woman, Erika Falck, who is an author, and one man, Falck's husband, Patrik Hedström, a police officer in the small town of Tanumshede, close to Fjällbacka on the west coast of Sweden, where the couple live and the novels are set. The two, who were childhood friends, become reacquainted in the first novel of the series, *Isprinsessan* (2003; *The Ice Princess* 2008; *La principessa di ghiaccio* 2010), and they are soon married and have a family. While Hedström in his official capacity is part of local murder investigations, Falck's curiosity tends to get her involved too, as she conducts re-

---

19   Bergman, 'Isolerad idyll', pp. 103–105.
20   Cf. ibid., pp. 107–109.
21   Kärrholm, 'Swedish Queens', pp. 138–141.
22   Ibid., p. 142.

search for one of her books, often related to some unsolved crime of the past. The two investigators then head off in different directions, until eventually past and present is united and the crime can be solved. Much page space is also dedicated to the couple's family life, of which the children are the centre, and whenever there is a character in one of Läckberg's novels who is not fond of or interested in children, he or she is certain to be the villain. Similar to Ystad on Sweden's south coast, where Mankell's Wallander novels are set, Fjällbacka, the setting of Läckberg's novels, has also turned into a popular site for crime fiction tourism. This is something that Läckberg has actively encouraged and contributed to, for example, by promoting the village on her website and by publishing two cookbooks with a strong local focus.[23]

While Nilsonne, Tursten, Jansson, Jungstedt, and Läckberg all belong to the police procedural genre, Inger Frimansson's, Karin Alvtegen's, and Åsa Larsson's novels can be better placed in the psychological thriller genre. Like Marklund and Jungstedt, Frimansson has a background in journalism, but she made her debut as a novelist as early as 1984. After writing mainstream fiction for many years, she published her first crime novel, *Handdockan* (1992, The puppet) in 1992, but it was not until 1998 that she had her big breakthrough as a crime writer with *Godnatt min älskade* (*Good Night, My Darling* 2007). For this novel she received the Best Swedish Crime Novel Award, The Golden Crowbar, by The Swedish Academy of Detection (Svenska Deckarakademin), an honour that was bestowed on her again in 2005 for *Skuggan i vattnet* (*The Shadow in the Water* 2008), and that few other women crime writers have received.[24] Frimansson is known for her psychological depth and her novels often portray strong characters, balancing on the edge of sanity and the law, who often have traumatic pasts that are used as the explanation for why they end up crossing the line. Many of Frimansson's crime novels address the issues of how far people can be pushed before they crack and what people are capable of if put to the test. But it is

---

23   Ethnologist Carina Sjöholm discusses the Läckberg tourism in *Litterära resor: Turism i spåren efter böcker, filmer och författare* [Literary journeys: Tourism tracing novels, films and authors] (Gothenburg/Stockholm: Makadam, 2011), pp. 87–119.

24   Since the award was instituted in 1982, the only other women writers to receive it are Kerstin Ekman in 1993, Aino Trosell in 2000, and Åsa Larsson in 2004 and 2012.

in the depiction of her complex characters that Frimansson's real strengths lie, something for which she has been widely acknowledged in Sweden, also by readers other than traditional crime fiction aficionados. Most of Frimansson's crime novels are set in or around Hässelby, a suburb on the outskirts of Stockholm. She uses the idyllic setting as kind of a microcosm, where anything might exist and be possible below the finely polished surface, and she investigates what could happen when people fail to conform to the implicit expectations of society.

Karin Alvtegen's novels also focus on protagonists who do not really fit into society, and who just happen to do something that turns out to be irrevocable and changes their whole world and, as in Frimansson's stories, it is mostly childhood experiences that have turned the individual into who he or she is today. Sometimes, as in *Skugga* (2007; *Shadow* 2009; *Ombra* 2010), it is even suggested that traumas and character traits can be inherited by successive generations. A Swedish literary critic has described Alvtegen as 'an investigative author who conducts fundamental psychological and social research, using the individual as an object of the study'.[25] This is a fitting description, as Alvtegen already from her debut novel, *Skuld* (1998; *Guilt* 2004), has created suspense by creating a web of lies and secrets that eventually almost take on a life of their own, leaving the characters of the novel helpless and scared, as they approach their breaking-point.

Åsa Larsson's novels are not as clear-cut psychological thrillers as Frimansson's and Alvtegen's crime novels mostly are. Instead Larsson mixes the psychological genre with elements taken primarily from the police procedural, and her novels always contain police investigations. In the first novel, *Solstorm* (2003; *Sun Storm/The Savage Altar* 2006; *Tempesta solare* 2005), Larsson's primary investigative protagonist, Rebecca Martinsson, who is a tax lawyer just like the author who invented her, returns to her roots in Kiruna, a small mining community in the very north of Sweden. In the novels, Martinsson also cooperates with another woman, the tough, local police officer Anna-Maria Mella, who as deuteragonist, receives somewhat

---

25 Marie Peterson, 'Hålla huvudet kallt: Karin Alvtegen (1965–)' [To keep a cool head: Karin Alvtegen (b. 1965)], in *Tretton svenska deckardamer* [Thirteen Swedish crime ladies] (Lund BTJ Förlag, 2009), pp. 31–46 (p. 35), my translation.

less space in most of the novels, but then comes to the fore in *Svart stig* (2006; *The Black Path* 2008; *Sentiero nero* 2009), as Martinsson has to spend time in a psychiatric ward, trying to recover from traumatic experiences in the two previous novels. Martinsson and Mella are both strong women, but they are also opposites in many ways. While Martinsson is the quiet loner, Mella is a much more boisterous and social character, and Larsson exploits their differences to create contrasts and to question expectations as to how women should be and behave. While all women in Larsson's novels tend to be strong, her male characters are often weaker and tend to be very lonely. Larsson's crime novels are all set in or around Kiruna, and many of them address issues stemming from life in a small, close-knit community, where religion and social expectations play an important part. Additionally, Larsson often lets her stories cross the boundaries of realism, and allows her dead to exist in a state of limbo, from where they can observe and comment on what happens, as well as provide the reader with additional information about what actually happened.[26] Other unexpected observers in the stories are birds, who can see both the dead and the living and who sometimes even actively try to direct the attention of the investigators towards things important for making the investigation move forward. Other animals are also given much attention, and both animals and nature in general are equipped with a soul in Larsson's novels. Furthermore, like Frimansson and Alvtegen, Larsson is a master of style, often praised for her innovative and complex language.

Aino Trosell, the remaining author who belongs to Marklund's generation, is also the most original of the group. Like Frimansson, Trosell had a long writing career behind her before turning to crime fiction. Trosell was one of the most successful Swedish authors in the genre of proletarian realism, a genre she had been writing in since the late 1970s, then made her debut as a crime writer with *Ytspänning* (1999, Surface tension). Unlike the other authors using women as investigative protagonists, Trosell is not providing her readers with an investigator who is slim and pretty and a successful professional in her late thirties or early forties and having previously had an academic education. Instead, from her second novel *Om*

---

26 This is a narrative tool extensively used also by Mons Kallentoft (b. 1968) in his police novels about Inspector Malin Fors and her colleagues at the Linköping police station.

hjärtat ännu slår (2000, If the heart still beats) onwards, Trosell has chosen a truly ordinary, middle-aged working-class woman as her investigator. In novels with a formal inspiration from the whodunit genre and a strong connection to the landscape and history of the province of Dalarna (Dalecarlia) in central Sweden, she lets her protagonist, Siv Dahlin, move in and out of unemployment and between different kinds of work. Whether as a tannery worker in *Om hjärtat ännu slår*, or working in the kitchen of a remote conference facility in *Järngreppet* (2008, The iron grip), Dahlin observes her surroundings from an underdog's perspective, while being almost invisible as a working class woman, mostly in the service industry (in other novels she works, for example, as a hotel cleaner or as a health visitor). Trosell's novels display a strong combination of feminist and class critique, unique in Swedish crime fiction.[27]

Many of the writers of Marklund's generation have shared a strong bond of solidarity, creating groupings and encouraging each other in a shared attempt to become an integrated part of the hitherto completely male-dominated Swedish crime fiction market, something, too, that many of these women authors have testified about in such affirmative terms. Parallel with these attempts on the part of the authors, however, is the fact that the Swedish media have also often tried to treat the women crime writers as one single group, often referring to them as 'The Crime Queens'. While perhaps beneficial for the emergence of such a strong presence of women on the Swedish market, this is simultaneously a way of creating anonymity and ignoring the specific qualities of each individual woman author. Meanwhile, the same Swedish media have always treated the male crime writers as individuals, thus accrediting each and every one of them with a stronger unique identity and importance on the Swedish literary scene.

The 'Daughters' of the Marklund Generation

The authors of Marklund's generation discussed above began their crime writing careers a little before or a little after the turn of the Millennium and have been active ever since, remaining prominent on the Swedish crime fiction scene and in the Swedish best-

---

27   Cf. Bergman, 'Beyond Stieg Larsson', p. 298.

seller lists. In the last few years, they have also been joined by a new, second generation of women crime writers, who towards the end of the first decade of the 2000s began to become an important part of Swedish crime fiction. Most notable among them – and being authors who seem to be here to stay – are Kristina Ohlsson (b. 1979), Carin Gerhardsen (b. 1962), the sister duo of Camilla Grebe (b. 1968) and Åsa Träff (b. 1970), and Katarina Wennstam (b. 1973).[28]

Ohlsson and Gerhardsen write quite traditional police procedurals set in urban Stockholm, but what makes them stand out are their police heroes, in particular the women officers of their police teams. Ohlsson is a political scientist with a background in intelligence work, and she lets her woman protagonist Fredrika Bergman share her academic perspective. Fredrika Bergman is a young criminologist who is brought in to work with the police in Ohlsson's first novel, *Askungar* (2009; *Unwanted* 2012; *Indesiderata* 2010). Unlike many of the woman heroes of Swedish police novels, Fredrika Bergman does not have a traditional family, but is engaged in a long-term relationship with an older, married man, while at the same time dreaming of having children. In *Tusenskönor* (2010; *Silenced* 2012; *Fiore di ghiaccio* 2012), she ends up becoming pregnant under less than ideal circumstances, as the older man who is the father of her child is implicated in a murder investigation. While her first three novels are firmly set in the police tradition, Ohlsson's fourth novel, *Paradisoffer* (2012, Victims of Paradise), belongs instead to the thriller genre, as the author draws on her experiences of working with counter terrorism in the OSCE (the Organization for Security and Co-operation in Europe).[29] By contrast, Carin Gerhardsen's woman officer, Petra Westman, is no academic, but shares the same outsider status held by Ohlsson's woman hero, in that she is something of a loner. In Gerhardsen's first novel, *Pepparkakshuset* (2008;

---

28   Many more could have been mentioned. In a more extensive survey, for example, Karin Alfredsson (b. 1953) would have been included. Alfredsson made her debut in 2006 and uses feminist perspectives as she writes about woman medical doctor Elin Elg in novels with diverse international settings. Also, one of the author's behind the recently very successful crime writer Lars Kepler (pen name for Alexander Ahndoril b. 1967, and Alexandra Coelho Ahndoril b. 1966) is a woman.

29   Ohlsson's most recent novel, *Davidsstjärnor* (2013, Stars of David), mixes the police genre with thriller elements.

The Gingerbread House 2012; *La casa di pan di zenzero* 2011), Westman is drugged and raped by a man she meets in a bar, and her own private attempts to solve this crime and to get revenge runs parallel to the different police investigations throughout Gerhardsen's series.

Following the success of Marklund's journalist detective, many authors of her generation followed her path by similarly depicting their women police officers as married with children, struggling to balance work pressures with family life. The women heroes of Ohlsson's and Gerhardsen's novels, however, both depart from this normative family situation, and this is a tendency visible in much of the Swedish crime fiction from the end of the first decade of the 2000s, a tendency most likely inspired by the many international examples of more hard-boiled and eccentric woman heroes from the 2000s, in conjunction with the success of Stieg Larsson's (1954-2004) Lisbeth Salander character. In her later novels, Marklund herself has also allowed her protagonist to become more and more lonely and eccentric, letting her go through a divorce and moving the focus away from her relationship with her children, and thus she can also be regarded as part of the trend to create more original women heroes in Swedish crime fiction.

The woman hero of Camilla Grebe and Åsa Träff's crime novels, psychologist Siri Bergman, can also be placed in this category of mostly single, somewhat eccentric women characters. Bergman has become a loner with serious commitment issues after her husband committed suicide. In the first novel of the series, *Någon sorts frid* (2009; *Some Kind of Peace* 2012; *Nel buio* 2011), she is also targeted by a violent stalker, and in each novel she ends up in trouble and involved in a criminal case as a result of something involving her clients. Grebe and Träff's novels belong primarily in the psychological thriller genre, and their use of the therapeutic session as a narrative element is relatively unique in the Swedish context, probably drawing on Åsa Träff's work experience as a psychologist specializing in cognitive behavioural therapy. From a feminist point of view, Grebe and Träff's second novel, *Bittrare än döden* (2010; *More bitter than death* 2013; *Trauma* 2013) is particularly interesting. There, Siri Bergman leads a support group for abused women, and the authors thus highlight the humiliation, violence, and sacrifices these women have been subjected to and put up with in the name of love – from date rapes and incest, to decades stuck in violent relationships. The main theme of the novel is the destructive power of 'love', and the mechanisms that make women prone to suffer this kind of abuse are thus criticized.

Even stronger feminist ambitions are to be found in the crime novels by former crime journalist Katarina Wennstam. In her trilogy of crime novels featuring district attorney Madeleine Edwards as the main detective, Wennstam explores power relationships and the abuse of power in traditionally male-dominated professions. Wennstam focuses particularly on men's power over women and their bodies. Her first crime novel, *Smuts* (2007, Dirt), deals with the legal profession, *Dödergök* (2008, Omen of death) with the police, and *Alfahannen* (2010, The alpha male) focuses on the film industry. Recently, Wennstam has also started another crime fiction trilogy with similarly feminist ambitions. *Svikaren* (2012, The quitter), the first novel in the new series, features two women protagonists, a lawyer and a police detective, and is a critical exploration of violence and intolerance in the world of male sports.

The success of this second generation of Swedish women crime writers thus seems to bode well for the future of women writers in Swedish crime fiction, in spite of the anti-feminist backlash that has permeated Swedish society in the last decade. The attempts made by these writers to develop the genre in fresh directions and to make feminism a more prominent feature of the genre – most likely a reaction spurred by the growing post-feminist tendencies in Swedish society – also augurs well for the genre in years to come. During the emergence of this generation of women writers, the Swedish crime fiction market has also begun to change again, not least as seen through the Swedish media. Now, rather than it being characterized by a division between men and women authors, there seems to be a strong focus on a new generation, consisting of authors of both sexes. Whereas the women writers of Marklund's generation were united in the ambition to create a place for themselves on a male-dominated crime fiction scene, this new generation appears to be equally supportive of their group, but the difference is that they share an ambition to conquer the world market, a market big enough for everyone, and where a larger number of visible writers can contribute to strengthening the 'trademark' of Swedish crime fiction, rather than create competition and exclusion. While the male authors of the previous generation still hold their single status, many of the women writers of Marklund's generation have tended to join and/or be included in this new 'crime writers' community', sharing the international ambitions of the new generation.

Despite the diversity of the Swedish women writers of the past decade and a half – in terms of sub-genres, characters, and agendas – a few common denominators can be identified among these authors. Many of them tend to follow in the footsteps of Marklund, portraying strong and independent women heroes. Although the struggle of balancing career and family life has been a persistent theme, there is also a recent tendency to leave this issue behind and create sovereign women heroes who struggle instead with being women in patriarchal work places and in patriarchal society, while simultaneously fighting their own personal demons.[30] Swedish society is still not gender-equal and Swedish women today are still vulnerable and abused within the patriarchal structures of society, where having children is still a trap for women, and where informal male networks are still a fundamental part of many workplaces. As late as the beginning of 2013, one of the main public debates in Sweden concerned the problem of massive hatred of, and severe threats towards, publicly visible and opinionated women in Sweden. Whether the Swedish women crime writers are intentionally addressing feminist issues or not, the image of being a woman in Sweden, as seen through the crime novels of both these generations of writers, is often still quite depressing.

Furthermore, psychological perspectives have been important for many of these authors, whether they explore the mind of criminals, as Inger Frimansson and Karin Alvtegen do in many of their novels, or explain criminal behavior as being a result of childhood traumas, as for example in Mari Jungstedt and Camilla Läckberg, or combine the two, as sister duo Camilla Grebe and Åsa Träff do in their novels about the psychologist Siri Bergman.[31] Additionally, many of the woman detective heroes, particularly in novels by the second gener-

---

30   Cf. Bergman, 'Lisbeth Salander', passim.
31   The psychological thriller is one of the only crime fiction sub-genres that has traditionally been a woman-dominated genre (cf. Stephen Knight, *Crime Fiction 1800–2000: Detection, Death, Diversity* (Houndsmills/New York: Palgrave Macmillan, 2004), p. 151), and many of the Norwegian and British woman authors who were popular in Sweden during the 1990s, and who have most likely inspired Swedish women writers, utilized the psychological thriller genre.

ation of women writers, evidently struggle with personal psychological traumas and issues.

As reflected throughout this book, there are many strong trends in Swedish crime fiction from the past decade, but *the* most notable trend is unquestionably the influx and presence of so many women crime writers, described in the present chapter.

V

STOCKHOLM – THE URBAN SPACE OF CRIME: *FROM STIEG TRENTER TO JENS LAPIDUS*

The urban setting traditionally characterizes the police novel, and Stockholm in particular has been a popular choice among Swedish crime writers. Today the capital city is also the scene of many of the most interesting developments in Swedish crime fiction, such as the hard-boiled novels of Jens Lapidus, narrated from the criminals' point of view. The focus of this chapter is on the use that Lapidus and other writers make of the urban space.

Stockholm, the beautiful Swedish capital located on a number of islands in Lake Mälaren, has always been important in Swedish literature. There are numerous authors famous for having portrayed the milieu of the city – from Carl Michael Bellman (1740–95) in the 1700s, August Strindberg (1849–1912), and Hjalmar Söderberg (1869–1941) around the turn of the 19th century, to Stieg Larsson (1954–2004) in the early 2000s. In Swedish crime fiction, the city has been particularly prominent, and many of the best-known authors associated with the city are in fact crime writers.[1] In recent decades, in particular, the prevalence of the capital metropolis as a favoured setting for crime fiction has stemmed naturally from the fact that the police procedural sub-genre has occupied such a privileged position in Sweden, the urban space being a typical setting for that genre and Stockholm being the nation's biggest city.[2]

---

1   This chapter builds primarily on my article, 'From National Authority to Urban Underbelly: Negotiations of Power in Stockholm Crime Fiction', in *Crime Fiction in the City: Capital Crimes*, ed. by Lucy Andrew and Catherine Phelps (Cardiff: University of Wales Press, 2013), pp. 65–84.

2   The Swedish preference for the police procedural is further discussed in chapter 2.

Discussing the importance of place in crime fiction, David Geherin notes that 'in realistic crime fiction, there is often an intimate
connection between crime and its milieu, which thus comes to play
a prominent thematic role in such novels'.[3] The detailed depiction of
setting has been a characteristic feature throughout Swedish literary
history, and it has even been considered one of the two most typical
elements of Swedish crime fiction, the other being the melancholic
detective with health problems.[4] In the introduction to *Following the
Detectives: Real Locations in Crime Fiction* (2010), Maxim
Jakubowski stresses that the city 'becomes an extra character in the
stories'.[5] This has certainly been true for Stockholm, in that it has
played an indispensable role in numerous Swedish crime novels.

Already in Prins Pierre's (pen name for Fredrik Lindholm 1861–
1938) *Stockholms-detektiven* (1893, The Stockholm detective), often considered to be the first Swedish crime novel, the city is established as a centre of power, authority, and the hub of investigative
skills, as a detective from the big city is called in to investigate what
lies behind a mysterious factory fire in the small town of Eskilstuna,
west of Stockholm. In her recent book on Stockholm-based crime
fiction, Alexandra Borg attempts to trace crime fiction set in the capital even further back, as she examines short stories published in
Swedish newspapers during the nineteenth century. Borg finds a
large number of sensationalist stories with crime elements: some depict the dubious nightlife of the big city in a way reminiscent of the
English Newgate novels, some are police memoirs, and others again
are primarily fictionalized accounts of real crimes.[6] Nevertheless,
although they all portray crime and criminality in Stockholm, the
majority of these texts can be regarded as belonging to sensationalist genres that preceded proper crime fiction, rather than actually be-

---

3   David Geherin, *Scene of the Crime: The Importance of Place in Crime
     and Mystery Fiction* (Jefferson, NC: McFarland, 2008), p. 8.
4   Bo Lundin, *The Swedish Crime Story*, trans. by Anna Lena Ringarp,
     Ralph A Wilson, and Bo Lundin (Bromma: Jury, 1981), pp. 8–10.
5   Maxim Jakubowski, 'Introduction: A Sense of Place', in *Following the
     Detectives: Real Locations in Crime Fiction*, ed. by Maxim Jakubowski
     (London/Cape Town/Sydney/Auckland: New Holland, 2010), pp. 12–13
     (p. 12).
6   Cf. Alexandra Borg, *Brottsplats Stockholm: Urban kriminallitteratur
     1851–2011* [Crime scene Stockholm: Urban crime fiction 1851–2011]
     (Stockholm: Stockholmia Förlag, 2012), pp. 89–105.

longing to the genre. Still, since the late nineteenth century, Stockholm has remained the city *par préférence* for many Swedish crime writers: Stieg Trenter (1914–67), Maj Sjöwall (b. 1935) and Per Wahlöö (1926–75), Liza Marklund (b. 1962), Stieg Larsson, and Jens Lapidus (b. 1974) being some of the best-known exponents. Today, Lapidus arguably provides the most interesting portrayal of Stockholm, as he uses new perspectives, so different from his many predecessors, thereby enabling his readers to see the city in a novel and distinctive light.

Crime in an Idyllic City: Trenter's Stockholm

One of the most influential forerunners of Lapidus in Stockholm crime fiction was Stieg Trenter, a leading crime writer during the Golden Age of the genre in the mid-twentieth century. Since his debut with *Ingen kan hejda döden* (1943, No one can stop death), Trenter has been regarded as one of the best Swedish authors of all times when it comes to describing Stockholm. He has also been named as the first Swedish writer to use the capital city as the setting for crime fiction in a truly successful manner, to the point that Bo Lundin calls the emphasis on setting in Swedish crime fiction as 'the "Trenter Syndrome" for [Trenter being] its foremost proponent'.[7] It has also been suggested that perhaps Stockholm 'is the true protagonist in [Trenter's] novels, rather than the detectives, victims, and murderers'.[8] Besides Stockholm, there are also two important detective protagonists in Trenter's novels, Harry Friberg who is a photographer, and his friend Detective Inspector Vesper Johnson. Trenter portrays Stockholm primarily through the eyes of the photographer, and the resulting image is of a city made up of details, lights, and shadows. Trenter did extensive research into the Stockholm locations, together with photographer Karl Werner Gullers (1916–98), who was also the major source of inspiration in the creation of the character of Harry Friberg. Trenter's Stockholm is an attractive and

---

7   Carl Olov Sommar, 'Stieg Trenter som stockholmsskildrare' [Stieg Trenter as a portrayer of Stockholm], in *Sankt Eriks Årsbok 1984* [Sankt Erik's yearbook 1984], ed. by Björn Hallerstedt (Stockholm: Samfundet S:t Erik, 1984), pp. 173–86 (p. 173); Lundin, p. 8.
8   Ibid., p. 175, my translation.

idyllic city, where well-known locations are often used for crime scenes, something that made the novels seem even more realistic to Swedish readers familiar with the scenery.[9] This was certainly a crucial factor behind Trenter's immense popularity.

Ulf Carlsson suggests that what makes Trenter's depiction of Stockholm unique is that he manages to combine the sense of a limited space central to the whodunit genre, with the depiction of Stockholm as a large, modern city.[10] Trenter was a big supporter of the modern Swedish welfare state, an ideological system that at the time could be well represented by the combination of the idyllic and the traditional with the new and the urban.[11] The novels are often set in summer, a time when the grittiness of the crimes can be contrasted with the glittering waters and the sunny green hills of the city. In portraying Stockholm, he uses a photographer's perspectives and often combines close-ups with descriptions of the view from the spot in question, thereby creating a more complex image of the location. The choice to make Friberg a keen driver allows panning shots of the city, described as it stretches out beyond his car windows.

Trenter used well-known locations in the centre of Stockholm for his novels, as did one of his most successful contemporaries, Maria Lang (pen name for Dagmar Lange, 1914–91). Whilst she mainly portrayed the Swedish countryside and small town life, Lang also set some of her most famous whodunits in Stockholm: *Intrigernas hus* (1969; The house of intrigues), which takes place in the Royal Opera House, and *Se, döden på dig väntar* (1955; *Death Awaits Thee* 1967) which is set in Drottningholm Palace Theatre, the sixteenth-century theatre building adjacent to Drottningholm Palace (the palace now home to the King and Queen of Sweden). Lang's novels contain excellent portrayals of these famous buildings, al-

9   Lundin, p. 21.
10   Ulf Carlsson, 'Stieg Trenter's 40-tal: Medelklassens hopp och ängslan' [Stieg Trenter's 1940s: The hope and fear of the middle class], in *Möten: Festskrift till Anders Palm* [Encounters: Festschrift in honour of Anders Palm], ed. by Karin Nykvist et.al. (Lund: Anacapri förlag, 2007), pp. 385–94 (pp. 388–89).
11   Cf. Sara Kärrholm, *Konsten att lägga pussel: Deckaren och besvärjandet av ondskan i folkhemmet* [The art of doing a jig-saw puzzle: The detective novel and the conjuring up of evil in the Swedish Welfare State] (Stockholm/Stehag: Symposion, 2005), p. 278.

though her descriptions of the city that surrounds them is less impressive and effective than Trenter's.

The City and the Disintegrating Welfare State: Sjöwall and Wahlöö's Stockholm

If Trenter truly put Stockholm on the Swedish crime fiction map, it was Maj Sjöwall and Per Wahlöö who made the city an internationally-renowned crime-fiction location. With their series of ten police novels, *Roman om ett brott* (1965–75; *The Story of a Crime* 1967–76; *Martin Beck indaga a Stoccolma* 1973–2011), they made Stockholm the number one setting for Swedish crime fiction for decades to come. Sjöwall and Wahlöö's ambition was to use the crime genre to highlight the disintegration of the Swedish welfare state.[12] Choosing the police procedural genre and the urban setting was a natural consequence of that ambition, and Sjöwall and Wahlöö's Stockholm displays the symptoms of a society that is far from well. The city is the epitome of the disintegrating welfare state, and its physical reconstruction and social degradation are said to be the result of the greed and corruption of its capitalist ethos. Bo Lundin has suggested that Sjöwall and Wahlöö 'achieve some of their most significant effects' by contrast: by alluding to the idyllic Stockholm of Trenter's novels, while simultaneously 'showing the old settings in a totally different light'.[13] Throughout the Sjöwall and Wahlöö series, there is a nostalgia for a lost past, often illustrated by the old Stockholm which is changing and disappearing. David Geherin has emphasized how the novels show the city's changes to be the consequence of an incompetent government, as '[i]rreplaceable old apartment buildings give way to sterile office monstrosities; lively neighborhoods are reduced to rubble', and the new 'city's hard naked surfaces of metal, glass, and concrete [embody] the dehumanization that inevitably accompanies the changes'.[14] This also affects the people of the city, and many of the descriptions of Stockholm found throughout Sjöwall and Wahlöö's series are provided as one of the characters observes the city from a

---

12   Sjöwall and Wahlöö's ambition to convey a political message to their readers is also addressed in chapter 2.

13   Lundin, p. 21.

14   Geherin, p. 164.

window, something that Alexandra Borg interprets as signifying the alienation of the modern city's inhabitants.[15]

Furthermore, as Alison Young has suggested, the setting in crime fiction is 'the scene of the interpretation of hierarchies of social groups'.[16] In Sjöwall and Wahlöö's case, it is clear that the Stockholm cityscape is used to convey the authors' analysis of the Swedish class system, as different areas of the city are repeatedly contrasted in order to illustrate class differences. In *Terroristerna* (1975; *The Terrorists* 1976; *Terroristi* 2011), it is primarily the district of Djursholm that represents the upper class, while the dilapidated buildings of Södermalm are associated with the working class and with Sweden's less privileged citizens. Specific homes are also made to illustrate these differences and to illustrate different political ideologies, as well. For example, the girlfriend of Martin Beck, the police protagonist of the series, runs a housing co-operative, something that demonstrates her socialist allegiance, whilst a porn producer, who is portrayed as one of the evil representatives of capitalism, lives in a modern, architect-designed home that has sharp angles and enormous glass windows. After the porn producer has been murdered, Beck visits his house and observes that it 'seemed bare and inhospitable, and the ultramodern and certainly extremely costly décor seemed designed more for show than for comfort and warmth'.[17] Furthermore, the man who killed the porn producer and the young woman who ends up shooting the Prime Minister of Sweden both live in old buildings and are associated with environmental consciousness and gardening, something that contributes to establishing them as essentially good people and victims of society, despite their crimes.[18] There is actually a general tendency throughout Sjöwall and Wahlöö's series for old buildings to be associated with virtue and nostalgia for the past, while modern glass and steel buildings tend to represent evil.[19] Contrasting present and new

---

15   Cf. Borg, p. 198.

16   Alison Young, *Imagining Crime: Textual Outlaws and Criminal Conversations* (London, Thousand Oaks and New Delhi: SAGE Publications, 1996), p. 90.

17   Maj Sjöwall and Per Wahlöö, *The Terrorists*, trans. Joan Tate (New York: Vintage Books, 2010), p. 75.

18   How these two murderers are established as fundamentally good people has already been discussed in chapter 2.

19   Stieg Larsson uses the same architectural symbolism in *Män som hatar kvinnor* (2001; *The Girl with the Dragon Tattoo* 2008; *Uomini che odiano*

with past and old, Sjöwall and Wahlöö use their Stockholm settings in order to accentuate both class differences and the moral status of the people who inhabit the city's various dwellings.

From the 1970s and up until the turn of the millennium, numerous Swedish authors have written crime fiction set in Stockholm containing social critique. Most of these authors might not have been as focused in their criticism as Sjöwall and Wahlöö, but their use of the police genre and of the capital city setting is often reminiscent of that of their predecessors. Some of these authors are Olof Svedelid (1932–2008), Leif G.W. Persson (b. 1945), Åsa Nilsonne (b. 1949), and Hans Holmér (1930–2002). Other authors have abandoned the police genre altogether but still use the Stockholm setting for their crime series, notably Jan Guillou (b. 1944) in his thrillers about Swedish special agent Carl Hamilton and Jan Mårtenson (b. 1933) in his whodunits about antiques dealer Johan Homan.

A City of Patriarchal Power Structures: Liza Marklund's Stockholm

As the turn of the millennium approached, the male dominance that had persisted among Swedish crime writers since the early days of crime fiction in the nineteenth century decreased, as the number of women writers in the genre grew substantially.[20] Liza Marklund is often regarded as a leading light for these developments, and in her crime novels about tabloid journalist Annika Bengtzon, Stockholm is the main location. During the time when Marklund was writing her first crime novel, *Sprängaren* (1998; *The Bomber* 2000/2011; *Delitto a Stoccolma* 2001), Stockholm was – unsuccessfully, as it turned out – applying to host the 2004 Summer Olympics. During the year of the application, violent attacks (among them a bomb explosion at Stockholm Stadium) were made against a num-

---

le donne 2008), cf. Kerstin Bergman,'From "The Case of the Pressed Flowers" to the Serial Killer's Torture Chamber: The Use and Function of Crime Fiction Sub-Genres in Stieg Larsson's *The Girl with the Dragon Tattoo*', in *Critical Insights: Crime and Detective Fiction*, ed. Rebecca Martin (Ipswich, MA: Salem Press, 2013), pp. 38–53 (pp. 48–49).

20   Cf. chapter 4.

ber of Swedish sports arenas, and *Sprängaren* was inspired by these real events. The novel depicts what could have happened if Stockholm had actually been selected to host the Olympics, and Marklund sets her novel in 2003, as the final preparations for the event are made in the Swedish capital.

As a consequence, the focus of Marklund's descriptions of Stockholm is to a great extent on sports arenas undergoing renovations and, in particular, on the (fictional) Olympic arena under construction.[21] Marklund thereby foregrounds the traditionally male-dominated construction business, and as two of the important characters of the novel are women in charge of construction projects related to the Olympic preparations, her focus is on how these women struggle to be respected, while being harassed by superiors and male employees alike. Maureen T. Reddy notes that in crime fiction with feminist ambitions it is common that when the villain is a woman, she is 'trying to end or avenge her own victimisation'.[22] Accordingly, the women in Marklund's novel, having fought patriarchal structures all their lives in order to reach the positions they are in, have evolved into merciless monsters. Parallel to the struggle of the two women, Marklund depicts similar problems that Annika Bengtzon experiences in the tabloid world. Luckily, however, Bengtzon has the committed support of her (male) editor-in-chief and, most of the time, of her family, something that prevents her from also turning monstrous.[23]

---

21   The English edition of Marklund's novel contains a map of central Stockholm where all the important locations of the novel are marked. See Liza Marklund, *The Bomber*, trans. by Neil Smith (London: Corgi Books, 2011), p. 6. The original Swedish novel contains no such map, as the Swedish readers are assumed to be familiar with the layout of the capital.

22   Maureen T. Reddy, 'Women detectives', in *The Cambridge Companion to Crime Fiction*, ed. by Martin Priestman (Cambridge: Cambridge University Press, 2003), pp. 191–207 (p. 198). That women heroes in crime fiction, despite constituting a progressive addition to the genre, still often need support by 'good' men in order to uphold their positions and be successful in their work, reflects that the world is still is to a large extent ruled by men.

23   In the later novels however, Bengtzon's relationships, both with her family and in the workplace, get increasingly complicated. Nevertheless, despite becoming increasingly lonely and eccentric, Bengtzon has remained an important feminist presence in Swedish crime fiction.

The close association between power and the cityscape in *Sprängaren* is foregrounded by the murderer's cherished relationship with buildings and architecture:

> Why did I choose to work with buildings? I love buildings! They speak to you in such an immediate, clear way. I love travelling, just to communicate with the buildings in new places, their shapes, their windows, their colours … their radiance. Inner courtyards give me a sexual thrill. Shivers run down my back when I travel through the Stockholm suburbs, washing hanging out to dry above railway lines, balconies leaning out.[24]

The murderer appears to have an intimate relationship with many of Stockholm's buildings, among them the City Hall, and these buildings seem to have the function of a calming, inner voice. Unfortunately, this voice is not strong enough, and in the end the murderer apologizes for blowing up the new Olympic arena while killing the women in charge of the Olympic preparations: 'That wasn't my intention, you understand. I didn't want to damage the stadium. Whatever had happened there wasn't the building's fault'.[25] Stockholm's physical manifestations are thus associated with benevolent qualities, while the people with power over them are characterized as villains.

This diverges both from Trenter's way of contrasting crimes with an idyllic Stockholm and Sjöwall and Wahlöö's way of letting the capital's spaces represent class differences and other evils resulting from capitalism. The latters' capitalist powers running the city are, in *Sprängaren,* replaced by patriarchal power systems, as Marklund uses the urban spaces primarily to discuss gender-related matters. Marklund's novels belong to the tradition of feminist adaptations of the hard-boiled crime genre, an urban genre where 'offenses in which the patriarchal power structure of contemporary society itself is potentially incriminated'.[26] Like Sjöwall and Wahlöö, Marklund explicitly uses the crime genre for critical purposes, stressing in a recent interview that 'I am absolutely a political writer. I use my novels to get a message across'.[27] The use of different Stockholm dis-

---

24 Marklund, p. 454.
25 Ibid., p. 475.
26 Priscilla L Walton and Manina Jones, *Detective Agency: Women Rewriting the Hard-Boiled Tradition* (Berkeley, Los Angeles and London: University of California Press, 1999), p. 4.
27 Quoted in Barry Forshaw, *Death in a Cold Climate: A Guide to Scandinavian Crime Fiction* (Basingstoke: Palgrave Macmillan, 2012), p. 90. For

tricts in order to illustrate class differences found in Sjöwall and
Wahlöö's novels, also characterizes in particular Marklund's later
novels, and most of her novels display an explicit critique of the
Swedish class system. This is particularly pertinent in the repeated
descriptions of how Annika Bengtzon with her working class background feels uncomfortable in the upper-class dwellings and con-
texts of her husband's family, while she simultaneously feels supe-
rior in relation to the artificiality of the same. And when, in *Nobels
testamente* (2006; *Last Will* 2012; *Il testamento di Nobel* 2009), she
buys her family a house in the affluent suburb of Djursholm, leaving
the apartment in central Stockholm behind, the contrast between
Bengtzon's class belonging and the alien and unfriendly character of
the new area and its inhabitants is striking.

Hide and Seek in the Urban Maze: Stieg Larsson's Stockholm

Power is commonly related to knowledge, and knowledge, in
turn, is generally dependent on the ability to access the whole picture. In crime fiction this is fundamental, not least when it comes to
the power held by detectives and criminals. The role of the urban
space is habitually used to illustrate, as well as to facilitate and/or to
obscure, the ability to establish knowledge through a full overview.
Leonard Lutwack concludes that in twentieth-century literature, the
streets of the city 'became a bewildering maze filled with the gro-
tesque horrors of a world dying of war, crime, and racial hatred'.[28]
The city as a maze is a common image used to illustrate the difficul-
ty of establishing knowledge and an overview, an image also frequently used in Swedish crime fiction. A recent and well-known example of this is Stieg Larsson's *Millennium* trilogy, where the urban
Stockholm cityscape is contrasted with the countryside. Larsson's
Stockholm is a veritable maze where people, and particularly Lisbeth Salander, one of the two investigative protagonists, can easily
hide and move around undetected, while the opposite is true of the
desolate island location used in *Män som hatar kvinnor* (2005, *The*

---

      more on Sjöwall and Wahlöö's purposes in using the crime genre, see
      chapter 2.
28   Leonard Lutwack, *The Role of Place in Literature* (Syracuse: Syracuse
      University Press, 1984), p. 234.

Girl with the Dragon Tattoo 2008; *Uomini che odiano le donne* 2008), of which the text provides a map, as if to make sure both readers and detectives know every nook and cranny of the island's geography, socially as well as physically.[29]

In crime fiction, the murderer can sometimes hide by blending into the city crowd.[30] However, as Alison Young notes, 'detective fiction subjects the hiding-places of the city and its crowds to the controlling gaze of the detective which ultimately allows no secret'.[31] In Larsson's novels, however, it is Salander, the enigmatic hacker detective, who can move around undetected in the city streets by blending into the crowd – whether in her youthful Goth outfit or dressed up to look like a plain business woman – or by using her various hiding places. The only person whose 'controlling gaze' can reveal Salander's secrets is her co-detective, Mikael Blomkvist. However, Salander's duality, her simultaneously being a detective and acting on the wrong side of the legal spectrum, explains how she is so successful in the hiding role. She is a child of the Stockholm streets, and these streets, using Young's words, consequently fulfil the 'promise to obliterate the details of the criminal in the crowd'.[32] Together, Blomkvist and Salander eventually divulge the bigger secrets of the city, as they expose the criminal activities and hide-outs of a clandestine faction of the Swedish security police, as well as the hidden illegal activities of two powerful Swedish businessmen.

A City Run by its Underbelly: Jens Lapidus's Stockholm

Until recently, Swedish crime writers have tended to depict Stockholm as a relatively isolated city, primarily of national interest.

---

29 Stieg Larsson, *The Girl With the Dragon Tattoo*, trans. by Reg Keeland (London: MacLehose Press/Quercus, 2008), pp. 101–104. The map is of course also a reference to the classical whodunit, a genre that Larsson explicitly evokes with the mystery set on the secluded island with its upper class inhabitants. In some English editions of Larsson's novels, Stockholm maps are also included, but these are not present in the original editions of the novels.

30 Gillian Mary Hanson, *City and Shore: The Function of Setting in the British Mystery* (Jefferson/London: McFarland, 2004), p. 6; Young, p. 86.

31 Young, p. 86–87.

32 Cf. ibid., p. 86.

This image is now changing: with globalization and growing migration, Swedish crime fiction has in the last decade increasingly addressed transnational, organized criminality. In Jens Lapidus's *Snabba cash* (2006; *Easy Money* 2011; *La traiettoria della neve* 2009), one of the Stockholm crime bosses explains:

> New times. New people. New ways of working [...]. Today, there are a lot more players on the Swedish field than there were when we began twenty years ago. Back then, it was just us and a couple of old bank robbers, Svartenbrandt and Clark Olofsson. But Sweden is different now. The MC gangs are here to stay. The youth and prison gangs are well organized; the EU dissolves the borders. Biggest change is that nowadays we're also competing with the Albanians, the Russian Mafia, a ton of nasty types from Estonia, just to name a few. It's not just Western Europe that's gotten smaller. The East is here. Globalization, yada yada.[33]

This new Stockholm and its new criminality represent the latest phase in the process of urban change depicted in modern Swedish crime fiction. The James Ellroy-inspired novels of Lapidus's 'Stockholm Noir' series – so far consisting of *Snabba cash*, *Aldrig fucka upp* (2008; *Never fuck up* 2013; *Mai far cazzate* 2010), and *Livet deluxe* (2011, Life deluxe; *Life deluxe* 2012) – keep a national focus in that they are centered on Stockholm, but Lapidus's way of depicting the city is still new to Swedish crime fiction and somehow places the city in a less isolated context. David Geherin stresses that in crime fiction, the city 'is often depicted as a center of corruption and decay, a place where crime, pollution, and general degradation of life are concentrated'.[34] This is an accurate description of Lapidus's Stockholm, where the majority of the protagonists are criminals. Furthermore, Lapidus's capital is a multi-cultural and multi-ethnic

---

33   Jens Lapidus, *Easy Money*, trans. Astri von Arbin Ahlander (London: Macmillan, 2012), p. 318. Lars-Inge Svartenbrandt and Clark Olofsson are two of Sweden's most notorious criminals. Svartenbrandt began robbing banks in the early 1960s, and is still active when not in prison – he has spent more than forty years in Swedish prisons ('Lars-Inge Svartenbrandt', in *Nationalencyklopedin* [The national encyclopedia] http://www.ne.se/lars-inge-svartenbrandt [accessed 21 February 2013]). Olofsson was charged in 1966 with the murder of a police officer, and has since been sentenced to more than fifty years in prison for different violent crimes ('Clark Olofsson', *Nationalencyklopedin* [The national encyclopedia] http://www.ne.se/clark-olofsson [accessed 21 February 2013]).

34   Geherin, p. 161.

city, and most of his main characters have their biological roots outside of Sweden. Nevertheless, the people of Stockholm are by no means presented as global citizens, as most of the main characters of Lapidus's novels actually have a very limited knowledge of the world outside of the Swedish capital.

What makes Lapidus's novels radically different from earlier Swedish crime fiction, however, is that he makes the members of Stockholm's criminal underbelly represent the 'norm' in the world of his novels. It is from *their* perspective that Swedish society is viewed, examined, and judged. 'Regular Swedes' are primarily presented as people to use and to swindle, simply as a source of income, while the police and society's other official authorities are mainly regarded as an annoyance. If possible, these official power structures are avoided and ignored by Lapidus's criminals, and when that is impossible, they are controlled and manipulated. Ultimately, if everything else fails, criminal networks and hierarchies are established in prison, from where they also continue to exhort power on the outside. When the Stockholm police in *Snabba cash* make increased efforts to come to terms with organized crime, the criminal networks respond by becoming even more organized themselves. They stop competing with each other, and instead start cooperating by dividing up areas and criminal activities amongst themselves, thus presenting a united front, helping each other to avoid police detection.

In Lapidus's Stockholm, the true power over the city is essentially in the hands of the criminals, and just as in Marklund's novels, this power is patriarchal. That only men are in possession of power is never questioned in Lapidus's novels, however, and not until *Livet deluxe* is the reader introduced to a woman character who is not solely presented as either a prostitute, or a girlfriend or family member of one of the male characters.[35] Lapidus's novels thereby express the recent anti-feminist backlash in Swedish society that is mirrored in much of the crime fiction from the early 2000s.[36] While the organized criminal networks run the city, some power is also ascribed to the privileged brats and yuppies ruling the exclusive bars and clubs in the Stureplan area. In many respects these 'high society' networks share an obsession with status, hierarchies, and money with the

---

35   In *Livet deluxe*, the main crime boss is killed, and eventually his daughter
       takes over and runs the business.
36   Cf. chapter 4.

criminal networks. Additionally, the area around Stureplan – characterized by designer shops, night clubs, and brat culture – is also
where younger criminals want to be seen and approved of, while
their older colleagues are attracted by the area's flourishing cocaine
market. Stureplan can be regarded the geographical hub of Lapidus's Stockholm, particularly in the first novel, *Snabba cash*. The
area is geographically delineated as Jorge Salinas Barrio, one of the
criminal protagonists, spies on one of the 'kings' of Stureplan, a
club host called 'Jet Set Carl':

> Jet Set Carl didn't venture far. Kept to his own pissed-in territory.
> Slipped into Café Tures in Sturegallerian, the exclusive indoor mall by
> Stureplan. Around 750 yards from where he lived. The geography
> within the golden rectangle was simple: Karlavägen-Sturegatan-Rid-
> dargatan-Narvavägen. The area practically had a velvet rope around
> it.[37]

Despite this limited central area, Lapidus' capital also extends to
include some of the suburbs where his protagonists live and/or originate. In particular, the poorer high-rise areas are frequently portrayed in these novels, but some of the more affluent villa suburbs
also appear on occasions. Like many of the crime writers cited here,
Lapidus uses the various districts to illustrate social class segregation, but also an ethnic segregation that few of the other authors
have described as poignantly. In Lapidus's novels the reader encounters people from all walks of life, from the homeless to the no-
bility. Jorge Salinas Barrio is well aware of the unwritten rules of
segregation, and the reader gets to share his thoughts on his Stureplan experiences:

> Jorge'd partied at the bars around there tons of times. Champagne-
> *chinga*'d *chicas*. Palmed some bills and the bouncer'd let him glide past
> the line. Bought some prime rib at the meat market. But still, something
> was missing. He saw the Swedish guys. No matter how much money he
> spent, he'd never be at their level. Jorge could feel it. Every *blatte* in the
> city could feel it. No matter how hard they tried, waxed their hair,
> bought the right clothes, kept their honor intact, and drove slick rides,
> they didn't belong with Them. Humiliation was always around the cor-
> ner. You could see it in the bouncers' gazes, the bitches' grimaces, the

---

37   Lapidus, p. 394.

bartenders' gestures. The message clearer than the city of Stockholm's segregation politics: In the end, you're always just a *blatte*.[38]

Although prevented by elements of racism from becoming fully integrated, Lapidus's criminals still easily negotiate the social ladder, with money opening all doors. Money is the ultimate source of power in Lapidus's Stockholm, and his portrayal of the city represents the very Sweden that Sjöwall and Wahlöö warned against in the 1960s and 1970s: a country corrupted by capitalism and greed. Although power has shifted hands from official to unofficial authorities, the governing principles still remain those motivated by money and greed. Lapidus's criminal underground has infiltrated every part and layer of Stockholm; it is operating just below the 'surface', thereby remaining relatively invisible to the casual observer. While Sjöwall and Wahlöö and Marklund represent the surface of Stockholm through buildings mirroring the state of society, Lapidus portrays the surface as just a veneer: the superficiality embodied by the importance of status and power symbols – cars, weapons, exclusive parties, designer clothes, et cetera.

In the crime novels discussed in this chapter, Stockholm's urban space is utilized in many different ways, but the primary result is generally that the cityscape is made to illustrate and represent the problems addressed in each author's work. Over time, the reader can observe how Sweden changes from being a relatively homogenous, isolated, and well-functioning welfare state in Trenter's oeuvre, to an individualistic and superficial country that is part of a globalized world, as in the Lapidus novels. The ultimate power exerted over the capital city is likewise shifted from capitalism in Sjöwall and Wahlöö, to patriarchy in Marklund, and finally, in Lapidus, to the criminal organizations representing both capitalism and patriarchy. Today, the utopian welfare state of Trenter's novels seems more and more distant, as the physical, moral, and ethical devastation of Stockholm continues. Although Stockholm is still presented as the nation's powerhouse in Swedish crime fiction, this has very different connotations today as compared to when Prins Pierre relied on the detective from the capital to solve the problems of society in the late nineteenth century.

---

38   Ibid., p. 321. *Blatte* is a Swedish slang word, referring primarily to Swedes of non-Caucasian ethnicities.

VI

THE NEO-ROMANTIC COUNTRYSIDE:
FROM MARIA LANG TO MARI JUNGSTEDT

In the early 2000s, an increasing number of Swedish crime writers moved away from the Sjöwall and Wahlöö tradition of social critique, creating instead police novels set in idyllic rural areas where almost all traces of globalization and threats from an external world are absent. These novels have been very successful with both the national and international audience. Mari Jungstedt's novels set on the island of Gotland constitute an emblematic example of this trend.

The Swedish countryside has always occupied a special place in Swedish crime fiction. This naturally stems from the central place which nature has occupied in Swedish literary tradition – from the evergreen landscapes of the medieval ballads, the scientifically detailed descriptions of nature found in botanist Carl von Linné's (1707–78) travel journals, the animated landscapes portrayed by the romantic poets in the early 1800s, the dramatic and deadly archipelago of August Strindberg's (1849–1912) *I hafsbandet* (1890; *By the Open Sea* 1985; *Mare aperto* 1986), and Selma Lagerlöf's (1858–1940) vivid geography lesson in *Nils Holgerssons underbara resa genom Sverige* (1906–07; *The Wonderful Adventures of Nils* 1907; *Il viaggio meraviglioso di Nils Holgersson* 1922), to the beauty of the poverty-stricken countryside found in the works of the proletarian realists of first half of the 1900s; the closeness to nature expressed in many of Astrid Lindgren's (1907–2002) children's books, and the elaborate nature metaphors used by poets like Gunnar Ekelöf (1907–68), Tomas Tranströmer (b. 1931) and Katarina Frostenson (1953) during the later parts of the century. Additionally, the Swedish natural landscape, with its deep forests, picturesque mountains, and other desolate places far from urban civilization, has long been regarded as a perfect contrast to the harsh reality of a brutal

murder.[1] One of the most successful authors of the twentieth century to use this contrast between the serenity of nature and the brutal-
ity of murder was Maria Lang (pen name for Dagmar Lange 1914–
91), Swedish master of the Golden Age whodunits. Lang set most of
her stories in and around the fictional small town of Skoga, loosely
based on Nora, in the wooded area of Bergslagen, north-west of
Stockholm. In Lang's more than forty clue-puzzle stories, from
Mördaren ljuger inte ensam (1949, The murderer does not lie alone)
to *Se Skoga och sedan* ... (1990, See Skoga, and then ...), the reader is familiarized with the dark beauty of the Swedish forest landscape, with its deep waters and moss-covered rocks, its flora and
fauna. As owls hoot, church bells toll in the night, and dead bodies
of beautiful women are found floating in peaceful forest ponds,
Lang's novels might even be seen to entertain a romantic flirtation

---

1   With its more than 520 000 km², stretching over 1572 km from the 69 par-
     allel in the north to the 55 parallel in the south, Sweden is a country with
     a very varied topography. The border towards Norway in the north-west is
     characterized by vast, barren mountains, the inland is filled with large for-
     ests consisting of mainly pine and fir trees, in the southern parts the old
     agricultural landscape is combined with lush mixed forests, and an archi-
     pelago borders most of the eastern and western coasts. Many lakes and
     rivers spread across the country, and in the Baltic Sea, off the east coast,
     two larger islands are located. With its 9.5 million citizens, of which 85%
     live in the urban areas of the south, Sweden is sparsely populated, and
     there are large areas of desolate landscape. The Swedish constitution
     grants the right to roam (*allemansrätten*), which allows Swedes and visi-
     tors access to the natural landscape – private as well as publicly owned
     land – all over the country, something that has without doubt contributed
     to making the Swedes a nature-loving people.
     The contrasting of beautiful scenery with brutal murder is of course found
     not only in Swedish crime fiction, but is common in many other crime fic-
     tion traditions as well. Most murderers tend to want to hide their crimes
     and corpses, and few places are more suited for the purpose than the out-
     doors. For example, Gillian Mary Hanson has explored the role of the
     coastal landscape in British mystery fiction in *City and Shore: The Func-
     tion of Setting in the British Mystery* (Jefferson/London: McFarland,
     2004), pp. 107–64. Still it seems to be especially common to make nature
     part of the intrigue in Swedish crime fiction, and Bo Lundin regards the
     focus on setting as one of the two major characteristics of the national tra-
     dition (Bo Lundin, *The Swedish Crime Story*, trans. by Anna Lena
     Ringarp, Ralph A. Wilson, and Bo Lundin (Bromma: Jury, 1981), pp.
     8–9).This is most likely due to the literary heritage described above, the
     sparsely populated countryside and the widespread love of nature among
     the country's inhabitants.

with the gothic tradition. Despite this, everything always has a natural explanation, one often rooted deep in the dark psyche of one of the seemingly innocent locals.[2] Romance and sexuality also play an important role in Lang's novels, and already in her debut novel from 1949 she lets the motive for murder stem from a lesbian woman's jealousy.[3] Her investigative protagonists, amateur detective Puck Bure and Detective Inspector Christer Wijk (called Wick in the English translations) also both experience love and passion during the series. Lang's combination of romance and murder proved to be a recipe for success, and from 1949, and well into the 1970s, her novels constantly featured on the Swedish bestseller lists. After the success of Maj Sjöwall (b. 1935) and Per Wahlöö's (1926–75) Stockholm police novels criticizing the Swedish welfare state in the 1960s and 1970s, however, urban spaces became the setting of choice for a majority of the Swedish crime writers. The small town and countryside locations became increasingly marginalized, and Maria Lang's popularity eventually faded.

The Swedish Countryside Rediscovered

The preference for the urban setting continued to dominate until the turn of the millennium, although the rediscovery of the Swedish countryside had already begun in the early 1990s when Henning Mankell (b. 1948) decided to set his police series about Inspector Kurt Wallander in and around the small town of Ystad, on Sweden's southern coast. Following Sjöwall and Wahlöö's pattern but wanting to portray a Sweden that was beginning to be affected by globalisation, the choice of Ystad, far away from the big city pulse of the Swedish capital, was not as unexpected as it might seem at first

---

2   Maria Lang has been widely translated, but still only three of her novels are available in English: *Inte flera mord* (1951; *No More Murders* 1967), *Se, döden på dig väntar* (1955; *Death Awaits Thee* 1967), and *Kung Liljekonvalje av dungen* (1957; *A Wreath for the Bride* 1966).

3   The use of sexuality in Lang's novels has been extensively discussed by Sara Kärrholm, for example in *Konsten att lägga pussel: Deckaren och besvärjandet av ondskan i folkhemmet* [The art of doing a jig-saw puzzle: The detective novel and the conjuring up of evil in the Swedish Welfare State] (Stockholm and Stehag: Symposion, 2005), pp. 149–58, 164–66, and 171–76.

glance. One of the southernmost cities in Sweden, Ystad is about as close as one could get to the European mainland, with an important port and numerous ferries linking it to the Polish port of Świnoujście. When Mankell initiated his series shortly after the fall of the Berlin Wall in 1989, Ystad was emerging as the gateway to the continent, making Eastern Europe suddenly seem more accessible and simultaneously more of a threat. Much of the transnational criminality that Wallander encounters, and that in the series he observes as changing the face of Sweden, has ties to Eastern Europe and the Baltic states.

Nevertheless, Mankell's use of the countryside and landscape around Ystad can in no way be regarded as romantic, as his main point is to show that violence and crime are no longer found only in the big cities, but that the threats present in a globalized society reach out everywhere. While Sjöwall and Wahlöö in *Terroristerna* (1975; *The Terrorists* 1976; *Terroristi* 2011) in the mid-1970s had their police protagonist, Martin Beck, experience increasing violence and an expanding drug scene in Stockholm, Mankell in 1991 describes the same development in rural Sweden. In the first Wallander novel, *Mördare utan ansikte* (1991; *Faceless Killers* 1997; *Assassino senza volto* 2001), Mankell lets the brutal murder of an elderly farming couple cause a wave of xenophobia. The racial hatred brought out into the open by the murder represents the fear of change and the unwillingness to accept being part of a globalized world, attitudes which reside in many local Swedish communities.[4] Despite using the beauty of the open landscape in southern Sweden to create a contrast with the viciousness of the killings, the countryside is viewed throughout Mankell's series as a metonymy of the Swedish welfare society that is changing and disintegrating – only to be gradually found no longer to exist. Mankell's nostalgia for the beauty and innocence of the landscape is thus simultaneously a nostalgia for an idyllic Sweden of the past, brutally contrasted with the dangers of the globalized world.

With the great success of the Wallander series – which was awarded several prizes from the outset – Mankell began to be regarded as

---

4   The theme of xenophobia in *Mördare utan ansikte* is further explored by
     Anna Westerståhl Stenport, in 'Bodies Under Assault: Nation and Immi-
     gration in Henning Mankell's *Faceless Killers*', *Scandinavian Studies*
     79.1 (2007), pp. 1–24 (passim).

the true heir of Sjöwall and Wahlöö, and his novels were soon perceived as the most important development in Swedish crime fiction since the mid-1970s. This led to a revitalization of the genre after the stagnation which characterized the preceding decade. Many new crime writers made their debut during the 1990s, and the popularity of Swedish crime fiction among Swedish (and eventually also international) readers increased substantially, until its peak in the early 2000s. Since then, the popularity of Mankell's small town Ystad and countryside locations began to inspire Swedish crime writers, who started 'colonizing' other parts of rural Sweden with their novels.

The 'Colonization' of the Swedish Countryside in the Early 2000s

Since the late 1990s, numerous Swedish crime writers have followed Mankell's example and set their novels far from the big Swedish urban areas. This amounts to a 'literary colonization' of Sweden, which saw a number of small towns, smaller cities, or rural locations become the setting for crime fiction stories. Much of Sweden, from Åsa Larsson's (b. 1966) Kiruna in the north, to Mankell's Ystad on the southern coast, from Camilla Läckberg's (b. 1974) old fishing community of Fjällbacka on the west coast, to Mari Jungstedt's (b. 1962), and Anna Jansson's (b. 1958) island of Gotland off Sweden's east coast, has now become established crime fiction territory. Each and every author takes advantage of the natural and cultural landscapes of 'their' little town or geographical area, thereby giving their novels a distinct local touch.

Camilla Läckberg has been particularly successful in putting the small, coastal village of Fjällbacka on the crime fiction map. Beginning with *Isprinsessan* (2003; *The Ice Princess* 2008; *La principessa di ghiaccio* 2010), her popularity has consistently grown. Today she is one of the best-known Swedish authors, at home and abroad, and during the first decade of the 2000s she is likely to be the Swedish author who has been most successful in terms of national sales.[5] Läckberg's novels have been particularly popular among women who can

---

5   Cf. Karl Berglund, *Deckarboomen under lupp: Statistiska perspektiv på svensk kriminallitteratur 1977–2010* [The crime fiction boom under the magnifying glass: Statistical perspectives on Swedish crime fiction 1977–2010] (Uppsala: Avdelningen för litteratursociologi, 2012), pp. 80–81.

identify with her woman protagonist, the author Erica Falk, a seemingly ordinary woman struggling with what are ordinarily considered everyday women's problems – such as weight issues, conflicts with her mother-in-law, and post-natal depression – and for whom family and children are always the first priority. In *Isprinsessan*, Falck returns to Fjällbacka where she grew up and is reunited with her childhood friend Patrik Hedström, who now works for the local police. Soon the two are a couple with a growing family, and together they solve the crimes that occur in Läckberg's (at the time of writing) nine Fjällbacka novels. The series is characterized by the small town life of the old fishing village on the west coast, where tourism has grown to become the main source of income, but where the people who have lived there for generations and seem to know everything about each other and have a knowledge of sea-faring, still set the norms for the dominant mentality. Despite her popularity, however, Läckberg has been one of the most controversial Swedish crime writers in recent years and is often cited as an example of what can happen when crime fiction takes over the book market at the expense of non-genre literature, considered to be of higher aesthetic value.[6]

An author who is untouched by critical controversies and receives universal praise is Åsa Larsson. She has Twice received The Golden Crowbar, the prize for best Swedish crime novel of the year awarded by The Swedish Academy of Detection: for *Det blod som spillts* (2004; *The Blood Spilt* 2007; *Il sangue versato* 2007) and for *Till offer åt Molok* (2012; *The Second Deadly Sin* 2013: *Sacrificio a Moloch* 2012). Additionally, both her debut novel, *Solstorm* (2003; *Sun Storm/The Savage Altar* 2006; *Tempesta solare* 2005) and *Till dess din vrede upphör* (2008; *Until Thy Wrath be Past* 2011; *Finché sarà passata la tua ira* 2010) were nominated for the same prize –

---

6   Often she is also accused of bad writing – even by her own fellow crime writers (cf. the 2007 attack by Leif GW Persson (b. 1945) and others, described in Sara Kärrholm, 'Swedish Queens of Crime: The Art of Self-Promotion and the Notion of Feminine Agency – Liza Marklund and Camilla Läckberg', in *Scandinavian Crime Fiction*, ed. by Andrew Nestingen and Paula Arvas (Cardiff: University of Wales Press, 2011), pp. 131–47 (p. 141)). Much of the critique against Läckberg can of course simply be considered 'sour grapes', due to her youth, success, and massive popularity among Swedish readers. Obviously readers not only in Sweden, but all over the world, find qualities in Läckberg's novels that well compensate for any potential literary or narrative flaws, or outdated gender patterns.

leaving only two of Larsson's novels un-nominated. *Solstorm* was also shortlisted for a Dagger Award for the best translated crime novel in 2007. Larsson's novels, centered on tax lawyer Rebecca Martinsson and Inspector Anna-Maria Mella in Kiruna, are characterized by the harshness of the cold, northern landscape. Most of the people populating Larsson's pages have lived in the Kiruna area for generations and are shaped by the small community where anonymity does not exist and conflicts can go on for decades, perhaps even centuries – something Larsson's novels have in common with Läckberg's. The Kiruna area is a landscape with long, dark winters and short, bright summers, a place where people and animals co-exist, dependent on each other for food, shelter and protection. Animals – dogs, in particular – also play important parts in Larsson's crime stories. Recently, another author, Tove Alsterdal (b. 1960), has moved in on Larsson's 'territory,' depicting a nearby northern setting in crime novels with a similar focus, for example *Kvinnorna på stranden* (2009, The women on the beach; *Corpi senza nome* 2011) and *I tystnaden begravd* (2012, In the silence, buried). The latter novel was nominated as the best Swedish crime novel of the year in 2012, when the award went to Åsa Larsson.

A completely different part of rural Sweden is found in Mons Kallentoft's (b. 1968) two series about Inspector Malin Fors in Linköping. The first series is themed around the seasons and contains five novels, from *Midvinterblod* (2007; *Midwinter Blood/Midwinter Sacrifice* 2011; *Sangue di mezz'inverno* 2010) to *Den femte årstiden* (2011; *The Fifth Season* 2014), and the later series is about the elements, starting with *Vattenänglar* (2012, Water angels). With almost 150, 000 inhabitants in the municipality, Linköping is not all that small by Swedish standards, although it is when compared to Stockholm or Gothenburg. Additionally, most of the events of Kallentoft's novels take place in the countryside surrounding the city, in the deep forests to the north and south, and in the open fields to the west and close to the city. Kallentoft lets the seasonal weather and temperature closely mirror the drama of his narrative. He also presents the nature of the area – especially the wooded areas of the north – as almost inherently evil. Such use of weather and nature has a long tradition in Swedish literary history. Among other crime writers, Henning Mankell is well-known for employing weather parallels in order to depict Wallander's state of mind and the progression of his cases. Identifying nature with evil is more uncommon in Swedish crime fiction, making Kallentoft's novels somewhat original. This symbiosis also serves to stress that evil is something fundamental and existing independently and, accordingly, when the series of torture, rape, and murder cases that run throughout Kallentoft's first Linköping series is finally solved in *Den femte årstiden*, there appears to be no motive behind the horrific deeds, as the man who committed them is found to have done so simply because he was able to.

The list of contemporary Swedish crime writers associated with specific Swedish rural locations and villages is almost endless, but a few more deserve a mention in addition to those already presented above: Aino Trosell (b. 1949),who writes about the region of Dalarna in central Sweden, and Karin Wahlberg (b. 1950), who sets her novels, among them *Matthandlare Olssons död* (2009; *Death of a Carpet Dealer* 2012), mainly in and around Oskarshamn on the east coast. Then there is Björn Hellberg (b. 1944), whose novels are set in a small, fictional town in the region of Halland on the west coast, and Kristina Appelqvist (b. 1968), who writes about life and death in Skövde, a small college city east of Gothenburg. Even more thriving in the international market is Johan Theorin (b. 1963), whose crimes take place on the island of Öland, off the east coast. For *Skumtimmen* (2007; *Echoes from the Dead* 2008; *L'ora delle tenebre* 2008) Theorin received both the prize for best Swedish crime fiction debut and a Dagger Award for best debut novel, and for *Nattfåk* (2008; *The Darkest Room* 2009; *La stanza più buia* 2011) he won The Golden Crowbar for best Swedish crime novel of the year, a Glass Key Award for best Scandinavian crime novel, and a Dagger for best novel in translation. Theorin's novels are characterized by their combination of close connections between past and present, moods bordering on the supernatural, and the harshness of the local Öland island landscape.

The rediscovery and 'colonization' of the Swedish countryside by recent crime writers has also brought with it a renewed interest in literary tourism.[7] If Henning Mankell was the one who initiated the

---

7   Sweden's main site of non-crime fiction literary tourism is the small town
     of Vimmerby in the region of Småland in south east Sweden, where the
     author Astrid Lindgren (1907–2002) had her roots and set many of her fa-
     mous children's stories, and where there is now even a theme park dedi-
     cated to her and her stories (cf. Carina Sjöholm, *Litterära resor: Turism i
     spåren efter böcker, filmer och författare* [Literary journeys: Tourism trac-
     ing novels, films and authors] (Gothenburg/Stockholm: Makadam, 2011),
     pp. 121–59). The first Swedish crime writer to be the target of literary

revival for rural settings in Swedish crime fiction, he was also the one whose Wallander novels – and the numerous films based on those novels and their characters – gave rise to the last decade's growing popularity for crime fiction tourism in Sweden.[8] Following the successful tourist promotion campaign in Ystad, tourist boards all over Sweden have followed suit and used 'their' crime writers in marketing the town or the area. The Läckberg tourism in Fjällbacka has been particularly flourishing, and Camilla Läckberg has actively taken part in promoting the coastal village, also outside the sphere of her fiction.[9] Additionally, following the international success of Stieg Larsson's (1954–2004) *Millennium* trilogy (2005–2007), Swedish crime fiction tourism has become increasingly popular not only in the countryside, but also in the big cities.[10]

The Isolated Rural Community

Perhaps the most emblematic example of the neo-romantic rediscovery of rural settings in Swedish crime fiction of late, is the oeuvre of Mari Jungstedt.[11] Since her debut with *Den du inte ser* (2003; *Unseen* 2006), her Gotland novels about Inspector Anders Knutas of the Visby police and television journalist Johan Berg have been increasingly popular. Jungstedt's novels display all the common characteristics of the typical Swedish rural police novels of the 2000s.

---

tourism was Maria Lang. The city of Nora (located in the wooded area of Bergslagen north-west of Stockholm and model for Lang's fictional town Skoga) has been visited by Lang readers for decades, and is still a popular venue for crime fiction tourism (cf. Sjöholm, pp. 40–42).

8   Swedish ethnologist Carina Sjöholm has studied the Wallander tourism and the strategic work behind promoting and enabling this tourism in and around Ystad, cf. Sjöholm, pp. 47–85.

9   Cf. ibid., pp. 87–119.

10   Cf. ibid., p. 42 on *Millennium* tourism.

11   Most of my thoughts concerning Jungstedt's novels presented in the following have previously been presented in Kerstin Bergman, 'Isolerad idyll och svart barndom: Marie Jungstedt (1962–)' [Isolated idyll and dark childhood: Mari Jungstedt (b. 1962)], in *Tretton svenska deckardamer* [Thirteen Swedish crime ladies] (Lund: BTJ förlag, 2009), pp. 96–111 (passim); and/or in 'The Well-Adjusted Cops of the New Millennium: Neo-Romantic Tendencies in the Swedish Police Procedural', in *Scandinavian Crime Fiction*, ed. Andrew Nestingen och Paula Arvas (Cardiff: University of Wales Press, 2011), pp. 34–45 (pp. 38–34).

Additionally, they have been widely translated, Nordic-German co-produced films for TV have been made from them, filmed in Gotland locations, and crime fiction tourists are now tracing the movements of Jungstedt's characters through Visby and all over Gotland. In many ways the emblematic qualities of Jungstedt's novels in the Swedish context also reach beyond the neo-romantic trend.

Jungstedt's Gotland is a beautiful and windswept island with a historically interesting past and it is small enough for everyone to know, or at least know of, everyone else – or at least their relatives. It is idyllic, and hardly anything is present that can really threaten this idyll: there is no organized crime, no contentious political issues, no Internet crime, and even no environmental issues. It is as if nothing really exists outside of the island and as if time stood still somewhere at the beginning of the 1950s. The only threat that exists stems from the ghosts of the past. This is typical not only of Jungstedt's novels, but of most of the Swedish crime novels of recent years set in the countryside. The focus on the local, the idyllic and isolated countryside, brings to mind the British crime fiction tradition as expressed in, for example, Caroline Graham's series about Chief Inspector Barnaby (1988–2004, filmed for television as *Midsomer Murders*, 1997–), rather than the Swedish police procedural tradition with its roots in the American, more hard-boiled, police novel.

Jungstedt's descriptions of the Gotland scenery are very thorough, and things related to the nature, culture, and history of the island are described in specific detail. Also thematically, Jungstedt often makes local connections, for example, when she lets the historical sites and archeological heritage of the island play an important role in *Den inre kretsen* (2005; *The Inner Circle/Unknown* 2008), or when she uses the utter isolation of Gotska Sandön (a smaller island off the coast of Gotland) as an important element of the story in *I denna ljuva sommartid* (2007; *The Dead of Summer* 2011; *In questa dolce estate* 2011). The local element also dominates in terms of characters. Most of the people populating Jungstedt's novels have been born and raised in Gotland and, whenever someone new is introduced, the reader – presumed to be an outsider – is told from which part of Gotland they come and where their relatives live. This contributes to the creation of Jungstedt's Gotland as a small and closed community where anonymity is impossible. The only exception is Johan Berg, the journalist protagonist, who is from Stockholm, but working on Gotland. Nevertheless, in the first novel, Berg falls in love with the island just as he does with resident primary school teacher Emma Winarve, and soon he dreams of living permanently on Gotland and becoming part of the local community. Through the character of Johan Berg, Jungstedt provides her readers from elsewhere an external point of observation easy to identify with and, as Berg explores the island, she lets her readers follow his impressions and the growing fascination he experiences as he encounters both the beauty of Gotland and the island's inhabitants. As an 'outsider', Berg also provides Jungstedt with a narrative strategy for explaining aspects of the local customs and environment to the reader.

The world outside of Gotland is rarely mentioned in Jungstedt's novels, and the reader gets the impression that the only thing that exists beyond the shores of the island is a distant Stockholm. The Swedish capital is vaguely sketched as a decadent and anonymous metropolis, in stark contrast to the intimate island community where everything is familiar. As almost all the murderers found in Jungstedt's novels are strongly linked to the island, and have been for generations, it is not the world outside –even the decadent Stockholm – that poses a threat towards the idyllic, Gotland community. The threat is rather internal, lurking among the picturesque medieval streets and the sunny beaches, in the individual past of a selected group of island inhabitants. The disintegrating welfare state found in novels by Sjöwall and Wahlöö and Mankell is nowhere to be seen on Jungstedt's Gotland, and criminality originating from globalization, increased migration, and developments in communication technology – characteristic of, for example, novels of Mankell, Arne Dahl (pen name for Jan Arnald, b. 1963) and Jens Lapidus (b. 1974) – is equally absent. Jungstedt's Gotland – as well as the Swedish countryside and the small towns in novels by so many of her fellow Swedish crime writers today – remains untouched by the developments that have taken place in society in recent decades.

Even with Gotland being geographically located a little further away from the European mainland than Mankell's Ystad, and even though it is an island naturally isolated by large bodies of water, Gotland still has an important central location in the Baltic Sea. The island has always been an important trading post, connected to Finland, the Baltic States, Poland, and Germany. Additionally, Gotland is one of Sweden's most popular tourist destinations, visited every year by hundreds of thousands of people from all over the world. Whilst there is no lack of options for credibly depicting criminals and criminality originating from the 'outside', Jungstedt has never-theless chosen to depict the island as being more isolated than it re-ally is, something that contributes to giving her novels an almost timeless quality and charm.

The Absence of Political Critique

Despite the strong tradition of social critique in Swedish crime fiction, it seems as if the distancing from the outside world in the new rurally-based crime novels has also brought with it a distancing from mainstream social and political critique. The Gotland police of Mari Jungstedt's novels do not ever complain about cutbacks or lack of resources in the force –probably one of the most commonly voiced criticisms in Swedish police novels. Instead, Knutas and his team appear to be satisfied with their situation and with the resourc-es they have available – and if occasionally they are not sufficient, they just call for reinforcements from Stockholm. While for exam-ple Wallander's attitude towards such reinforcements – and towards the capability of the Stockholm police in general – is dominated by negative feelings and fears that 'they' will take over his cases, Knu-tas actually welcomes any help and has no territorial issues.

In the Swedish crime fiction tradition, it is common for protago-nists to express their critical thoughts and discuss political issues. In addition to having insufficient police resources, a common target of criticism in the last decades has been media ethics. Tabloid journal-ism in particular has been extensively criticized – perhaps this is most rife in the novels by Liza Marklund and Stieg Larsson. Even though Jungstedt has made one of her protagonists a journalist, the discussions of media ethics found in her novels are not especially in-cisive. They are generally limited to Berg occasionally thinking that the television company he works for ought to be a little more restric-tive when it comes to interviewing children and victims of crimes. The critical potential of the journalist character is thus barely uti-lized. Among the police officers who appear in the novel too, the critical comments are few, and are mostly limited to the occasional irritation over journalists being 'pushy'. The most explicitly politi-cal comments of the series are found in *I denna stilla natt* (2004; *Unspoken* 2007), when Karin Jacobson, a woman police officer, suddenly bursts out in an emotional speech about society's injustices. Her comments are, however, quickly dismissed by her colleagues: 'Do you have to turn everything into a political issue? asked Knutas, sounding annoyed. We're in the middle of a murder investigation here'.[12] It is obvious that the Gotland police station is no forum for political discussion, and that such discussions simply have no place in Jungstedt's novels either, but this quote could easily be attributed to almost any of the Swedish crime writers portraying small, rural communities today.

A consequence of the isolation and absence of politics in the rurally-based novels is that the motive for murder cannot be portrayed as a result of society failing, or attributed to foreign crime syndicates. Jungstedt's novels are constructed according to a relatively strict pattern: someone is found murdered or is reported missing, Knutas' team begin their investigation, Berg finds out and starts his own investigation by interviewing neighbours, relatives, and Knutas. Berg then discovers something the police missed, and this annoys Knutas. The case proves to be more complicated than it seemed at first, at least one more crime – often a murder – is committed, and then suddenly, after the investigation has been halted for a while, everything happens at once and it ends with a dramatic denouement as someone from the local community is revealed to be the murderer. Since many pieces of the puzzle do not fall into place until the finale, an epilogue usually follows where everything is fully explained. This is a pretty common pattern for a police novel, though in Jungstedt's case the variant is the presence of two different detectives – the police and the journalist – and the fact that Berg's love life is given unusually extensive page space. All in all, the extended romantic motive has been an increasingly common occurrence in Swedish crime fiction in the early 2000s, characterizing not only the neo-romantic, countryside novels, but in fact most Swedish crime fiction.

Both murderers and murder victims are locals in Jungstedt's novels. Leif Almlöv, the murderer in *I denna stilla natt*, is said to come 'from a family of fishermen who for generations had fished the

---

12   Mari Jungstedt, *Unspoken*, transl. by Tiina Nunnally (New York: St. Martin's Minotaur, 2007), p. 108. In the Swedish original (Mari Jungstedt, *I denna stilla natt* (Stockholm: Bonniers, 2004), p. 155), the last part of the quote reads 'Här sysslar vi med mordutredningar', which rather means 'what we do is murder investigations', thereby creating a stronger opposition between murder investigations and politics than what comes across in the English translation.

stormy Baltic along Gotland's coast', and many other murderers and victims are described in similar terms.[13] Often the crimes originate from some family tragedy and are explained as being motivated by events in the murderer's childhood or youth. The rare exception to the latter scenario is in fact Almlöv in *I denna stilla natt*, who kills to hide the fact that he once had a relationship with an underage girl. A common feature shared by most of Jungstedt's murderers is that they are men from the lower middle class, who kill in order to hide family secrets, or to get revenge for things done to them or their relatives in the past, or because of mental illness. The murderers are caught or killed during the dramatic finale, except in *I denna ljuva sommartid*, where the murderer – who is actually a woman – is allowed to escape, following an intense climax.

Detective Combos and Gender Issues

Many of the new novels set in the Swedish countryside are police novels, their authors thereby aiming to repeat the success of so many previous Swedish writers who have employed that sub-genre. Instead of being traditional police procedurals, where the focus tends to be equally shared between all members of the police team, these new rurally-based police novels are rather an expression of today's more individualistic society, as they often focus mainly on one police character or combine a police protagonist with someone other than a police officer in the leading roles. The combination of police and amateur detectives was also popular in Sweden even before Sjöwall and Wahlöö's time, some of the most successful duos being Stieg Trenter's Detective Inspector Vesper Johnson and photographer Harry Friberg, and Maria Lang's Detective Inspector Christer Wijk and amateur detective Puck Bure.

Mari Jungstedt follows in the path of these predecessors as she lets Inspector Anders Knutas compete for page space with television journalist Johan Berg. Knutas and Berg are not exactly collaborating as such, but occasionally they share information as they take turns in finding new clues and drawing their own separate conclusions. In fact Knutas and Berg endure a complicated relationship common between police and media representatives in

---

13   Jungstedt, *Unspoken*, p. 242.

crime fiction: Knutas believes that Berg tends to run off in directions that might harm the case and he is frustrated when Berg refuses to divulge his sources or finds out things the police do not already know. Knutas is often impressed by how much Berg manages to find out, and his opinion of the journalist is summarized in *I denna stilla natt*, when he concludes that if Berg had not 'become a journalist, he would have made an excellent police detective'.[14] Berg, for his part, is constantly frustrated that Knutas refuses to share information with him concerning the progress of the police investigations, but he still invariably respects the professional capabilities of the Inspector. Other popular detective combos that feature in the recent novels based in small towns are Camilla Läckberg's police officer Patrik Hedström and author Erica Falck in Fjällbacka, Karin Wahlberg's (b. 1950) police officer Claes Classon and medical doctor Veronika Lundborg in Oskarshamn, Kristina Appelqvist's police officer Filip Alexandersson and university rector Emma Lundgren in Skövde, and Ingrid Kampås' (b. 1957) police officer Åke and District Nurse Mari Johansson in the small (fictional) village of Sundsby, located in the region of Halland on Sweden's west coast – just to mention a few.[15]

The presence of women – writers as well as characters – has increased substantially in Swedish crime fiction since the late 1990s.[16] Nevertheless, Jungstedt has chosen two men for the leading roles, and it is them and their perspectives that dominate her novels. The only woman police officer in the series is Karin Jacobson, Knutas' closest colleague, but she is given only marginal space throughout the series. Knutas considers Karin his friend – and he is also somewhat attracted to her – but he is also aware that he knows almost nothing about her private life and he perceives her as mysterious.[17] In *Den inre kretsen*, she is said to have a fierce temper and to be 'a splash of color and a bundle of energy' in an otherwise grey police environment.[18] Berg's camerawoman, Pia Lilja who has an even

---

14   Ibid., p. 121.
15   Åke's last name is never mentioned.
16   Cf. chapter 4.
17   Following Jungstedt's practice, I call the women by their first names in what follows.
18   Mari Jungstedt, *The Inner Circle*, transl. by Tiina Nunnally (New York: St. Martin's Minotaur, 2008), p. 14.

smaller role in the series, is described in a similar way: as being temperamental, colorful, and focused on her career.

In addition to Karin and Pia, the two other main women characters of the series are Knutas' wife Line, and Emma Winarve, with whom Berg soon initiates a relationship. Line is a midwife and described as a passionate and voluptuous redhead. Being Danish, she is exoticized and described as a colorful butterfly in the grey Swedish society. Knutas thinks she is a miracle, but sometimes also a mystery. Line's primary function throughout the series is to take care of the couple's children and to be a warm embrace for Knutas to return to and shelter in whenever his professional world seems too cold and cruel. Emma is a primary school teacher and, when the series begins, a mother of two. She is beautiful and her passionate side is illustrated by how quickly she falls in love and throws herself into a relationship with Berg, although she is already married and has a family. When she accidentally gets pregnant she decides to have the baby, despite the uncertain nature of her relationship with Berg. Emma's function as a mother is constantly emphasized, and out of consideration for her first two children, she is hesitant to really let Berg into her life, even after her divorce settlement. Berg perceives Emma as a beautiful goddess, perfect in every way. In *Den du inte ser* he thinks that: 'Her very being enchanted him. Her power terrified and enticed him'.[19] Nevertheless, Emma is a mystery to him, and he cannot understand why she keeps her distance from him for so long – something that does not keep him from following her every whim, eagerly awaiting her attention, until she eventually makes up her mind and they end up getting married.

Karin, Line, and Emma thus all seem mysterious to the male protagonists. Line and Emma in particular are also presented as pretty and passionate in a manner evoking traditional gender stereotypes and they are heavily associated with motherhood and children in both their professional and private lives. Even though they could perhaps be categorized as the kind of women who in Swedish crime fiction follow a Liza Marklund-type pattern of struggling with balancing family and careers, in fact, Line's and Emma's work lives are hardly more than mentioned in passing and in this way they are further reduced to being just caring mothers, wives, and lovers. But Karin is different, as she is por-

---

19   Mari Jungstedt, *Unseen*, transl. by Tiina Nunnally (London: Corgi Books, 2008), p. 296.

trayed rather as 'one of the guys' in her male dominated workplace.[20]
Nevertheless, when on duty the police occasionally encounter children, it is still hinted that Karin has suppressed maternal feelings, and at the end of *I denna ljuva sommartid*, it is revealed that in her teens, she was forced to give up a daughter – who was the result of a rape – for adoption. Karin and Pia both work solely with male colleagues and, despite the fact that Knutas and Berg sometimes find them mysterious, there is really not much to distinguish them from their male colleagues. Clearly, if Jungstedt had made them male instead, the novels would not have changed in any significant way. In conclusion, gender roles are quite conservative in Jungstedt's novels, something that is never questioned – more than perhaps by the fact that Line eventually leaves Knutas. The gender stereotypes are also something Jungstedt's novels have in common with a majority of the other Swedish crime novels from the first decade of the 2000s.

With their neo-romantic portrayal of the Swedish countryside, their isolated location, the timeless qualities, the absence of political critique, the dynamic police-amateur detective duo, and the gender stereotypes, Jungstedt's novels are quite simply emblematic of one of the most popular trends in Swedish crime fiction today. In stark contrast to the Sjöwall and Wahlöö tradition of primarily urban-based police procedurals filled with social and political criticism, these neo-romantic novels constitute both a new trend and a revival of the Swedish Golden Age: a pre-Sjöwall and Wahlöö crime fiction tradition. In times of change – in the light of the rapid globalization and digital revolution of recent decades – the attractiveness of the nostalgia for the well-known past that these novels expresses is perhaps only natural, and in a national literary tradition that has always valued the importance of setting and detailed descriptions of nature and landscape, the success of these new crime novels is hardly surprising.

---

20   John Scaggs notes that 'there are few police procedurals written by women that actually interrogate the position of women, rather than tacitly accepting it by "becoming one of the guys" in order to succeed in the still largely male world of law enforcement' (John Scaggs, *Crime Fiction* (London/New York: Routledge, 2005), p. 102).

VII

THE INTERNATIONAL SUCCESS STORY: *STIEG LARSSON*

Although Swedish crime fiction has been translated into many different languages since the early twentieth century, the first large-scale international breakthrough came with Stieg Larsson's Millennium *trilogy (2005–2007). Larsson's novels also finally broke the dominance of the police procedural in Sweden and paved the way for increased variation and genre hybridization. The focus of this chapter will be on what makes Larsson's trilogy different, causing its international and national impact.*[1]

Swedish crime fiction, Scandinavian crime fiction, Nordic Noir – there are many different names for describing what has been a remarkable success story in the world book market in recent years. Crime fiction from Sweden and the other Nordic countries has become a major export industry, and collectively its authors and novels have become a phenomenon usually associated with good quality, exotic locations, and dark moods. Today these crime novels are marketed and sold internationally with labels such as *Schwedenkri-*

---

1   This article builds to a great extent on my previous articles on Stieg Larsson: 'Lisbeth Salander and her Swedish Crime Fiction "Sisters"': Stieg Larsson's Hero in a Genre Context', in *Men Who Hate Women and Women Who Kick Their Asses: Stieg Larsson's Millennium Trilogy in Feminist Perspective*, ed. by Donna King and Carrie Lee Smith (Nashville: Vanderbilt University Press, 2012), pp. 135–144; 'From "The Case of the Pressed Flowers" to the Serial Killers Torture Chamber: The Use and Function of Crime Fiction Sub-genres in Stieg Larsson's *The Girl with the Dragon Tattoo*', in *Critical Insights: Crime and Detective Fiction*, ed. by Rebecca Martin (Ipswich, MA: Salem Press, 2013), pp. 38–53; and 'Genre-Hybridization – A Secret Behind Hyper-Bestsellers? The Use and Function of Different Fiction Genres in *The Da Vinci Code* and *Millennium*', *Academic Quarter*, 7 (2013).

mi, *polar polaire*, and *Nordic Noir* – premium concepts that alone can boost sales and guarantee fame. The success of crime fiction from the Nordic countries is, of course, no isolated phenomenon: crime fiction has been in the last couple of decades the fastest growing and probably the most popular genre worldwide, and a revitalization and popularization similar to that seen in Sweden has been experienced by many other national and regional expressions of the genre. Translating crime novels is clearly not a new phenomenon either. As early as in the first decades of the twentieth century, Swedish crime writers such as Frank Heller (pen name for Gunnar Serner 1886–1947) and S.A. Duse (1873–1933) were widely translated, and in the 1960s and 1970s, there were few avid crime fiction readers around the globe who had not read the novels by Maj Sjöwall (b. 1935) and Per Wahlöö (1926–75). The latter are today available in over thirty languages, almost as many as Stieg Larsson (1954–2004), and have recently had an international (and national) revival along with the general upswing for Swedish crime fiction. Until Stieg Larsson, however, Swedish crime fiction was mostly known outside of Sweden only by true aficionados.

Today most quality Swedish crime writers get translated as, due to the general popularity of Nordic crime fiction, international publishers seem to regard the Swedish authors as a relatively safe investment, but this has not always been the case.[2] In the 1990s, the international circulation of crime fiction from Sweden began to grow, expanding out of the traditional recipient market of the Nordic region and into the German market first and that of a few other European countries. Germany is still one of the principal markets for Swedish crime fiction, and most new Swedish crime fiction today is immediately translated into German.[3] These days, the rights to many

---

2   Another important factor contributing to Swedish crime writers getting attention by international publishing houses, is that most authors today are represented by skilled and knowledgeable literary agents, working hard to get the crime novels translated and sold abroad. Having a literary agent was not common at all among Swedish writers only ten years ago, the agents are a relatively recent phenomenon in Sweden.

3   In 2011, the Swedish tabloid *Expressen* published a top ten list of how well Stieg Larsson's *Millennium* trilogy had sold abroad. After the US (17,300,000), and England (11,000,000), Germany was in third place with 6,500,000 copies sold, followed by France, Sweden, Spain, Italy, The Netherlands, Canada, and Norway (Roland Johansson, 'Milenniums miljonsuccé' [Millennium's million success], in *Expressen*, 23 June 2011

of these novels are often sold abroad even before the author's first novel has been released and reviewed in Sweden: 'sold to five countries' is a relatively common sales pitch also for new crime writers.[4] While the German market has been receptive to the Swedish authors for a relatively long time, the English-speaking markets have proved much more resistant. For example, Henning Mankell's novels about Inspector Kurt Wallander have been translated into English since the 1990s, and already then efforts were made to launch them in the USA. Although the response from the crime fiction fans there was enthusiastic, the wider audience did not catch the Wallander fever immediately. It was first in the wake of Stieg Larsson's success that Mankell had his major breakthrough in the English-speaking world, and now Wallander is just as well-known as many of the established British and American crime fiction protagonists.

In the case of Liza Marklund (b. 1962), the story is similar. She was first translated into English in the early 2000s, but her novels were not successful. Since 2010, however, new translations have been made of her first novels, she is being re-launched in the USA, and the rest of her novels are being translated at a fast pace. Marklund's major breakthrough in the English-speaking market came in 2010, after bestselling American author James Patterson asked her to co-write a novel with him, *Postcard Killers* (2010; *Cartoline di morte* 2011), which was released at the same time and with the same title in English and Swedish. That Patterson chose to work with the Swedish writer illustrates the status and prestige of Swedish crime fiction at the time. In addition to Mankell and Marklund, some of the Swedish authors most successful internationally today are Camilla Läckberg (b. 1974), Mari Jungstedt (b. 1962), Helene Tursten (b. 1954), Jens Lapidus (b. 1974), Håkan Nesser (b. 1950), Johan Theorin (b. 1963), Kristina Ohlsson (b. 1979), Karin Alvtegen (b. 1965), Kjell Eriksson (b. 1953), Åsa Larsson (b. 1966), and Lars Kepler (pen name for Alexander Ahndoril b. 1967, and Alexandra Coelho Ahndoril b. 1966). Further-

---

http://www.expressen.se/noje/milleniums-miljonsucce/ [accessed 1 March 2013]).

4   For example, when Carin Gerhardsen's (b. 1962) first crime novel, *Pepparkakshuset* (2008; *The Gingerbread House* 2012; *La casa di pan di zenzero* 2011) was published, it was stressed in the marketing material that it was already sold to four countries.

more, some established authors who are just rising to international acclaim are Inger Frimansson (b. 1944), Arne Dahl (pen name for Jan Arnald b. 1963), and Åke Edwardson (b. 1953). This list does not include those many authors who are successful in some countries, for example in Germany, but not as known to the extensive English-language market.[5]

Stieg Larsson's Success Story

The real international breakthrough for Swedish crime fiction, which essentially means breakthrough in the English-speaking markets, came with Stieg Larsson and the enormous attention his *Millennium* trilogy (2005–2007) received worldwide. Larsson's novels – *Män som hatar kvinnor* (2005; *The Girl with the Dragon Tattoo* 2008; *Uomini che odiano le donne* 2008), *Flickan som lekte med elden* (2006; *The Girl Who Played with Fire* 2009; *La ragazza che giocava con il fuoco* 2008), and *Luftslottet som sprängdes* (2007; *The Girl Who Kicked the Hornets' Nest* 2010; *La regina dei castelli di carta* 2009) – had been translated into at least thirty-seven languages already in 2011, and sold more than 60 million copies worldwide.[6] That was even before the American remake of the Swedish film based on the first novel was released.[7] Three Swedish adaptations – *Män som hatar kvinnor* (2009, directed by Niels Arden Oplev), *Flickan som lekte med elden* (2009, directed by Daniel Alfredson), and *Luftslottet som sprängdes* (2009, directed by Daniel Alfredson) – had already been made, and following the popularity of the novels they attracted sizeable audiences abroad, considering they were Swedish films. The first American remake, *The Girl with*

---

5   Cf. 'Autoren: Schweden' [Authors: Sweden], in *Schwedenkrimi* [Swedish crime fiction] http://www.schwedenkrimi.de/autoren_schweden.html [accessed 27 February 2013], where over a hundred Swedish crime writers, all translated into German, are listed.

6   Sales figures are notoriously unreliable, these from 2011 are from an article in the Swedish book market trade magazine (Lars Schmidt, 'Stieg Larssons böcker sålda i 60 miljoner exemplar'[Stieg Larsson's novels sold in 60 million copies], in *Svensk Bokhandel* [Swedish book trade magazine], 9 June 2011 http://www.svb.se/nyheter/stieg-larssons-b-cker-s-lda-i-60-miljoner-exemplar [accessed 28 March 2013].

7   The American film version was released at Christmas 2011.

the Dragon Tattoo (2011, directed by David Fincher) premiered in 2011, and although it did not do as well at the box office as had been hoped (with the consequence that the making of the two following films was postponed), the film made Stieg Larsson and his novels popular also to people who had not yet read the novels. Today there is also a comic book version based on the first novel, *The Girl with the Dragon Tattoo* (volume 1: 2012, volume 2: 2013, text by Denise Mina, illustrations by Andrea Mutti and Leonardo Manco) and, second only to Dan Brown's *The Da Vinci Code* (2003; *Il codice da Vinci* 2003), Stieg Larsson's trilogy is probably the most successful crime fiction phenomenon worldwide in the last decades, and perhaps ever.[8]

In 2010, *The Economist* wrote that: 'The quality and popularity of [Nordic] crime fiction has given Nordic novelists a prestige that [crime fiction] authors from other countries do not enjoy'.[9] This might be a bit of an exaggeration, but what is interesting is that the stamp of quality put on the Nordic authors in the international context tends to apply to *all* Nordic crime writers. From a Swedish perspective, it is obvious that the growing popularity of national crime fiction has resulted in a rise in the publication of some poorly written Swedish crime fiction. Not all is of high quality. Additionally, although there is still the occasional Swedish crime novel judged not fit for translation, a great deal is being translated, and not only the top echelon. It is thus likely that translators make important contributions to the quality of many of the Swedish crime novels that reach an international audience. It might also work the other way around, as the English translation of the *Millennium* novels is generally acknowledged to be sloppy. After comparing the English versions with Stieg Larsson's original Swedish texts, John-Henri Holmberg concludes:

> The English translation shows no feeling and no respect for Stieg Larsson's style or intentions. There are innumerable misinterpretations, wrongly selected words, misunderstandings and textual changes. Surprisingly often, the translation seems smugly to correct the author; clarifications and indications of mood and character are cut or abbreviated.

---

8   Bergman, 'Genre-Hybridization', passim.
9   'Scandinavian Crime Fiction: Inspector Norse', in *The Economist*, 11 March 2010, http://www.economist.com/node/15660846 [accessed 28 February 2013] (the article is anonymously written).

Slang words and phrases and typical Swedish idioms are misinterpreted. Stieg's humor, often expressed by continuously repeating the same word or phrase but inferring slightly different meanings, is often erased since the translation avoids all repetition, obviously never suspecting that it may serve a purpose. In short, the English translation is stilted, reads badly, is full of unwarranted cuts, deletions, changes, and misunderstandings, and gives no true impression of the style, atmosphere, or storytelling 'voice' of Stieg Larsson's novels.[10]

It is quite obvious that the *Millennium* novels have qualities that transcend the language and the misinterpretations found in the English text.[11]

In the article in *The Economist*, the author establishes that there are three factors behind the success of the Scandinavian crime writers: 'language, heroes and setting'.[12] With reference to Niclas Salomonsson, a Swedish literary agent representing many of the most prosperous and a number of up-and-coming writers, it is concluded that the 'plain, direct writing, devoid of metaphor' used by the Scandinavian authors, 'suits the genre well', that the detectives of the Nordic crime novels are 'often careworn and rumpled', but that '[m]ost important is [the] setting'.[13] The conclusion concerning language describes well most of the Swedish crime writers, although there are definite exceptions – such as Åke Edwardson, who tends to use a much more poetic language – and also, for example, Henning Mankell, whose Wallander novels exhibit a straightforward language (only enhanced by an extensive use of weather metaphors), whilst a novel such as *Kennedys hjärna* (2005; *Kennedy's Brain* 2007; *Il cervello di Kennedy* 2007) is written in a much more elaborate style. In terms of heroes, *The Economist*'s writer is also fairly accurate. Most detective protagonists of Swedish

---

10   John-Henri Holmberg, 'The Novels You Read are not Necessarily the Novels Stieg Larsson Wrote', in *The Tattoed Girl: The Enigma of Stieg Larsson and the Secrets Behind the Most Compelling Thrillers of Our Time*, by Dan Burstein, Arne de Keijzer, and John-Henri Holmberg (New York: St. Martin's Griffin, 2011), pp. 29–41 (p. 40).

11   Regarding the critique of the English translations, see Holmberg, p. 34–41, and Donna King and Carrie Lee Smith, 'Introduction', in *Men who Hate Women and Women who Kick Their Asses: Stieg Larsson's Millennium Trilogy in Feminist Perspective*, ed. by Donna King and Carrie Lee Smith (Nashville, TN: Vanderbilt University Press, 2012), pp. xiii–xix (p. xvii).

12   'Scandinavian Crime'.

13   Ibid.

crime fiction are far from perfect, and they have generally been shaped by different personal hardships – from Wallander's divorce and near-death experience, as he was once stabbed, to Lisbeth Salander's traumatic childhood in Stieg Larsson's novels. The article writer seems, however, primarily to have the Wallander-type characters – the care-worn middle-aged, male police detectives – in mind, as the other examples mentioned are the Icelandic Arnaldur Indridason's (b. 1961) Inspector Erlandur, and the Norwegian Jo Nesbø's (b. 1960) Inspector Hole.[14] In 1981, Bo Lundin noted that in combination with a strong sense of setting, this type of detective character was the most characteristic feature of Swedish crime fiction.[15] It might be added that it *had been* the most common detective type in Swedish crime fiction until the early 2000s, and only in the last few years has there been greater diversity and more women among Swedish investigative characters.[16] In terms of setting, the article from *The Economist* refers to Scandinavian crime novels showing the 'dark underside' hidden beyond the welfare system.[17] This is something that has been characterizing Swedish crime fiction tradition, thus promoting social and political critique, inspired by the police novels of Maj Sjöwall and Per Wahlöö from the 1960s and 1970s.[18] Today however, many of the Swedish authors most acclaimed abroad– for example Camilla Läckberg, Mari Jungstedt, and Johan Theorin – do not write in this crime fiction tradition, and their novels do not examine any 'dark underside' of the welfare state.[19] Actually, in the novels by the few more critically inclined among the Swedish crime writers today, there are only remnants of the welfare system left, and the 'underside' is no longer hidden, but spun out into

---

14   Ibid.
15   Bo Lundin, *The Swedish Crime Story*, trans. by Anna Lena Ringarp, Ralph A. Wilson, and Bo Lundin (Bromma: Jury, 1981), pp. 8–10.
16   Cf. Kerstin Bergman, 'Beyond Stieg Larsson: Contemporary Trends and Traditions in Swedish Crime Fiction', in *Forum for World Literature Studies*, 4.2 (2012), pp. 291–306 (p. 297–302); and 'Lisbeth Salander and her Swedish Crime Fiction 'Sisters': Stieg Larsson's Hero in a Genre Context', in *Men Who Hate Women and Women Who Kick Their Asses: Stieg Larsson's Millennium Trilogy in Feminist Perspective*, ed. by Donna King and Carrie Lee Smith (Nashville: Vanderbilt University Press, 2012): 135–144 (passim).
17   'Scandinavian Crime'.
18   Cf. chapter 2.
19   Cf. chapter 6.

the open.[20] The Swedish welfare system is something which belongs to the past; today only fragments remain, but the idealized images of a well-functioning Sweden still circulate abroad.

Is the combination of the language, the worse-for-wear detectives, and the setting of a dying – or already defunct – welfare system what really makes Swedish (and Nordic) crime fiction successful abroad? Yes and no. An uncomplicated and easily accessible language characterizes most crime fiction, not only within the Nordic sphere; for this has always been part of the genre's attraction, the straightforward language contributing to a suspenseful and fast-pace read. Although the Wallander-type characters have much in common with well-known detectives of other countries' crime fiction series – for example Inspector Morse and his many equally melancholic and lonely colleagues of the British crime fiction tradition – Inspector Wallander, with his ulcers, his diabetes, and his bad judgment when drinking has enjoyed particular popularity worldwide. The fallibility of Mankell's hero makes him perhaps more human than some of the similar international examples, something that has most likely contributed to his triumphs. Nevertheless, with Stieg Larsson's Lisbeth Salander definitely being the most successful Swedish crime fiction hero in the international market in the last decade, and with Camilla Läckberg now ranking third in terms of novels sold abroad (after Mankell and Stieg Larsson), it is clear that having a Wallander-type hero is not a prerequisite for a Swedish crime novel to succeed abroad. When it comes to the disintegrating welfare system, this has already been addressed above and, additionally, the argument for Läckberg's success is valid here too, as her novels are not concerned with political critique. Nevertheless, there is some evidence to suggest that those novels where the 'underside' of the welfare society is still an issue are popular abroad. Perhaps many international readers gain a sense of malicious pleasure from reading about a Sweden that is not flawless: that is, not living up to the standards of being the perfect socialist utopia it is reputed to be.

This is by no means the whole truth behind the Swedish crime fiction wonder and behind Stieg Larsson's unusual success, however. First, more importance is attached to the setting than to the disintegrating Swedish welfare state. Swedish crime writers are

---

20   Many socially and politically conscious Swedish crime writers today also
       examine international and transnational phenomena, cf. chapter 8.

prone to extensive description of the physical environment of their novels, whether it be the changing skies over Stockholm, or the landscape and nature of the Swedish countryside. Sweden (and the other Nordic countries) is a part of Europe that few have actually visited, and to many people the vast spaces of this large but sparsely populated country in the far north holds an almost exotic allure. In the last decades this interest has for example manifested itself in many foreigners – in addition to Norwegians and Danes, primarily people from Germany and The Netherlands – acquiring summer houses in the Swedish countryside. The image of beautiful Swedish nature with the midnight sun in the summer and long dark and snow-filled winters has also been spread, for example, by the films of Ingmar Bergman (1918–2007). Combined with notions of 'Swedish sin' and a generally liberal attitude towards sexuality, a mental image of an exotic and fascinating country has been created, that many people abroad are curious about. Crime fiction, in that it mostly provides relatively realistic images of contemporary society, gives readers an opportunity to satisfy at least some of this curiosity.

Secondly, although most Swedish crime fiction can hardly be described as feminist, to international readers from many countries, these novels still provide a represention of a place with relative gender equality.[21] Even though many novels portray rather outdated gender relations and a hierarchical subjugation of women, the majority of women heroes in Swedish crime fiction are at least strong, have a career, and are reasonably respected by their male peers. Although relatively rare, the work of some authors like Stieg Larsson and Liza Marklund also offers an outspoken feminist critique. In Larsson's case, this has most likely been a contributing fact in the success of his trilogy – something to which we will return. Thirdly, Stieg Larsson's popularity is also to a great extent based in his playful mixture of different crime fiction sub-genres and elements, something that has made genre-hybridity and increased genre variety a strong trend in Swedish crime fiction in the last few years.

---

21   For a more extensive discussion of to what extent Swedish crime fiction can be considered feminist, see chapter 4.

Having Fun with Genre

The *Millennium* trilogy is characterized by a diverse mix of genres, crime fiction sub-genres and other genres of popular fiction.[22] This is particularly noticeable in the first novel, *Män som hatar kvinnor* (2005; *The Girl with the Dragon Tattoo* 2008; *Uomini che odiano le donne* 2008), the novel that initiated the trilogy's success. The novel begins as journalist Mikael Blomkvist takes time off from the *Millennium* magazine, having lost a libel case brought against him by powerful millionaire Hans-Erik Wennerström. As soon as he steps down from *Millennium*, Blomkvist is hired by wealthy industrialist Henrik Vanger, ostensibly to write the Vanger family history, in reality to solve the mystery of the disappearance of young Harriet Vanger in the 1960s. Reluctant at first, Blomkvist takes on the case and moves to the remote island which is home to the Vangers and from which Harriet vanished. He soon realises that he is dealing with a serial killer and hires Lisbeth Salander, a computer hacker-cum-freelance investigator with a private security firm, to help him. Salander is entrusted by the State to legal guardians since childhood. The latest appointed guardian, lawyer Nils Bjurman, sexually abuses her. Eventually Blomkvist and Salander close the Vanger case – solving the mysteries of both the missing girl and the serial killer; Salander overturns the power relationship she has with Bjurman; and the two gather evidence against Wennerström so that Blomkvist can be exonerated from the accusation with which the story had started.

In terms of genre, *Män som hatar kvinnor* can first and foremost be categorized as a fusion of an intellectual whodunit mystery and a suspenseful serial killer thriller. Initially, the clue-puzzle genre associated with Harriet's disappearance from the isolated island dominates, but eventually it is the psychological thriller associated with the serial killer case that takes over. The shift from one genre to the other is gradual, but with the turning-point clearly marked by several genre-related features, for example, an increase in tempo and suspense, the threat inherent in the killing and mutilation of Blomkvist's cat, and weather metaphors associated with an approaching storm. After Blomkvist is chased by a gunman, even the characters become aware that their world is switching genres, and Salander declares: 'This may

---

22   I have previously explored this at length in Bergman, 'Pressed Flowers', passim, and this section is primarily based on that article.

have started out as a historical mystery', but now 'we can be sure we're on somebody's trail', thus indicating that their adventure is no longer primarily about a disappearance in the 1960s, but has now put them in the midst of something very present and dangerous.[23] As the thriller genre becomes gradually more dominant, the suspense also escalates, thereby making it increasingly difficult for the reader to put the novel down. In addition to these two dominating genre affiliations, the novel also aligns itself with a number of other fiction genres and sub-genres, which include: the American hard-boiled detective novel (particularly as Salander works in the manner of a PI associated with this genre, and by her lone wolf status), the children's detective story (primarily by its explicit and implicit references to authors and novels of this genre, and by playful elements within the narrative), and the action thriller (Salander turns more and more into an action hero, and throughout the trilogy her main inspiration comes from women action heroes of popular culture). The novel follows at times the conventions of the police novel (for example, the cold case scenario and the interview with the officer in charge of the disappearance in the past), and of the financial thriller (the Wennerström affair and the sections relating to journalism and the media). It also pays tribute to the horror genre (Mikael's naïve visit to and final showdown with the serial killer), to the journalistic detective novel (with Blomkvist as protagonist and his manner of investigation, the importance of *Millennium* magazine), and contains features of 'true crime' (through its explicit references to real Swedish crimes, criminality, and 'real crime' books).

One crucial aspect in turning Larsson's trilogy into such a success is that the novels managed to reach an audience beyond that of traditional crime fiction readers. That Larsson not only played with the crime genre, but also with other popular fiction genres, definitely contributed to making the novels attractive to a wider audience. In addition, his experiments with different crime genres have been paramount in expanding his readership. Readers who normally dismiss crime fiction as being too formulaic might find the utter complexity of these novels intriguing compared with more emblematic novels of the genre. Additionally, crime fiction aficionados who generally prefer only certain sub-genres, might find reasons to expand their

---

23   Stieg Larsson, *The Girl with the Dragon Tattoo*, trans. Reg Keeland (New York: Knopf, 2008), p. 331.

horizons as their favoured sub-genre is combined with others.[24] It is obvious that Larsson enjoyed himself, employing his extensive genre knowledge as he wrote the trilogy, and that millions of readers worldwide have since appreciated his efforts.

Stieg Larsson's Message

In the introduction to *Men who Hate Women and Women who Kick their Asses: Stieg Larsson's Millennium Trilogy in Feminist Perspective* (2012), editors Donna King and Carrie Lee Smith write:

> What struck us in our own readings of Larsson was the unexpected combination of familiar crime fiction devices – rape, murder, mayhem, etc., often at women's expense and described in excruciating detail – served up with a distinctly feminist flavor and with some remarkable feminist characters. The juxtaposition was jarring, yet strangely compelling.[25]

Even if the intricate play with genre is likely to have been the main key to Stieg Larsson's success, other factors mentioned above – and not least the feminist message encoded in his novels – should not be underestimated.[26] The Swedish title of Larsson's first novel, *Män som hatar kvinnor*, literally means 'men who hate women', and

---

24   Even if Larsson's intricate combination of elements from so many genres
      was crucial for his novel's reaching such a wide audience, this is of course
      not the only reason behind his success. In order to become an internation-
      al bestseller, both external factors associated with marketing, timing and
      the publishing business, and text-internal factors such as the feminist mes-
      sage of the novels and the attractiveness of the Lisbeth Salander character
      (the latter is also to a great extent related to the mixing of conventions
      from different popular genres). For a more extensive discussion of the rea-
      sons behind Larsson's international success, see Bergman, 'Genre-Hy-
      bridization'.
25   King and Smith, p. xiii.
26   The feminism of Larsson's novels has been questioned, mainly by femi-
      nist factions arguing that the novel cannot be feminist due to the explicit
      portrayal of violence against women, which is considered to be anti-fem-
      inist by default. Abby L. Ferber makes a balanced account of the ambiva-
      lent feminist approaches to the violence against women in Larsson's tril-
      ogy in 'Always Ambivalent: Why Media Is Never Just Entertainment', in
      *Men who Hate Women and Women who Kick Their Asses: Stieg Larsson's
      Millennium Trilogy in Feminist Perspective*, ed. by Donna King and Car-

that is a strong indication of what the novel – and the following two novels – are about. With *Män som hatar kvinnor*, Larsson aims to criticize and raise awareness of structural and physical violence towards women. This continues to be a prevailing theme throughout the trilogy, perhaps most explicitly represented in the serial killer case of the first novel and in the story about Salander that runs through all three. Abby L. Ferber stresses how '[p]art of the appeal of Larsson's novels is his direct and repeated refutation of [...] postfeminist assertions', that he regards violence against women 'as an urgent social problem threatening women's lives and well-being' even today.[27] While the media in general tend to promote postfeminist ideas, assuming that 'gender equality has now been achieved and oppression of women is largely a thing of the past', Ferber finds the rejection of any such claims to be one of the most attractive things about the *Millennium* trilogy.[28] As Sweden is a country with a reputation of being a beacon of gender equality, the realization for international readers that this is not the case, that even Sweden is still not equal, might be a surprising, particularly fascinating and perhaps shocking revelation. That Larsson also supports his narrative by quoting statistics about the violence against women in Sweden at the outset of each of the four parts of *Män som hatar kvinnor*, further increases the likelihood that readers will connect the fictional story with present reality. While most people today are aware that physical violence against women is a problem, realizing that structural violence against women is still also a major issue – even in a 'country of gender equality' like Sweden – might constitute an eye-opener for supporters of the postfeminist positions in this regard.

The fact that Larsson's feminist ideas and perspectives are still not too radical probably enables a wider audience to find his novels refreshing, without having to readjust their tolerance threshold. Ferber notes that what makes Larsson's novels remarkable is that 'he does not reduce the issue [of men's violence against women] to simply the actions of a few bad men. Instead, he presents it as a systemic, institutional system of inequality'.[29] While most products of popular fiction

rie Lee Smith (Nashville, TN: Vanderbilt University Press, 2012), pp. 3–14.
27   Ferber, p. 5.
28   Ibid., p. 5.
29   Ibid., p. 6.

– not only crime fiction – tend to point a finger at one man or select a number of specific villains, Larsson shows gender inequality and violence against women to be a fundamental, structural problem in modern society. This makes the problem even more difficult to come to terms with, and thereby perhaps also easier to ignore, but what Larsson aims to do is at least to raise awareness of the problem by showing his readers the many forms taken by the oppression of and violence towards women. Furthermore, he sets examples by portraying characters of strong and successful women, but also of good men who regard women as equals and who strive for gender equality.

In some ways, it can be argued that Larsson inverts traditional gender stereotypes, by providing Mikael Blomkvist with more traditionally female traits, and letting Lisbeth Salander be the action hero as she finally rescues the captured Blomkvist from the serial killer.[30] After the two of them start working together half-way into the novel, they do, however, appear to take an equal share in solving the mystery, right up until the very end. Indeed, that their working relationship tends to be gender equal is likely to be part of the novel's attraction, and something an international audience might also expect, and accept, from a modern Swedish novel. Lisbeth Salander has been the main focus of both the marketing and the reception of Larsson's trilogy in the English-speaking markets, and that the feminist message of Larsson's novels is closely connected with her popular character should also be taken into account. Salander is based primarily on the women action heroes of popular films, but the novel format provides an opportunity to create a portrait of a more complex woman, enabling Larsson to make Salander strong but at the same time human and vulnerable. In addition to woman action heroes, the Salander character builds on a tradition of strong women heroes in Swedish literature in general, and in Swedish crime fiction from the last decade and a half in particular.[31] It can be argued that Larsson's novels, at least to some extent, challenge the male paradigm traditionally dominating the

---

30   Cf. Sara Kärrholm, 'Is Mikael Blomkvist the Man of the Millennium? A Swedish perspective on Masculinity and Feminism in Larsson's Millennium Trilogy', in *Men who Hate Women and Women who Kick Their Asses: Stieg Larsson's Millennium Trilogy in Feminist Perspective*, ed. by Donna King and Carrie Lee Smith (Nashville, TN: Vanderbilt University Press, 2012), pp. 145–54 (p. 151).

31   Cf. Bergman, 'Lisbeth Salander', passim.

crime genre and advocate more progressive ideas about gender equality, while at the same time criticizing structural violence and suppression of women in society. The reasons behind the recent international bonanza for Swedish crime fiction in general, and for Stieg Larsson's novels in particular, thus lie in a combination of numerous factors: Nordic crime fiction's reputation for being of quality, having some accomplished translators, the use of a straightforward language, the depiction of human, complex and fallible heroes, the critique of the disintegrating Swedish welfare system, the 'exotic' elements of the Swedish setting, the relative feminism and/or gender equality portrayed and expressed in many of the novels, the genre hybridization, and successful marketing. One can only speculate on how long the success story will continue, but since many of the really better quality Swedish crime writers have only just begun to become available through translation in the large, English-speaking markets, it is likely that the triumphs will continue well into the foreseeable future. In Sweden the number of crime writers still grows steadily and, although the quality of the work of some of the new authors is questionable, there are also many really good new writers emerging. So far, the national popularity of Swedish crime fiction has shown no signs of decreasing, but has remained pretty stable since the turn of the millennium.[32] As Jan Arnald (Arne Dahl) explains in an interview:

> I will probably always dabble in the crime genre somehow. Crime fiction provides a therapeutic process, a kind of healing process. You get answers and truths that you don't get in your everyday life. It brings with it a promise of creating order and coherence out of disorder and chaos. Herein lies the enticement and the pleasure of crime fiction, and this is why the genre will not die.[33]

---

32 Swedish crime fiction has continuously dominated the Swedish bestseller lists in the last decade, occupying an average of 60% of the top ten positions 2004–2010 (cf. Karl Berglund, *Deckarboomen under lupp: Statistiska perspektiv på svensk kriminallitteratur 1977–2010* [The crime fiction boom under the magnifying glass: Statistical perspectives on Swedish crime fiction 1977–2010] (Uppsala: Avdelningen för litteratursociologi, Uppsala universitet, 2012), p.162).

33 Sanna Torén Björling, 'Sanna Torén Björling möter Jan Arnald' [Sanna Torén Björling meets Jan Arnald (interview with Jan Arnald)], *Dagens Nyheter*, 13 June 2011, my translation.

Nevertheless, it is difficult to foretell the consequences of the recent increase in genre-hybridization. Swedish crime writers today intermingle not only different crime fiction sub-genres, but also many other popular fiction genres, for example those of romance, horror, and fantasy. If this continues to an extreme, perhaps the crime genre will eventually turn insipid, and merge into some general mish-mash of popular fiction, thus losing many of those characteristic elements making it so popular today, nationally as well as internationally.

VIII

THE EUROPEAN TURN: *ARNE DAHL*

Towards the end of the first decade of the 2000s, increasing attempts have been made to introduce European (and global) perspectives into Swedish crime fiction. National identity is now contrasted with notions of European identity, many novels include settings beyond the Swedish national borders, and international crime syndicates are colonizing Sweden. An emblematic example of these developments is Arne Dahl's recent Europol crime series, which is the focal point of this chapter.

The Swedish crime fiction tradition characterized by social and political critique and awareness that followed the example set by Maj Sjöwall (b. 1935) and Per Wahlöö (1926–75) in the 1960s and 1970s, often displayed a strong national focus.[1] The primary object of criticism was the disintegrating Swedish welfare state, in many cases in combination with a discussion of media ethics and limited police resources. The novels and writers of this tradition tended to combine a critique of a present Swedish reality with nostalgia for a functioning welfare state that increasingly appeared to be a thing of the past. In the 1990s, authors associating themselves with this tradition, perhaps most notably Henning Mankell (b. 1948), started to depict a Sweden that was not only threatened by internal disintegration, but also from the outside, by a new organized criminality following in the wake of a growing globalization.[2] Anna Westerståhl Stenport notes how already in his first crime novel, *Mördare utan ansikte* (1991; *Faceless Killers* 1997; *Assassino senza volto* 2001), Mankell 'posits Sweden as a recent and uneasy member of a global network of nations open to

---

1   This is further explored in chapter 2.
2   Cf. chapter 3.

unwanted large-scale migration'.[3] In this first Inspector Wallander novel, 'porous national borders' are presented as a major threat, and 'Sweden's collective mourning for a lost paradise' is important to the national state of affairs.[4] This focus on international threats to an established, national whole is typical for much of the Swedish crime fiction from the 1990s and early 2000s, exhibiting social and political awareness. In particular, despite the end of the Cold War there seems to be a strong threat coming from the east, and organized crime with ties to Eastern Europe, often related to human-trafficking and the drug trade, becomes a staple in much of Swedish crime fiction. Still, Sweden is regarded as an enclosed and perhaps rather naïve society in comparison with the distant places beyond its borders where the new criminality originates.

One author, who throughout his crime fiction oeuvre has striven to engage with current social and political issues, is Arne Dahl (pen name for Jan Arnald, b. 1962). Starting out as an author of mainstream fiction under his real name in 1990, Arnald made his debut as a crime writer under the pseudonym of Dahl in 1998 with *Ont blod* (*Bad Blood* 2013; *La linea del male* 2006).[5] It took four more Dahl novels before the author's real identity was revealed, and the mystery contributed to creating media attention for the new crime series.[6] Following the pattern established by Sjöwall and Wahlöö, Dahl's ambition was to write a series of ten police novels. Nevertheless, his attitude towards social and political critique has always been different from that of his predecessors:

> There are of course many things in society today that upset me: a fixation with money, media stupidity, indoctrination inherent in advertising, dehumanization, and the lack of thinking, of empathy, of culture, and of history. But the ideological criticism is never primary – in that respect I

---

3   Anna Westerståhl Stenport, 'Bodies Under Assault: Nation and Immigration in Henning Mankell's *Faceless Killers*', *Scandinavian Studies* 79.1 (2007), 1–24 (p. 6).

4   Ibid., pp. 7 and 20.

5   In addition to *Ont Blod*, so far only one of Dahl's novels, *Misterioso* (1999; *Misterioso/The Blinded Man* 2010; *Misterioso* 2009), is available in English translation, but this is likely to change in the near future.

6   Svante Lidén, 'Gåtan Arne Dahl är löst: Nu träder den hemliga deckarförfattaren fram' [The riddle of Arne Dahl is solved: The secret crime writer comes forward (interview with Arne Dahl/Jan Arnald)], *Aftonbladet*, 12 April 2002.

feel a difference between me and Sjöwall/Wahlöö. To me it is much more important to write well than to write politically.[7]

Dahl has succeeded in becoming known for being a good writer, but also he has come across as one of the most political Swedish crime writers of recent years, providing a well-researched and relevant analysis of contemporary society in his police novels.[8] A decade after the statement above, Dahl stresses in another interview that 'I might not criticize the system as much as I try to show how it changes and how we change with it'.[9] This is in itself an implicit form of criticism.

Dahl's first police series – consisting of ten police novels plus an eleventh, aptly called *Elva* (2008, Eleven), a Decameron-like novel where the police collective of his previous novels is reunited for one night, and take it in turn to tell a story over dinner – is set mainly in Stockholm. It follows a national police task force, in Swedish called *A-gruppen*, the A-Group, but in English translation so far alternately referred to as the Intercrime Group, the A-team and the A-unit, tasked to deal with violent criminality with international ties. Dahl's Intercrime Group is centered around the character of Paul Hjelm, a man who in many respects is reminiscent of Sjöwall and Wahlöö's Martin Beck and Mankell's Kurt Wallander, but who throughout the series shares the foreground equally with nine colleagues with whom he works closely. The novels of the Intercrime series can be described as true police procedurals in that they portray the efforts and the working processes of the whole team, rather than making Hjelm the sole hero. Although the team is part of the national Swedish police, and although they spend most of their time investigating crimes committed in the Swedish capital, the international elements in the work of the Intercrime Group are prominent.

---

7   Kerstin Weigl, 'Att bli känd är inget mål i sig' [To become famous is not a goal in itself (anonymous interview with 'Arne Dahl')], *Aftonbladet*, 10 November 2001, my translation.

8   The aesthetic qualities of Dahls novels have been studied primarily by Peter Kirkegaard, *Blues for folkhemmet: Næranalyse af Arne Dahls Europa Blues* [Blues for the welfare state: A close reading of Arne Dahl's Europa Blues] (Aalborg: Aalborg Universitetsforlag, 2013).

9   Sanna Torén Björling, 'Sanna Torén Björling möter Jan Arnald' [Sanna Torén Björling meets Jan Arnald (interview with Jan Arnald)], *Dagens Nyheter*, 13 June 2011, my translation.

During the time of the series – taking place from 1997 to 2007 – the group deals with, for example, terrorism, organized crime, the drug trade, Internet crime, trafficking, hostage situations, robberies, and even an American serial killer visiting Sweden. The stories of many of the novels of the Intercrime series are anchored in history as well as in Swedish reality at the time when they are set, and readers encounter everything from the Swedish financial crisis in the 1990s to the new surveillance society and recent cultural controversies. Despite having a primarily Swedish focus, the international aspects of the criminality fought by the Intercrime Group together with the increasing effects of globalization visible in Swedish society, give Dahl's series a somewhat transnational outlook. Some tendencies towards highlighting the impact of Europeanization are found already in the Intercrime series. For example, the appropriately titled *Europa Blues* (2001, Europe blues; *Europa blues* 2012) starts out as one of the many crime novels from the last decades which examine Sweden's past during the Second World War and the fate of the Swedish Nazi collaborators, but it soon turns into an investigation of a past and present that is not only Swedish but increasingly European, with important parts of the novel set in Germany, Italy, and the Ukraine.[10]

Beyond the National Borders

Towards the end of the first decade of the twenty-first century, an increasing number of Swedish crime writers have not only presented Sweden as being infiltrated and colonized by international criminals, but also started to set their novels beyond the national borders. One of the best examples of this is Karin Alfredsson (b. 1953), who uses international settings throughout her whole series with the medical doctor Ellen Elg in the investigative role: from southern Af-

---

10   Concerning Swedish crime novels dealing with Swedish Nazi collaboration, among them Dahl's *Europa Blues* and Mankell's *Danslärarens återkomst* (2000; *The Return of the Dancing Master*, 2004), see Kerstin Bergman, 'The Good, The Bad, and the Collaborators: Swedish World War II Guilt Redefined in 21st Century Crime Fiction', in *The Individual Confronts the Masses: Life in Mass Dictatorships in Literature and Cinema*, ed. by Michael Schoenhals and Karin Sarsenov (New York: Palgrave, 2013), pp. 183–210 (passim).

rica in *80 grader från Varmvattnet* (2006, 80 degrees from Varmvattnet), through to novels set in Hanoi, Poland, and India, to the
most recent *Pojken i hiss 54* (2011, The boy in elevator 54), set in
Pakistan and Dubai. Alfredsson is a journalist and has dedicated her
work mainly to women's rights issues, working nationally as well as
internationally. This devotion also emerges in her crime novels. The
whole series depicts the situation of women in different parts of the
world and, for example, *Klockan 21:37* (2009, 9:37 PM) caused
controversy in Poland for its critical portrayal of anti-abortion sentiments within the Catholic Church. Throughout the series, Alfredsson's reputation as a crime writer has grown, and today she is recognized as one of the Swedish authors worth paying attention to. Other
Swedish crime writers who have recently set their novels, or at least
parts of their novels, abroad, are Henning Mankell (Europe and Africa), Ola Wong (b. 1977, Asia), Henrik Tord (b. 1969, Asia), Åsa
Nilsonne (b. 1949, Africa), Liza Marklund (b. 1962, Europe and Africa), Åke Edwardson (b. 1953, Europe), and Håkan Nesser (b.
1950, Europe), amongst others. In most cases the milieus used are
either those familiar to many Swedes – as is the Spanish coast in
novels by Edwardson and Marklund – or places used in order to
raise awareness of inequalities in the world, as in novels by Alfredsson, Mankell, Tord, and Nilsonne. Recently, however, it has been increasingly common to use European settings to create a sense of fa-
miliarity and to take the focus away from national borders in times
of European Union membership, where people are becoming increasingly European.

The internationalization in Swedish crime fiction is not only
about settings and international criminals, but also about cultural
identity and identification.[11] In Henning Mankell's *Den orolige
mannen* (2009; *The Troubled Man* 2011; *L'uomo inquieto* 2010), the
final novel of the Inspector Wallander series, Mankell shows that
national identity and national perspectives are in the process of becoming obsolete, and that the way forward is for new generations to
identify themselves as Europeans rather than as Swedes. The nation-
ally-oriented police hero represented by Wallander is portrayed as
ageing and becoming a figure of the past, no longer able to deal with
the new, modern criminality. Instead Wallander works as a private
investigator while his daughter, Linda Wallander, is made out to be

---

11   This is further addressed in chapter 3.

a representative of a more modern and European generation, more suited to handle the new and future criminality.[12] The most striking example of the Europeanization trend in Swedish crime fiction is, however, the new police series by Arne Dahl, a series that in many senses continues where Dahl's Intercrime series left off, and which also attempts to put into practice what Mankell suggested in *Den orolige Mannen*.

Europeanization in Practice: Arne Dahl

After finishing his Intercrime series in 2008 with *Elva*, Arne Dahl returned to crime fiction with a new series, starting with *Viskleken* (2011, Chinese whispers), which was announced to be the first of a quartet of new crime novels.[13] So far, the first instalment – which was awarded The Golden Crowbar for best Swedish crime novel of the year by the Swedish Academy of Detection in 2011 – has been followed by *Hela havet stormar* (2012, Musical chairs) and *Blindbock* (2013, Blind man's buff). The new series portrays an investigative police team connected to Europol: the 'Opcop' group is a secret, operative test unit within the European police agency, and consists of a number of police investigators located in The Hague, as well as a number of smaller, local/national units, connected to the main team.[14] Dahl has brought along some of his favorite characters from the Intercrime series to work in The Hague: Paul Hjelm is once again found in the leading role and, additionally, some of the remaining Intercrime members now work for the local Stockholm Opcop-unit, thus also appearing in the new series. In addition to the Swedish characters, Dahl has created officers from all over Europe

---

12   This is extensively analyzed and discussed in Kerstin Bergman, 'Initiating a European Turn: Negotiation of European and National Identities in Mankell's *The Troubled Man* (2009)', in *Scandinavica*, 51.1 (2012), pp. 56–78.

13   The following analysis of Dahl's *Viskleken* builds primarily on my article, Kerstin Bergman, 'Beyond National Allegory? Europeanization in Swedish Crime Writer Arne Dahl's *Viskleken*', forthcoming.

14   Opcop officially stands for 'Overt Police Cooperation', but really means 'Operating Cops', thus stressing the operative aspects of their work (Arne Dahl, *Viskleken* (Stockholm: Bonniers, 2011), p. 37–38).

in order to provide a complex and truly European cast of characters for his new series.

The members of the Opcop team come from Germany, Poland, Romania, Sweden, the UK, Lithuania, Greece, France, Spain, and Italy, and they are said to represent the biggest countries as well as the different regions of EU Europe.[15] However, when initially presented in a whodunit-inspired list at the beginning of the novel, it is not the nationalities of the team members that are stressed, but rather the cities or regions they come from and the type of criminality they have previously had to deal with. Six of the nine new officers are actually located in Europe by city rather than by country, for example, 'MAREK KOWALEWSKI: desk officer from Warsaw, who has a background in fighting economic criminality in Eastern Europe' and 'CORINE BOUHADDI: Muslim drug squad cop from one of Europe's roughest cities, Marseilles'.[16] Already here the national borders of Europe are thus somewhat blurred by being ignored in the textual presentations.

Nevertheless, the initial descriptions of the characters do build on national stereotypes, or at least on national stereotypes as seen from a Swedish perspective.[17] At first, the members of the Opcop team are also said to all struggle with their common language of communication, the 'EUnglish', 'this strangely flat linguistic repertoire that was used within the EU.[18] A hundred pages into the novel, however, the leader of the team notes that the group has overcome all language barriers. Thirty pages further along the German officer is seen thinking in EUnglish, and as the novel progresses the members of the team nonchalantly mix words and expressions from each other's languages.[19] National stereotypes also become nuanced as the teammates learn to respect and like each other.[20] The settings of Dahl's

---

15 Cf. Dahl, p. 39–41. Of the local/national Opcop representatives very few have active roles in the novel, and only the Swedes appear in the initial list of characters.

16 Ibid., p. [5], my translation.

17 Cf. ibid., pp. 33–36.

18 Ibid., p. 35, my translation.

19 Ibid., p. 101 and 137. The language barriers seem to disappear as soon as the team members are actually working together, in contrast to when they are initially mostly pushing papers, unsure of what the purpose of the group really is.

20 For example, half way into the novel, Kowalewski, the Pole, cannot stand Polish Bison Vodka, said to be 'European nowadays' (Dahl, p. 270, my

novel similarly illustrate the transnational perspective. Key events take place in The Hague, London, Berlin, Basilicata (in Southern Italy), Riga, Stockholm, and New York and, as with the Opcop characters, nationality is not focused on in the description of places either; instead the locations – except for New York – are portrayed as being just part of a largely undifferentiated Europe.

The creation of Opcop is presented as a necessity, as it is impossible nowadays to catch big criminals without crossing national borders.[21] Symbolically, Dahl's embryonic transformation of Europol into a European FBI coincides with moving the Europol headquarters from a cosy old school building, into a modern 'bureaucratic high-rise'.[22] This is a clear reference to how Sjöwall and Wahlöö, in the last novels of their series, contrasted their old Stockholm police offices with the new, modern headquarters under construction. The latter was taken to represent the corruption, militarization, and bureaucratization of the Swedish police in Sjöwall and Wahlöö's novels.[23] While their police protagonists were associated with the old buildings and posited as the last outpost of sanity in a police organization gone mad, Dahl's European police team are now instead part of the new times and fit well into the modern building and the Europol organization – an organization that, despite remaining relatively anonymous, is not negatively connoted.[24]

At the London G-20 Summit held in April 2009, support for struggling banks embroiled in the financial crisis was discussed, and this is an important point of departure for many chains of events in the novel. When the meeting is described, much of the emphasis is put on the protests against it. The protests are said to be organized over the Internet by use of Twitter, in a way structured along biblical lines, with the Four Horsemen of the Apocalypse representing

---

translation), and when at dinner the team discusses the different food cultures of Europe as they tend to, they suggest untraditional cross-kitchen mixes, some seriously and others mostly joking, but the food mixes all become images of their cross-European cooperation (ibid., pp. 194–97). Cf. also the more extensive descriptions of the team in ibid., pp. 101–06.

21   Ibid., p. 44.
22   Cf. ibid., p. 31, my translation.
23   Kerstin Bergman, 'From National Authority to Urban Underbelly: Negotiations of Power in Stockholm Crime Fiction', in *Crime Fiction in the City: Capital Crimes*, ed. by Lucy Andrew and Catherine Phelps (Cardiff: University of Wales Press, 2013), pp. 65–84 (p. 70).
24   Cf. ibid.,' p. 70.

four different areas of criticism against the G-20 Summit.[25] The transnational character of the Internet and the biblical references serve to associate the events of the novel both with a common present-day reality and with a shared European cultural heritage: that is, to bonds and structures reaching far beyond national borders.[26]

Just as biblical references are used in order to create a common European past, so too is the use of Greek mythology. In Dahl's novel, the myth of Ariadne and Theseus and how they tricked the Minotaur in the maze is particularly significant: Dahl's Ariadne is a woman searching for the truth, but ends up as a murder victim, her death investigated by the Opcop team, while Dahl's Minotaur is personified as an elusive villain banker. Elements of a historical past are brought up in order to illustrate a common European identity as well.[27] Additionally, more recent trans-European phenomena are used to the same end. The digital communication between The Hague headquarters and the local Opcop representatives is a constant source of information as well as amusement, as when the agents in Rome and Riga call and the latter announces: 'This is Riga', one of the Opcop officers whispers to another: 'This is like the fucking Eurovision Song Contest'.[28] The common televisual reference is thus used to illustrate how the different parts of Europe already share a common culture today.

In *Viskleken*, Europe is portrayed as 'kind of framed', in between the Russian and the Italian mafia, but as these criminal organiza-

---

25   Dahl, pp. 12–13. The image of the Four Horsemen of the Apocalypse is found in chapter six of 'The Book of Revelations'. The Horsemen are said to bring about the Apocalypse and the Last Judgment, and are commonly interpreted as representing war, death, conquest and famine, respectively. Dahl lets his protesters arrive from four different directions, dressed in four different colours (the red, green, silver, and black of the biblical Horsemen), each procession led by a doll representing one of the Horsemen – and the four processions in turn symbolize the different "threats" represented by the G-20 meeting: war, environmental crimes, financial crimes and the closed borders of the EU.

26   The Internet is described as 'being' the present and during the novel it becomes an image for the fluidity and the networks of the globalized world (ibid., p. 12).

27   For example, Dahl digresses to talk about Latvian amber, once 'more valuable than gold', and at one point famous in both ancient Greece and Rome (ibid., p. 187, my translation).

28   Ibid., p. 181, my translation.

tions are no longer nationally confined, their tentacles reach right through the EU and beyond.[29] As in the presentation of the characters, nationality is not often used when referring to mafia organizations either.[30] In the greater scheme of things, Dahl's novel also shows Europe as 'framed' between the USA and China, as these superpowers are the outposts of economic crime in the novel.[31] The London Summit officially connects the two in Europe and, furthermore, the Minotaur – the villain banker – is revealed to be hiding somewhere in Europe, controlling the Chinese-American money.[32] Dahl's narrative construction thereby makes Europe the centre of the metaphorical maze that is the new society. In the novel, it is also stressed how criminality is changing not only in terms of geography, but also by type. Economic crime is said to be on the increase, and violent crime to be decreasing in the new Europe.[33] As if mirroring the backdrop of the financial crisis, money is also what lies behind all the crimes occurring in the novel. Reiterated throughout the novel is how the mafia is 'buying up the world', that '*within ten years, Europe will be owned by the mafia*', and that 'all criminality is related'.[34] Dahl creates a picture of organized crime slowly seizing control over everything, from business to politics, locally as well as worldwide. The financial crisis that struck Europe and North America in 2008 acts as an ever-present backdrop to the events in *Viskleken* and contributes to making all aspects of society an easy prey for the mafia. Underneath the official power structures lies another, unofficial network that will soon wield all the power unless something is done about it.[35] Although Dahl presents stopping these developments as 'a mission impossible', it is still stressed how essential it is

---

29   Ibid., p. 116, my translation.
30   Instead the Opcop group talks primarily about the Ndrahgheta and La Santa (organizations originating from Calabria in Southern Italy).
31   Cf. Dahl, pp. 394–395, 421.
32   Ibid., p. 344.
33   Ibid., p. 116.
34   Ibid., pp. 110–111, 117, my translations. Not until page 134, does the realization about how the mafia is truly international really begin to sink in (ibid., p. 134).
35   This is reminiscent of how Swedish crime writers Jens Lapidus (b. 1974) in his Stockholm Noir series portrays Stockholm as completely run by criminal organizations, present everywhere, just under the official surface of society (cf. chapter 5, and Bergman, 'From National Authority', pp. 75–78).

to at least put up a fight against them, and this is where the Opcop team comes in. The group's transnational composition mirrors the transgressive structure of the mafia networks, and thus Opcop is said to have at least a reasonable chance of understanding and gaining knowledge about the criminal organizations.

The new type of transnational criminality differs from the old criminality insofar as the criminals are harder to identify and track down. Over and over again members of the Opcom team note that they detect a large number of crimes, but are still unable to find any criminals. "'I fear this is the criminality of our times", said Paul Hjelm. "The decision-makers are never seen. We are fighting ghosts, shadows – something as elusive as an era"'.[36] Perhaps it is the remnants of and roots in national perspectives among the members of the Opcop team that cause the new criminals to be invisible to them? One of the Swedish police officers asks: 'How could we confront criminality where none of the essential players are national, unless we become international ourselves too?'[37] It seems that national police officers need to become integrated as Europeans before they are able actually to identify the criminals. However, even when the Opcop team is beginning to figure out how everything fits together and who at least some of the villains are, they continue to complain that they are still 'not *catching* any criminals'.[38] Not even at the end of the novel do they have any major players in custody, as these either remain elusive or are killed, and the only criminals caught are the smaller fry who could simultaneously be regarded as victims.

The only ones who seem to have some kind of control, or at least an overview, of the new world are the people behind a security company called Asterion, people who seem to be conducting business in every nook and cranny of the maze-like world and who, as it turns out, are some of the main villains of the novel. Nevertheless, the Asterion people are never caught, but vanish completely at the end of the novel. As one of the Opcop team members conclude: Asterion 'let themselves become extinct in order to reappear eventually in a new form, as demanded by the era'.[39] Towards the end of the novel, one of the minor criminals also asks: 'Will the justice system from

---

36 Dahl, p. 309, my translation. Also see Dahl, p. 377.
37 Ibid., p. 399, my translation.
38 Ibid., p. 434, my translation, my emphasis. Also cf. ibid., p. 494–95.
39 Ibid., p. 495, my translation.

now on *always* be weaker than the international crime syndicates?'[40]
He thus formulates a question that underlies Dahl's novel as a whole.
Is the new criminality growing so strong and powerful, that there is
no longer a way to confront it? Is perhaps corruption saturating all
strata of the judicial system, so that fighting it will be a futile effort
from now on? Dahl still provides the reader with a sense of hope, as
he lets his team members believe in what they do, and even though
they do not capture all the villains, at least they gain some knowledge about the criminal organizations, and they do solve the murders they are faced with. In the end, the experimental Opcop team is
also incorporated as a permanent – if still secret – feature of the Europol organization.

In trying to summarize the Opcop group's first case and identify
what it was really about, the team members conclude that it was all
about 'the future'.[41] This observation is applicable to Dahl's novel in
several ways, in that it describes the new transnational criminality
and the European cooperation and identification represented by the
Opcop team. The developments and the new Europe are also summarized, as Hjelm suggests that they replace the European map with
the team's case 'map' on their digital whiteboard, a 'completely mad
and completely logical map of a continent in mental shambles: an
unlikely constellation of connections between dying body parts. A
nervous system drugged by money. A horrifying diagram of spiritu-
al decay and cultural polish'.[42] Following Mankell's predictions in
Den orolige mannen concerning the need for European perspectives
and the obsolescence of the national police tradition, in *Viskleken*
Dahl thus outlines a possible future police organization and new
methods of detection applicable to the criminality of the future, a
criminality that to a great extent is already here. Nevertheless,
Viskleken ends with a reference to the ending of Sjöwall and
Wahlöö's Decalogue, namely the last page of their novel *Terroristerna* (1975; *The Terrorists* 1976; *Terroristi* 2011).[43] The reference
indicates that beyond the new world portrayed in *Viskleken*, the novel still has a strong and close bond with the social and political crit-

---

40   Ibid., p. 484, my translation.
41   Ibid., p. 487, my translation.
42   Ibid., p. 497, my translation.
43   Ibid., p. 500; Maj Sjöwall and Per Wahlöö, *The Terrorists*, transl. by Joan
        Tate (New York: Vintage, 2010), p. 280.

icism of the Swedish crime fiction tradition. Accordingly, capitalism is still pointed to as being what is destroying – not only Sweden as in Sjöwall and Wahlöö's novels, but now also Europe and the world.

The European (and global) tendencies have increased in Swedish crime fiction in the last few years, and as crime fiction tends to portray the society of its time, it is likely that there will be even more Europeanization of the genre in years to come. This is the direction that the politically conscious Swedish crime fiction is inevitably taking today, in total contrast to, in particular, the neo-romantic novels, with their focus on local, close-knit, rural communities exhibiting few connections to the surrounding, contemporary world beyond.[44] While Sweden is a country increasingly affected by Europeanization and globalization, the strategies of dealing with this in Swedish crime fiction are thus either to try to keep up with the pace – or perhaps even to keep abreast, ahead of the new developments – or to just pretend nothing is happening, and that everything is just as it used to be.

---

44   The neo-romantic novels are discussed in chapter 6.

IX

THE NORDIC NEIGHBOURS

This chapter introduces the crime fiction traditions of Sweden's Nordic neighbours: Denmark, Finland, Iceland, and Norway. The focus is on the recent decades and on similarities and differences between these national crime fiction traditions as compared with the Swedish tradition.

Crime fiction traditions in the Nordic countries have followed a relatively similar path. This is to a great extent the result of the genre in all five countries finding its main influences from the same traditions: the Anglo-American tradition and the crime fiction of their Nordic neighbours. In the introduction to *Scandinavian Crime Fiction* (2011), Paula Arvas and Andrew Nestingen also highlight the welfare state system and the common political movement from a Social Democratic dominance during a major part of the twentieth century to a growing Neoliberalism from the 1980s onwards as factors accountable for creating similarities between the Nordic crime fiction traditions.[1] These common traits have been especially pronounced since the 1960s, as Swedish Maj Sjöwall (b. 1935) and Per Wahlöö (1926–75) with their *Roman om ett brott* (1965–75; *The Story of a Crime* 1967–76; *Martin Beck indaga a Stoccolma* 1973–2011), their ten police procedurals filled with social critique, became immensely influential not only in Sweden, but also in the other Nordic countries. I choose to talk about 'Nordic' here rather than 'Scandinavian' because the use of the latter term generally only includes Sweden, Denmark, and Norway, thus excluding Finland and

---

1   Paula Arvas and Andrew Nestingen, 'Introduction: Contemporary Scandinavian Crime Fiction', in *Scandinavian Crime Fiction*, ed. by Andrew Nestingen and Paula Arvas (Cardiff: University of Wales Press, 2011), pp. 1–17 (pp. 8–9).

Iceland, something that would limit the perspective and overlook some of the most interesting developments in and authorships of Nordic crime fiction. Still, it should be mentioned that Swedish crime fiction – perhaps mainly because of Sjöwall and Wahlöö – has become quite predominant in the Nordic context, something that is highlighted, too, by the recent international interest in Nordic crime fiction, where Swedish authors have played a central role. Nevertheless, the gathering of crime novels from Sweden, Denmark, Finland, Iceland and Norway under common terms such as *Nordic Noir*, *Scandinavian Crime Fiction* or *Schwedenkrimi*, tends to overlook the differences between the national traditions, instead stressing a homogeneity that is only there to a certain extent.

In an academic Scandinavian Studies context – a context that, despite its name, actually also often includes Finnish and Icelandic studies – there has been a commonly-held desire to trace the history, or at least the influences of Nordic crime fiction back to the heritage of the Icelandic/Old Norse Sagas and their violent narratives. The Sagas are the common origin of all Nordic literature, and their influences have been pivotal in the development of the different national literary traditions. Whether tracing this heritage is really relevant for crime fiction, a genre developing in the Nordic countries in the nineteenth century, could be opened to debate, even though many elements found in contemporary crime fiction from the region have their parallels in the very first Nordic literature. These would include, for example, the plain language, the strong women characters, the violence, the gloomy moods, and the 'exotic' Nordic setting. Still, this is not specific enough to motivate one to look back to the early Middle Ages for a starting-point for a Nordic crime fiction history. It makes much more sense to focus on the early examples of Nordic crime fiction found in the mid-nineteenth century.

Denmark, Norway, and Sweden all had crime stories quite similar to those of Edgar Allan Poe, stories combining rational logic and Gothic elements, that actually more or less pre-dated Poe's *The Murders in the Rue Morgue* (1841; *Il doppio assassinio in via Morgue* 1863). In Sweden's case, it was Carl Jonas Love Almqvist's (1793–1866) short story 'Skällnora Qvarn' (1838, Skällnora mill) with its murderous intrigue; in Denmark, Steen Steensen Blicher's (1782–1848) novella *Præsten i Vejlbye* (1829; 'The Pastor of Vejlbye' 1996); and in Norway, Maurits Hansen's (1794–1892) novel *Mordet på maskinbygger Roolfsen: Criminalanecdot fra Kongsberg*

(1839, The murder of engineer Roolfsen: Crime anecdote from Kongsberg). The origins of crime fiction in Finland and Iceland are of a somewhat later date. Over time, the different national crime fiction traditions of the Nordic countries have developed their own distinct specificities and genre preferences. Arvas and Nestingen point to a number of historical, political, and cultural developments that have given rise to these differences. In particular, they stress the importance of the historical power relationships between the countries: each country's situation and experiences during the Second World War, and the varied relationships to the European Union and, prior to that, the European Common Market.[2]

Denmark: International Thrillers and Nordic-style Police Novels

The publication of Steen Steensen Blicher's novella *Præsten i Vejlbye* (1829; 'The Pastor of Vejlbye' 1996) is often referred to as the point of origin of Danish crime fiction, though it took a while before the genre got established in Denmark. Palle Rosenkrantz's (1867–1941) novel *Hvad skovsøen gemte* (1903, What was hidden in the forest lake) is still generally regarded as the first proper Danish crime novel, and in 2003, the centennial birthday of Danish crime fiction was celebrated.[3] Rosencrantz was thus considered a pioneer of Danish crime fiction and, with *Hvad skovsøen gemte*, which is a classic whodunit, he made the genre popular. Rosenkrantz has also had his name attached to the most prestigious Danish crime fiction prize, The Palle Rosenkrantz Prize, which since 1987 has been awarded annually to the best crime novel published in Denmark, but rarely to Danish crime novels, repeatedly going to novels by foreign authors in Danish translation.[4]

Despite its early beginnings, Danish crime fiction kept a relatively low profile up until the 1970s. After the success of Maj Sjöwall and Per Wahlöö in Sweden, the duo also soon grew influ-

---

2   Ibid., pp. 8–9.
3   Cf. Harald Mogensen, *Mord og mysterier: Den danske krimis historie* [Murders and mysteries; The history of Danish crime fiction] (Viby: Centrum, 1983), p. 9.
4   Since 2007, there is also a prize for the best Danish crime novel each year, called the Harald Mogensen Prize, named after Danish crime fiction expert Harald Mogensen (1912–2002).

ential with regard to Danish crime fiction. Some of the Danish writers following in the wake of the Swedish duo as early as in the 1970s were Torben Nielsen (1918–85), with a series of police novels about Inspectors Jens Ancher, Aage Brask, and Hans Rieger in Copenhagen; and then there was Poul Ørum (1919–97) with his series about Inspectors Jonas Mørck and Knut Ejnarsen. Mørck and Ejnarsen are incidentally also based in Copenhagen, but work throughout the country. Nielsen and Ørum were then followed by thriller writers Leif Davidsen (b. 1950) and Jan Stage (1937–2003), both making their debuts in the genre in the 1980s and continuing their output in the following decades. Davidsen has primarily written international political thrillers, among his best known being *Den russiske sangerinde* (1988; *The Russian Singer* 1991; *La cantante russa* 1992) and *Den sidste spion* (1991, The last spy), both about the end of the Soviet era, and *Lime's billede* (1998; *Lime's Photograph* 2002; *Quando il ghiaccio si scioglie* 2001). Stage's novels are also primarily spy thrillers, from *Fare, fare krigsmand* (1985, Danger, danger warrior) to *Den cubanske fælde* (2002, The Cuban trap). Despite the use of the thriller genre, Davidsen and Stage both show clear inspiration from Sjöwall and Wahlöö's use of leftist political criticism.

Recently, the writing duo Christian Dorph (b. 1966) and Simon Pasternak (b. 1971) have also written a series of socially critical police novels explicitly inspired by Sjöwall and Wahlöö, with Inspectors Erik Rhode and Ole Larsen as the main investigators.[5] While most authors with similar inspiration tend to describe and criticize their contemporary society and reality, Dorph and Pasternak have chosen instead to reexamine the recent Danish past. Their novels are set starting in 1975 with *Om et øjeblik i himlen* (2005, In a moment in heaven) and so far have reached 1985 with the third novel in the series, *Jeg er ikke her* (2010, I am not here). In addition to Sjöwall and Wahlöö, Dorph and Pasternak are also inspired by James Ellroy's hard-boiled writing style and his ways of

---

5   They begin their series on the very date on which the Swedes completed their last novel and by quoting Sjöwall and Wahlöö (cf. Karsten Wind Meyhoff, 'Digging into the Secrets of the Past: Rewriting History in the Modern Scandinavian Police Procedural', in *Scandinavian Crime Fiction*, ed. by Andrew Nestingen and Paula Arvas (Cardiff: University of Wales Press, 2011), pp. 62–73 (pp. 63–64)).

portraying the urban environment. Karsten Wind Meyhoff has noted that, although the police procedural has also been a popular genre in Denmark, most Danish authors using the genre are still less focused on social and political criticism, as compared with their Swedish counterparts. Instead, the Danish writers of police novels have busied themselves with 'the psychological and existential aspects of the crime'.[6]

The American hard-boiled tradition has also had its Danish disciples. During the 1980s, Dan Turèll (1946–93) wrote a series of ten novels and two short story collections set in Copenhagen, commonly referred to as *Mord-serien* (The murder series), featuring a journalist detective protagonist. From *Mord i mørket* (1981, Murder in the dark) to *Mord i San Francisco* (1990, Murder in San Francisco), Turèll provides a complex and sharp image of 1980s Copenhagen, and his crime novels have been described as pastiches of American hard-boiled detective fiction.[7] The hard-boiled baton was also picked up by Flemming Jarlskov (b. 1947), who since 1989 has written crime novels about the private investigator Carl Kock, and these are likewise set in the Danish capital.

Additionally, just like Sweden and Norway, Denmark has seen an increasing number of women crime writers emerge in recent decades. An important forerunner in women-authored crime fiction in Denmark was Kirsten Holst (1936–2008), who made her entry into the crime genre as early as in 1976 with the thriller *De unge, de rige og de smukke* (The young, the rich, and the beautiful), and who continued to be a prolific crime writer far into the 2000s.[8] Among the most successful women crime writers who entered the genre a few decades later than Holst are Elsebeth Egholm (b. 1960), Gretelise Holm (b. 1946), Sara Blædel (b. 1964) and Susanne Staun (b. 1957). Egholm and Holm have both chosen women journalists-cum-detectives as their protagonists, and have been productive since the early 2000s. Egholm's journalist Dicte Svendsen is active in Aarhus (Denmark's

---

6   Karsten Wind Meyhoff, *Forbrydelsens elementer: Kriminallitteraturens historie fra Poe til Ellroy* [The elements of crime: The history of crime fiction from Poe to Ellroy] (Copenhagen: Informations Forlag, 2009), p. 310, my translation.

7   Ibid., p. 309.

8   An even earlier Danish woman crime writer, Else Fischer (1923–76), was a very popular writer of whodunits in the 1960s and 1970s, but is relatively forgotten today (cf. Mogensen, p. 92).

second largest city, located on the Jutland peninsula) and the main character of Egholm's feminist crime novels from *Skjulte fejl og mangler* (2002, Hidden defects) to *Vold og magt* (2009, Violence and power). Then in *Tre hundes nat* (2011; *Three dog night*, 2013), Egholm introduces Svendsen's son, Peter Boutrup, as her new protagonist and her novels turn more action-driven and less feminist in style. Right from Holm's second crime novel, *Paranoia* (2002, Paranoia), journalist Karin Sommer, who works for *Sjællandsposten*, a daily newspaper from the southern part of the Danish island of Zealand, has been the main investigative protagonist. Holm's novels are characterized by social critique in the tradition of Sjöwall and Wahlöö, despite not being police novels as such. Blædel does, however, write about a woman police officer, Louise Rick, and her colleagues in Copenhagen, first introduced in *Grønt støv* (2004, Green dust).

Staun is perhaps the most original of the Danish women crime writers. She maintains a humorous distance from the genre and its conventions, and her woman protagonist, the glamorous Danish behavioural psychologist Fanny Fiske, works as a profiler for the 'European Federal Bureau of Intelligence' in the fictional area of Cornwell-Grafton, located somewhere between England and France. Fiske also cooperates with forensic pathologist Lisa Selander – named so years before the appearance of Lisbeth Salander in Stieg Larsson's (1954–2004) *Millennium* trilogy. Fiske and Selander actually appear in five novels, from *Som arvesynden* (1999, Like original sin) to *Før jeg dør* (2009, Before I die). Additionally, Staun has recently written a thriller trilogy – *Døderummet* (2010, Room of death; *Il bosco della morte* 2012), *Hilsen fra Rexville* (2011, Greetings from Rexville), and *Helt til grænsen* (2013, To the very limit) – featuring another forensic pathologist, Maria Krause, who tends to get personally involved in the murder cases she investigates.

The most internationally renowned Danish crime writer of recent years is Jussi Adler-Olsen (b. 1950), who made his debut as a crime writer in 1997 with the international thriller *Alfabethuset* (The alphabet house) and published two more thrillers before turning to the police procedural genre in 2007. Today Adler-Olsen is primarily renowned for his police series about Inspector Carl Mørck, his assistant Hafez el-Assad, and their colleagues in Department Q of the Copenhagen police, beginning with *Kvinden i buret* (2007; *Mercy/The Keeper of Lost Causes* 2011). So far,

Adler-Olsen has published five novels about Department Q, the most recent being *Marco effekten* (2012, The Marco effect). The series consists of traditional police procedurals, in which social critique typical of the Sjöwall and Wahlöö tradition is displayed. What is exceptional about Adler-Olsen's Department Q series, however, is the cast of unique characters that really stand out in the Nordic context, making the author one of the most interesting additions to the police procedural genre in recent years. A great international success was also Peter Høeg's (b. 1957) *Frøken Smillas fornemmelse for sne* (1992, *Miss Smilla's Feeling for Snow/Smilla's Sense of Snow* 1993; *Il senso di Smilla per la neve* 1994), a psychological thriller. Høeg is a well-established mainstream Danish author, and *Frøken Smillas fornemmelse for sne,* his only real crime novel, about Smilla Jaspersen's adventures in Copenhagen and Greenland, is often held up as an example a mainstream author using elements from popular genres in his fiction.[9]

In Denmark, the political/spy thriller has thus enjoyed a greater success compared to the situation in Sweden. Together with the police procedural, this has been – and still is – the most popular sub-genre in Danish crime fiction, something that can in all likelihood be attributed to Denmark's political history. During the Second World War, the Danish authorities initially cooperated with the German Nazi's, but in order to counteract the presence of a strong Danish resistance movement, Denmark was put under German rule in 1943. Following the war, in 1949, Denmark became one of the founding members of NATO (together with Norway and Iceland), and in 1972, by becoming a member of the EEC, Denmark was the first Nordic country to take part in pan-European cooperation.

Other Danish crime writers who would be mentioned in a longer survey are: Anders Bodelsen (b. 1937), Henning Mortensen (b. 1939), Georg Ursin (1934–2013), writer duo Lene Kaaberbøl (b. 1960) and Agnete Friis (b. 1974), and Christian Jungersen (b. 1962).

---

9   Cf. Magnus Persson, 'High Crime in Contemporary Scandinavian Literature: The Case of Peter Høeg's *Miss Smilla's Feeling for Snow*', in *Scandinavian Crime Fiction*, ed. by Andrew Nestingen and Paula Arvas (Cardiff: University of Wales Press, 2011), pp. 148–58 (p. 148).

Finland: Realist Police Novels and Russian Neighbours

In Finland the crime fiction tradition starts a little later than in the Scandinavian countries.[10] The first Finnish crime novel is said to be *Min första bragd* (1904, My first exploit) by Harald Selmer-Geeth (pen name for Werner August Örn, 1853–1913). Örn came from the Swedish- speaking minority in Finland and hence wrote in Swedish. The first original crime stories in the Finnish language were written by Rikhard Hornanlinna (pen name for Rudolf Richard Ruth, 1889–1957), who in 1910 published two collections of detective short stories, titled *Kellon salaisuus* (The clock secret) and *Lähellä kuolemaa* (Close to death). Just as in Sweden, most of the early crime fiction in Finland was inspired by the Sherlock Holmes stories; but the Finnish stories were to an even greater extent self-reflexive, the fictional detectives actually reading detective stories 'for instructions in precarious situations'.[11] The 1910s and 1920s were a fruitful time for Finnish popular literature in general, often referred to as a Golden Age, but it still took a little longer before crime fiction had its breakthrough.[12] Paula Arvas and Andrew Nestingen explain that it was first during the war years of 1939–1944, when Finland was fighting the Soviet Union, that the national output and consumption of crime fiction peaked, and Finland experienced its first Golden Age of the genre. During this time, the classic whodunit was the dominant subgenre in Finnish crime fiction.[13] Still, even as early as this there were certain police officers occupying important roles, as in Mika Waltari's (1908–79) series about Inspector Frans J. Palmu.[14]

---

10   I am very grateful to Paula Arvas for insightful comments on this part on Finnish crime fiction.

11   Kristina Malmio, '"He Strongly Envied Sherlock Holmes. But He Decided Not to Take Him to His Model": A Discursive Approach to the "Self" in an Early Self-Reflexive Finnish Detective Novel', *Scandinavian Studies* 80.4 (2008), 455–76 (pp. 455–56). Also see Kristina Malmio, *Ett skrattretande (för)fall: Teatraliskt metaspråk, förströelselitteratur och den bildade klassen i Finland på 1910- och 1920-talen* [A laughable decline/case: Theatrical meta-language and the educated class in Finland during the 1910s and 1920s] (Helsingfors: Helsingfors universitet/Meddelanden från avdelningen för nordisk litteratur, 2005), p. 37.

12   Malmio, 'He Strongly Envied', p. 455.

13   Arvas and Nestingen, 'Introduction', p. 4.

14   Some additional information in English about the early Finnish crime fiction tradition is found in George J Demko, 'Mysteries in Finland', *Mys-*

Of all the things that distinguish Finland from the other Nordic countries, one of the most important is its 833 mile-long border with Russia, and Paula Arvas has noted how Russians have always been regarded as the main Other of Finnish crime fiction.[15] Although Russians and other Eastern Europeans have also extensively frequented other Nordic countries' crime fiction, their role in Finnish crime fiction has been particularly prominent. Arvas notes how Russians already in the 1930s were portrayed as 'cruel, beastly and barbaric Bolsheviks', and during the Second World War they continued to be portrayed as spies and criminals. After the war, however, they disappeared for a long time from Finnish crime fiction, only to reappear after the end of the Cold War. In the post-Cold War period, crime fiction has actually been one of the main sources contributing 'to the images of Russia in the popular imagination' in Finland.[16] After the Cold War, the Russian criminals motivated by ideology have been replaced by a Russian criminality fundamentally anchored in money and greed.[17] Since the late 1990s, the international action/political thriller genre has flourished in Finland, and Ilkka Remes (pen name for Petri Pykälä, b. 1962), Taavi Soininvaara (b. 1966), and Tero Somppi (b. 1972) have been particularly important in the development of this crime fiction sub-genre. In their novels, Russians share the villainous roles with criminals primarily from the Middle East and, with this scenario, Finnish reality and history is put into the context of an international, global reality. Another author providing an interesting perspective on Finland's relation to Russia is Matti Rönkä (b. 1959), who has written

---

tery Readers Journal: Scandinavian Mysteries, 23.3 (2007), 25–27.

15   Paula Arvas, 'Next to the Final Frontier: Russians in Contemporary Finnish and Scandinavian Crime Fiction, in *Scandinavian Crime Fiction*, ed. by Andrew Nestingen and Paula Arvas (Cardiff: University of Wales Press, 2011), pp. 115–27 (p. 116).

16   Ibid., pp. 115–16.

17   Ibid., p. 125. Arvas concludes that since the early 1990s there have been three main types of Russian characters in Finnish crime fiction. First, the 'agents of death', 'military professionals trained by the Red Army, who typically sell their services on the black market' and function as killers. Second, the '"beautiful, powerless, and abused" Russian woman, typically the enslaved prostitute working in the West', and, third, the 'middle man', a figure who in contrast to the two former types 'underscores the positive elements of Russian culture and its complicated relationship to Finland and the Scandinavian world' (Arvas, 'Final Frontier', p. 117).

a series featuring petty criminal, Viktor Kärppä, in the investigative role. Kärppä is constantly negotiating between Finnish and Russian cultures, he himself belonging to both, and Rönke thus provides a more nuanced image of the Russian Other than the majority of the other Finnish crime writers.[18]

While many Finnish crime writers have been extensively translated into German, the only ones who have had any success in a broader international context are Matti Joensuu (1948–2011), Jarkko Sipilä (b. 1964), and Leena Lehtolainen (b. 1964). Three of Joensuu's novels about Inspector Timo Harjunpää have been translated into English and three of Sipilä's Inspector Kari Takamäki novels have as well, while still only one of Lehtolainen's novels, about Inspector Maria Kallio, is available in English: *Ensimmäinen murhani* (1993; *My First Murder* 2012; *Il mio primo omicidio* 2010). All three authors write urban police novels, the most popular sub-genre in Finland, and the fact that Joensuu, Sipilä, and Lehtolainen are the Finnish authors who have been most successful abroad might be related to the strong position of this sub-genre in the Nordic tradition in general.[19] Nordic crime fiction is often associated with Swedish Sjöwall and Wahlöö's police novels, and the tradition Sjöwall and Wahlöö initiated has also spread to the other Nordic countries.

The most successful of all the Finnish crime writers in recent decades is incontestably Matti Joensuu. Voitto Ruohonen suggests that the 'contemporary society-oriented crime novel in Finland can be seen to be epitomized in Matti Yrjänä Joensuu and his ten novels featuring Detective Sergeant Timo Harjunpää'.[20] From the first Harjun-

---

18 Ibid., pp. 117–125. Arvas also suggests that having a petty criminal as a protagonist is a relatively common feature of Finnish crime fiction, more so than in crime fiction from the other Nordic countries (cf. Paula Arvas, 'Contemporary Finnish Crime Fiction: Cops, Criminals and Middle Men', *Mystery Readers Journal: Scandinavian Mysteries*, 23.3 (2007), 4–8 (p. 4).

19 Most Finnish crime fiction is set in the three big cities of Helsinki, Tampere, or Turku (Arvas, 'Contemporary Finnish', p. 7).

20 Voitto Ruohonen, 'English Summary', in *Paha meidän kanssamme: Matti Yrjänä Joensuun romaanien yhteiskuntakuvasta* [The evil within us: The image of society in the novels of Matti Yrjänä Joensuu] (Helsinki: Kustannusosakeyhtiö Otava, 2005), pp. 557–63 (p. 557). Joensuu published an eleventh Harjunpää novel in 2010, *Harjunpää ja rautahuone* (Harjunpää and the iron room; *La stanza di ferro* 2013).

pää novel from the mid-1970s, *Väkivallan virkamies* (1976, The officer of violence), Joensuu has been seminal to the development of the police genre in Finland.[21] His novels are typical of the Finnish tradition, as they provide realistic depictions of society, ordinary people, and collective police work, and feature hard-working, idealistic, and morally conscious police officers. As in so much Swedish crime fiction from recent decades, the motives for the murders in Joensuu's novels tend to be traced back to the characters' childhoods. Often the victims are presented as scapegoats of society and their family situation, rather than just simply victims of crime, and for their part, the criminals often seem to 'drift into crime' almost by accident.[22] Harjunpää is the character through whose perspective Finnish society is critically viewed and judged, and it is a 'grim and pessimistic' view of society that dominates. Rouhonen even characterizes the society of the Harjunpää novels as 'a society of isolated individuals, a modern dystopia in which social life and authentic love and interaction between individuals have disappeared'.[23]

If Jouensuu is the most successful and influential, Lehtolainen is perhaps the most unique author of recent Finnish crime fiction. While writing quite traditional police novels, she is one of few authors sporting a strong woman investigative protagonist. Women crime writers have not been as successful as their male counterparts in Finland, but in addition to Lehtolainen, some names worthy of note are Outi Pakkanen (b. 1946) and Sirpa Tabet (b. 1943). Lehtolainen made her crime fiction debut in 1993 with *Ensimmäinen murhani* (*My First Murder* 2012; *Il mio primo omicidio* 2010). As the title(s) suggests, this was when readers were first introduced to Maria Kallio, who at the time was new to the police force. During the series, Kallio becomes a tough and independent Helsinki police officer, who both starts a family and matures in her professional role. *Ensimmäinen murhani* has been followed up by thirteen more Kallio novels to date, and in most of these Kallio also functions as the narrator – a trick that serves to bring readers

---

21 *Harjunpää ja pyromaani* was Joensuu's second crime novel, the first (not featuring Harjunpää) being *Possu ja paavin panttivangit* (1977, The pig and the pope's hostages). Joensuu also worked as a police officer until his retirement, and often uses genuine crimes as inspiration for his novels (Rouhonen, p. 559).

22 Cf. ibid., pp. 560–62.

23 Ibid., p. 562.

closer to her thoughts and perspectives, but this tactic is quite rare in the police genre. As with many other Finnish crime writers, Lehtolainen also mixes the police genre with elements from the whodunit.[24] The general realist thrust of Finnish crime fiction has provided a strong foundation for social critique, a tendency that seems to have increased over time, and Lehtolainen's novels also give space to examine current issues in Finnish society. For example, *Minne tytöt kadonneet* (2010, Where did the girls disappear?) deals with racism and prejudices in Finland, and in particular with the difficult situation for young girls from immigrant families who end up getting caught between two cultures. The focus on the consequences of increased globalization in this and other novels connects Lehtolainen to current trends in other Nordic crime fiction today. There are also clear feminist aspects to Lehtolainen's novels, something that makes her stand out in the Finnish context, and, additionally, Lehtolainen represents one of the things that distinguishes Finnish crime fiction from other Nordic crime fiction, and that is the unimpeachable character of the police. In the Finnish tradition, corrupt police officers are very rare, unlike in, for example, Swedish crime fiction where it is quite common to portray high-ranking police officers, in particular, as corrupt and to make them into villains.

Some additional popular Finnish crime writers are Tapani Bagge (b. 1962), Seppo Jokinen (b. 1949), Pentti Kirstila (b. 1948), Reijo Mäki (b. 1958), Markku Ropponen (b. 1955), and Harri Nykänen (b. 1953).

Iceland: A New Tradition Linking Past and Present, Local and Global

Just as in many of the other Nordic countries, Sherlock Holmes was also an important point of reference for the early crime fiction of Iceland. The story generally credited with being the first Icelandic crime story was even called 'Íslenzkur Sherlock Holmes' (1910; *An Icelandic Sherlock Holmes* 1994), and was written by Jóhann Magnús Bjarnason (1866–1945). Bjarnason was an Icelandic immigrant in Canada, and this is also mirrored in the story, as it features

---

24   Cf. Arvas, 'Contemporary Finnish', pp. 5–6.

an Icelandic immigrant, Hallur Þorsteinsson, as the detective.[25] Bjarnason's story, however, never contributed to the development of any Icelandic crime fiction tradition at the time. The first Icelandic crime story in the novel format might be Einar Skálaglamm's (pen name for Guðbrandur Jónsson, 1888–1953) *Húsið við Norðurá* (1926, The house by Norðurá).[26] In the 1930s and 1940s, there was a brief wave of Icelandic crime fiction, for example represented by Ólafur Friðriksson (1886–1964), whose novel *Allt í lagi í Reykjavík* (1939, All is well in Reykjavik) is about a robbery and includes some political critique.[27] Nevertheless, the genre did not take off. In the 1960s and 1970s, Sjövall and Wahlöö did not have the same impact in Iceland as in the other Nordic countries – although they were widely read there, too – and some argue that 'Icelandic crime fiction was virtually non-existent until the late 1990s'.[28]

It is clear that despite the few early examples, Icelandic crime fiction remained pretty much dormant throughout most of the twentieth century.[29] This can probably be explained with the high status of national literature in Iceland, in combination with a small population where a limited number of authors have upheld the prestigious profession. Or, in other words, writing crime fiction was not really an option for an Icelandic author who wanted to be respected in society and by his or her peers. Additionally, criminality used to be extremely low in Icelandic society, and crime fiction set in Iceland was thus not regarded as realistic and believable. There were of course exceptions. One of them being Viktor Arnar Ingólfsson (b. 1955), who in the late 1970s and early 1980s wrote two crime novels before he abandoned the genre, only to return to it almost two decades

---

25   Cf. Katrín Jakobsdóttir, 'Meaningless Icelanders: Icelandic Crime Fiction and Nationality', in *Scandinavian Crime Fiction*, ed. by Andrew Nestingen and Paula Arvas (Cardiff: University of Wales Press, 2011), pp. 46–61 (p. 46). Bjarnason's authorship is described at length in Daisy L Neijmann, *The Icelandic Voice in Canadian Letters: The Contribution of Icelandic-Canadian Writers to Canadian Literature* (Carleton: Carleton University Press, 1997), p. 146–58.
26   Norðurá is the name of a river in central west Iceland.
27   Cf. Arvas and Nestingen, p. 4.
28   Norðfjörð stresses that all Icelandic crime novels might not fit into his three categories, but still most of them do. Cf. Björn Norðfjörð, '"A Typical Icelandic Murder?" The "Criminal" Adaptation of *Jar City*', *Journal of Scandinavian Cinema*, 1.1 (2010), 37–49 (p. 40).
29   Cf. Jakobsdóttir, p. 47.

later with *Engin spor* (1998; *House of Evidence* 2012), after which he has continued his successful crime writing career.[30]

Björn Norðfjörð divides today's Icelandic crime fiction into three types, one being the police procedural inspired mainly by Swedish writers such as Henning Mankell (b. 1948) and Sjöwall and Wahlöö. In the most Nordic tradition, Norðfjörð includes the authors Arnaldur Indriðason (b. 1961) and Ævar Örn Jósepsson (b. 1963).[31] Indriðason made his debut as a crime writer in 1997 with *Synur duftsins* (Sons of dust) and has since become the most successful of the Icelandic crime writers in both the national and the international market. Indriðason's primary hero, Inspector Erlandur Sveinsson, belongs in the category of melancholic, divorced, fallible, and lonely police officers similar to Sjöwall and Wahlöö's Inspector Martin Beck and Mankell's Kurt Wallander, a type of hero so typical of Swedish and Nordic crime novels.[32] To a great extent, Erlandur epitomizes the history and traditions of Iceland, but he is counterbalanced by his more modern co-workers, Elínborg and Sigurdur Óli, representing the new, in contrast to the old.[33] Icelandic crime fiction is almost always characterized by the dichotomies of 'the difference between past and present, city and country and the status of Iceland as a peripheral society'.[34] This is made particularly clear in Indriðason's novels, and throughout his Inspector Erlandur series the reader is familiarized with conflicts originating in difficulties of uniting the traditional with the new and modern in Iceland. Peter Rozovsky describes Erlandur's investigations almost as archeological excavations, as the Icelandic investigator digs into the past both metaphorically and literally.[35] As compared with Indriðason, Jósepsson is more explicitly political and satirical in his police novels about officers Stefán and Árni and their colleagues, beginning with *Skítad-*

---

30   Cf. ibid., p. 48.
31   Norðfjörð, p. 40.
32   Bo Lundin, *The Swedish Crime Story*, trans. by Anna Lena Ringarp, Ralph A. Wilson, and Bo Lundin (Bromma: Jury, 1981), pp. 8–10.
33   Cf. Norðfjörð, p. 41. In accordance with Icelandic tradition, I have used first names when referring to the characters, while I have kept to international practice and used last names when indicating the authors.
34   Jakobsdóttir, p. 47.
35   Peter Rozovsky, 'Arnaldur Indridason & Erlandur's Iceland', in *Following the Detectives: Real Locations in Crime Fiction*, ed. by Maxim Jakubowski (London/Cape Town/Sydney/Auckland: New Holland, 2010), pp. 56–65 (pp. 56–57).

jobb (2002, A shitty job). Jósepsson's most political novel so far is *Blóðberg* (2005, Blood rock/Wild thyme) which is centred on the controversial construction of the power plant Kárahnjúkar, built in 2002–07 close to the glacier Vatnajökull in the south-eastern part of Iceland.[36]

In the same year Indriðason published *Synur duftsins*, another Icelandic crime writer also made his debut. That was Stella Blómkvist (a woman's pen name for an author whose identity to date is unknown) and her first novel was called *Morðið i stjórnarráðinu* (1997, Murder in the ministry). Together the two authors lay the foundation for what has now become a vivid contemporary crime fiction scene in Iceland. Blómkvist's fiction – as well as that by Árni Þórarinsson (b. 1950) – belongs to the second type of Icelandic crime fiction as described by Norðfjörð; crime novels inspired by the American hard-boiled tradition.[37] Þórarinsson actually published his first crime novel already in 1989, but then returned to the genre first in 2000, continuing his series about the investigative journalist Einar.[38] Like Einar, Stella Blómkvist's detective hero is also a hard boiled loner, a woman lawyer who also goes by the name of Stella Blómkvist. In true hard-boiled fashion Stella (the character) is the first person narrator of Blómkvist's novels: novels that show a strong affinity with the feminist hard-boiled crime fiction of authors like Sara Paretsky and Sue Grafton, often scrutinizing corruption and abuse of power in the patriarchal structures of Icelandic society.

Although the author hiding behind the pen name of Stella Blómkvist might not actually *be* a woman, there are currently a number of successful women writers in Icelandic crime fiction. Most well-known is Yrsa Sigurðardóttir (b. 1963), who has made a name for herself far beyond the shores of Iceland.[39] Sigurðardóttir's first crime novel was *Þriðja táknið* (2005; *Last Rituals* 2007; *Il cerchio del male* 2006), which introduced another woman lawyer protagonist, Þóra Guðmundsdóttir, who is kept busy solving murders originating from

---

36   Jakobsdóttir, pp. 50–51.
37   Norðfjörð, p. 40.
38   So far, the only novel by Þórarinsson to be translated into English is the fourth novel in the series, *Tími nornarinnar* (2005; *Season of the Witch* 2012).
39   Another very popular Icelandic woman author is Birgitta H Halldórsdóttir (b. 1959), who in her novels mixes romance with the thriller genre.

the judicial cases she works on – cases often related to property claims and wills. This is a concept that gives Þóra a reason to dig far into the past of the people involved, and enables Sigurðardóttir to depict Icelandic society both in the past and in the present. Sigurðardóttir's novels belong to the last of the three categories specified by Norðfjörð: more escapist and adventurous novels 'based on a fanciful plotting in the mould of Dan Brown's *The Da Vinci Code* (2003; *Il codice da Vinci* 2003) – often written with translation in mind'.[40] Besides Sigurðardóttir, Óttar M Norðfjörð (b. 1980) also belongs in this category. His novels are international thrillers often only partly set in Iceland, and in them, Biblical mysteries, Viking mythology, and conspiracy theories are frequent components. Some of Óttar M Norðfjörð's novels also include political elements, as for example in both *Áttablaðarósin* (2010, The eight pointed rose) and *Lygarinn* (2011, The Liar), the privatization of national natural resources following the Icelandic bankruptcy is discussed.

The Icelandic crime fiction tradition can thus be regarded as a more recent phenomenon than its Nordic sister counterparts. Proportionately, the police procedural has played a somewhat smaller part than in the other Nordic countries, despite being the genre preferred by Iceland's most prolific crime writer, Indriðason. Nevertheless, Icelandic crime fiction shares the Nordic interest in social and political critique, and it plays an important part in the current international success of Nordic crime fiction.

Norway: Hard-Boiled Influences, Private Investigators, and Police Novels

Maurits Hansen's (1794–1892) novel *Mordet på maskinbygger Roolfsen: Criminalanecdot fra Kongsberg* (1839, The murder of engineer Roolfsen: Crime anecdote from Kongsberg) is generally mentioned as the first real example of Norwegian crime fiction.[41]

---

40   Norðfjörð, p. 40. *Ég man þig* (2010; *I Remember You* 2012; *Mi ricordo di te* 2012) is a thriller where Sigurðardóttir brings in a new protagonist.

41   Other earlier examples that could perhaps aspire to the title are discussed in Willy Dahl, *Dødens fortellere: Den norske kriminal- og spenningslitteraturens historie* [Storytellers of death: The history of Norwegian crime and suspense literature] (Bergen: Eide Forlag, 1993), pp. 13–19.; and in Bjørn Carling, *Norsk kriminallitteratur gjennom 150 år*

Despite the early start, the country's crime fiction production was relatively sparse throughout the remainder of the nineteenth century. Nevertheless, the 1910s and 1920s were often considered to be a first Golden Age in Norwegian crime fiction.[42] The leading crime writer during that time was Stein Riverton (pen name for Sven Elvestad, 1884–1934). Riverton was the first really important author in Norwegian crime fiction, and it is also after him that the Riverton Prize is named: The Golden Revolver that has been awarded annually since 1972 to the best work of Norwegian crime fiction (all media and formats are eligible, but the prize is generally given to novels). Riverton/Elvestad made his debut in 1902 and published around a hundred crime novels over almost thirty years (some of them under the pen name of Kristian F. Biller). Many of these novels were about the private detective Asbjørn Krag, who has a past in the police force, or else about the police detective Knut Gibb. Riverton's best known novel is *Jernvognen* (1909; *The Iron Chariot* 2005). Another writer from this first Golden Age was Fredrik Viller (pen name for Christian Sparre, 1859–1940), who created what is thought to be the first serial hero in Norwegian crime fiction, private detective Karl Monk: pre-dating Riverton's Krag and Gibb, Monk first appeared 1897.[43] Yet another early Norwegian crime fiction hero was the adventurer and criminal Jonas Fjeld, who appeared in more than twenty violent – and quite racist – adventure thrillers by Øvre Richter Frich (1872–1945), from *De knyttede næver* (1911, The fists) to *Menneskejegerne* (1935, Man hunters).

A second Golden Age in Norwegian crime fiction came during the Second World War, when Norway was occupied by the German Nazis (1940–45).[44] At that time there was a great demand for escapist literature in Norway, and in addition to being escapist, much of the crime fiction published during this time was also at least implicitly somewhat revolutionary – something that naturally increased its popularity. Most of the Norwegian crime fiction from these years

---

[Norwegian crime fiction during 150 years] (Oslo: Gyldendal, 1976), pp. 14–18.

42 Arvas and Nestingen, p. 4.

43 Cf. Nils Nordberg, 'Stedfortredere i underverdenen: Forord' [Underworld representatives: Preface], in *De nye krimiheltene: 12 noveller* [The new crime fiction heroes: 12 short stories], ed. by Nils Nordberg (Oslo: Gyldendal, 2002), pp. 7–18 (p. 9).

44 Cf. Arvas and Nestingen, p. 4.

was set in Oslo during the 1930s.[45] Some of the important crime
writers during the years of German rule were Hans Brückenberg
(pen name for Torolf Elster, 1911–2006), Bernhard Borge (pen
name for André Bjerke, 1918–85), and Stein Ståle (pen name for
Trygve Hirsch, 1912–92), and perhaps the most famous crime novel from this time is Brückenberg's *Historien om Gottlob* (1941, The
story of Gottlob), a novel that contains strong – although relatively
implicit – anti-Nazi sentiments.[46]

By contrast, from the end of the Second World War and leading
up to the 1970s, the world was mostly seen in Cold War black and
white in Norwegian crime fiction, and the perspectives were quite
conservative.[47] Despite the two above-mentioned Golden Age peri-
ods, however, Nils Nordberg concludes that there are few memora-
ble detective heroes in Norwegian crime fiction before the 1970s,
but that a new and interesting wave of Norwegian crime fiction began in 1973.[48] Hans H. Skei agrees, noting that in the early 1970s
'Norwegian crime fiction changed so radically, that in terms of focus, interest, and quantity, it became something completely different
than prior to 1972'.[49] Skei attributes the changes at least partly to the
inspiration of international crime fiction being translated into Norwegian, as well as a more favourable attitude towards crime fiction
from the publishing industry, but also to the growing, radical political interest in the early 1970s, amongst other factors.[50] In 1973, and
inspired by the Swedish Maj Sjöwall and Per Wahlöö, David Torjussen (pen name for Tor Edvin Dahl, b. 1943) published *Etterfor-
skning pågår* (1973, Investigation in progress), the first proper Norwegian police novel, a novel that received that year's Riverton

---

45   Cf. Dahl, pp. 120–21, and 124.
46   Ibid., pp. 126–29. After the war, Elster continued to write crime novels
     under his own name up until the turn of the Millennium.
47   Cf. Hans H. Skei, *Blodig alvor: Om kriminallitteraturen* [Bloody serious:
     On crime fiction] (Oslo: Aschehoug, 2008), p. 166.
48   Nordberg, pp. 9–10.
49   Skei, p. 165, my translation.
50   Ibid., p. 167–68. The most important change in the book market condi-
     tions was provided by *Den svarte serien* (The black series) initiated by
     Gyldendal publishing house in 1967. The series promoted quality crime
     fiction, initially publishing primarily international classics in translation,
     but during the 1970s to an increasing extent also new Norwegian crime
     novels.

Prize.[51] With the ambition to create truly realistic crime novels, Torjussen wrote five more police procedurals where all the members of the police collective are equally prominent, much more so than in the novels by Sjöwall and Wahlöö – but then Torjussen is a little less political than his Swedish colleagues.[52] In 1981, Torjussen started a new series with one main protagonist, Anders Reknes, who despite being a police officer strongly resembled the lone, hard-boiled private detectives of the American tradition.[53] Since the late 1990s, Tor Edvin Dahl has been writing another popular crime series under his own name, featuring the woman priest Pernille Linde and her transvestite friend Roger/Rosalinde in the detective roles.

Two other writers who made their debut in the 1970s were Jon Michelet (b. 1944) and Gunnar Staalesen (b. 1947), who both used the police genre and have remained important figures on the Norwegian crime scene ever since. Michelet started with *Den drukner ei som henges skal* (1975, He who is born to be hanged shall never be drowned), where Vilhelm Thygesen – Michelet's police detective hero in numerous crime novels to come – was first introduced. The debut novel was filled with political critique and set in a newspaper environment. Michelet has been awarded the Riverton Prize twice, for *Hvit som snø* (1980, White as snow) and for *Den frosne kvinnen* (2001, The frozen woman). Staalesen, although initially producing police novels characterized by political satire, soon started writing novels about the hard-boiled private detective Varg Veum, beginning with *Bukken til havresekken* (1977, The goat to (mind) the oats). Veum has a past, working in social services, and behind a tough surface he possesses strong morals and integrity and is motivated by an idealistic drive to help people.[54] The Veum novels are set in Bergen, a small city on the south west coast of Norway, and they are the main reason for Straalsen's fame today. Staalesen's move from the police genre to the hard-boiled genre, and to a sharper focus on a private detective, is illustrative of Norwegian crime fiction, where the influence

---

51   Skei, p. 168. Skei and Nordberg both acknowledge the influence of
       Sjöwall and Wahlöö, while simultaneously playing down their importance
       for Norwegian crime fiction (ibid., p. 171; and Nordberg, p. 10–11).
52   Dahl, p. 166.
53   Nordberg, p. 10.
54   Cf. Skei, p. 179.

from Sjöwall and Wahlöö has been important – although not as tra-
dition-transforming as in some of the other Nordic countries – and
where the American hard-boiled tradition has been a great influence.[55] Nevertheless, similar to the Swedish context, leftist political perspectives have been fundamental to Norwegian crime fiction from the 1970s onwards.[56]

Up until 1992, almost all Norwegian detective heroes and crime
writers were men.[57] This changed, however, as Anne Holt (b. 1958),
Kjersti Scheen (b. 1943), Pernille Rygg (b. 1963), Unni Lindell (b.
1957), and Karin Fossum (b. 1954) made their debut in the 1990s,
and joined Kim Småge (b. 1945) who had started publishing in
1983. Additionally, some of the male writers – Telma B.S. Hansen
(woman's pen name for Idar Lind b. 1954) and Tor Edvin Dahl –
started featuring woman heroes in their books during this decade.[58]
Skei notes that the quality of Norwegian crime fiction also improved
substantially in the mid-1990s, something he attributes to the many
new writers in the genre, women and men, and the 1990s is often described as a new Golden Age in Norwegian crime fiction.[59] That
many of the women writers, Holt and Fossum in particular, soon became successful also internationally, gives at least some indication
of the quality of their novels. Both Holt and Fossum have made use
of the police genre, Fossum to a great extent, mixing it with the psychological thriller. In novels by most of the Norwegian woman writers, feminist traces can be found. Additionally, many of them focus
on 'child welfare and violence against women'.[60] Since the 1990s,
however, very few new women writers have joined the genre.[61]

55   Cf. Nordberg, p. 11. Staalesen's police novels did already show influenc-
      es from the American, hard-boiled tradition (Skei, p. 178).
56   Ibid., p. 182.
57   Nordberg mentions authors Ella Griffiths Ormhaug (b. 1926–90) and Kim
      Småge (b. 1945) as the only exceptions, along with Småge's hero, hobby
      diver Hilke Thorhus who appears in two of Småge's early novels (Nord-
      berg, s. 12). Skei and Dahl have found a few more, but not many (Skei, p.
      77–81; Dahl, p. 154–58, and 196).
58   Cf. Nordberg, pp. 12–13.
59   Skei, pp. 165 and 195–97.
60   Ellen Reese, 'Straight Queers: Anne Holt's Transnational Lesbian Detec-
      tive Fiction', in *Scandinavian Crime Fiction*, ed. by Andrew Nestingen
      and Paula Arvas (Cardiff: University of Wales Press, 2011), pp. 100–14
      (p. 101).
61   Skei, p. 216.

When Anne Holt made her crime fiction debut with *Blind gudinne* (1993, *Blind Goddess* 2012; *La dea cieca* 2010), she simultaneously introduced the first lesbian investigative hero into Norwegian crime fiction, police detective Hanne Wilhelmsen.[62] Ellen Reese has concluded that in addition to 'a focus on lesbian and gay identity', what makes Holt's novels unique among the works of the Norwegian women crime writers is 'a strong pro-immigration political stance; and a seemingly paradoxical pro-American attitude on the part of her protagonists'.[63] Additionally, Reese stresses that 'Holt's crime fiction is transnational in the sense that she focuses particular attention on the ways in which Norwegian society has changed in the face of globalization, as well as how individual life experiences have become increasingly transnational'.[64] This juxtaposition of the national with the global has been important in crime fiction emanating from all the Nordic countries in the past decades. Furthermore, during this time, Norwegian crime fiction has been characterized by an increased genre hybridity – notable also in Holt's novels – and by a growing interest in writing fast-paced crime thrillers with international settings.[65]

Apart from featuring women detectives, Norwegian police novels have tended to favour primarily middle-aged, male police detectives similar to the protagonists of Sjöwall and Wahlöö's and Henning Mankell's novels. Before the 1970s, the journalist detective was the most common hero of Norwegian crime fiction, but today (s)he is a rare type.[66] Private and amateur detectives of different professions are still of common occurrence, however. In Jo Nesbø's (b. 1960) violent novels the protagonist, Harry Hole, is a combination of the Swedish style, melancholic police detective and the hard-boiled private detective.[67] Hole has been described as a mix-

---

62 Wilhelmsen is still the most well-known lesbian detective in Nordic crime fiction. Swedish Stieg Larsson's (1954–2004) Lisbeth Salander is of course more famous, but she is bisexual. In Swedish crime fiction Inger Jalakas' (b. 1951) police detective Margareta Nordin was for a long time the only lesbian protagonist in Swedish crime fiction, but recently she has been joined by, for example, police detective Charlotta Lugn in Katarina Wennstam's (b. 1973) new crime series.

63 Reese, p. 101.
64 Ibid., p. 101.
65 Skei, p. 227.
66 Nordberg, p. 14. Also cf. Carling, p. 12.
67 The explicit use of graphic violence in Nesbø's novels has been discussed in Berit Åström, 'Over Her Dismembered Body: The Crime Fiction of Mo

ture of Varg Veum, Kurt Wallander, and John Rebus.[68] Hole, who is a police detective with a strong intuitive streak, made his initial appearance in *Flaggermusmannen* (1999, *The Bat* 2012), a novel set in Australia. Nevertheless, the major part of Nesbø's series – like the majority of Norwegian crime fiction – has been set in Oslo.[69] Nesbø's protagonist is an alcoholic and loner, not one for cooperating with his colleagues or adapting to police regulations. Sometimes during the series he gets suspended on account of drinking or for overstepping the rules of his profession, and occasionally the reader is even in doubt as to whether he will actually survive. Presently, Nesbø has published ten novels about Hole, some of the most acclaimed being *Rødstrupe* (2000; *The Redbreast* 2006; *Il pettirosso* 2006) and *Frelseren* (2005; *The Redeemer* 2009; *La ragazza senza volto* 2009), and with the most recent being *Politi* (2013; *Police* 2013).

Norwegian crime fiction has had a stronger tradition of hardboiled private detectives compared to the other Nordic countries, something that can probably be traced back to distrust of the police that had its roots in the Nazi occupation during the Second World War. Despite the early start in 1839, and despite the success of Stein Riverton in the first decades of the twentieth century, the national crime fiction tradition really takes off first in the early 1970s. In the 1990s, the many strong women writers and women heroes make Norwegian crime fiction truly stand out in the Nordic context. Today, however, the resurgence of woman writers seems to have stagnated, and the most celebrated writer is Jo Nesbø. Some of the many other Norwegian crime writers who would have been presented in a longer survey are Fredrik Skagen (b. 1936), Audun Sjøstrand (b. 1950), Knut Faldbakken (b. 1941), Kjell Ola Dahl (b. 1958), Tom Egeland (b. 1959), Magnhild Bruheim (b. 1951), and Tom Kristensen (b. 1955).

Hayder and Jo Nesbø', in *Rape in Stieg Larsson's Millennium Trilogy and Beyond: Contemporary Scandinavian and Anglophone Crime Fiction*, ed. by Berit Åström, Katarina Gregersdotter, and Tanya Horeck (Houndsmills: Palgrave Macmillan, 2013), pp. 97–113.

68   Meyhoff, *Forbrydelsens elementer*, p. 323, my translation.

69   Starting in the 1990s, the Norwegian countryside has been an increasingly common setting for Norwegian crime fiction (Skei, p. 187), even though the Oslo settings still dominate (cf. ibid., pp. 195 and 199).

Nordic Coherence and Variation

As this brief survey of the different crime fiction traditions of Sweden's Nordic neighbours shows, there are strong grounds for talking about Nordic crime fiction as a common, regional phenomenon. The important role of the police procedural, the focus on (leftist) social and political critique and/or consciousness, the preference for realism, the importance of setting, the melancholic male detectives, and the strong women detectives, are all aspects supporting such an inclusive grouping. The close geographical, historical, cultural, and political connections between the Nordic countries also give reason for communal perspectives, and there is even a Nordic prize for crime fiction called *Glasnyckeln* (The Glass Key Award), which since 1992, has been awarded annually by *Skandinaviska Kriminalsällskapet* (SKS, Crime Writers of Scandinavia) to the best Nordic crime novel or short story collection of the year. Still, all the national crime fiction traditions display their own specificities and preferences – often based on national historical conditions rather than on mainstream literary history – differences that are often overlooked in the international marketing and reception of these authors and novels. In surveying the international translations, it is also clear that a very large portion of what is referred to when Nordic Noir and Scandinavian Crime Fiction is mentioned actually consists of works originating from the hands of Swedish crime writers.

EPILOGUE

Since the 1990s, Swedish crime fiction has grown substantially in terms of both quantity and prominence. In addition to the sheer volume of crime novels published and the number of new authors making their debuts in the genre every year, some of the most notable changes of recent years have been the growing number of women crime writers as well as a burgeoning international audience for crime fiction from Sweden. However, the heritage of crime writers Maj Sjöwall (b. 1935) and Per Wahlöö (1926–75) from the 1960s and 1970s – that is, the popularity of the urban police procedural and the propensity for attempting to convey social and political critique – is still strong. Nevertheless, in the wake of Stieg Larsson's (1954–2004) *Millennium* trilogy (2005–07), Swedish crime fiction has shown tendencies to outgrow this genre model that has dominated since the 1970s, and today the genre displays increased variation in terms of genre-mixes, heroes, and settings.

The three most visible trends of recent years have been, first, genre hybridization, the merging of different crime fiction subgenres, as well as the progressive introduction of more elements from, for example, the horror, action, and romance genres; second, increased Europeanization and globalization – today Sweden, as it is presented in crime fiction, is a country greatly influenced by the effects of globalization, and more crime novels are increasingly set outside Swedish territory, primarily in Europe, but also in, for example, Africa and Asia, while, additionally, the criminality and the social and political issues addressed in today's Swedish crime fiction have taken on more and more of a transnational character; third, perhaps to counter globalization and growing transnational links, there has been a growing number of crime novels set in rural areas, such as in small towns located in the Swedish countryside or on the coast: many of these novels also tend to avoid political critique and the mention of current national and international events, instead they promote bourgeois family values and conservative gender roles in novels set in environments isolated from the wider world. As part of my work as a member of the Swedish Academy of Detection, I am currently reading all the new Swedish crime novels from 2013, and can attest that these three trends are persisting and, in fact, on the rise. Another tendency – and one that bodes well for the future – is the growing feminist awareness expressed in novels by many of the most recent authors, in particular in the novels by those women crime writers that I have referred to here as the second generation of women writers, or the 'daughters of Marklund's generation'.

The national and international popularity of Swedish crime fiction shows no signs of abating. Although I am certain that many of the crime writers who have made their debut in the last few years will soon be forgotten, others – not least the ones mentioned in the chapters of this book – will certainly find further fame and popularity, and be regarded as important names in future accounts of the history of Swedish crime fiction. Furthermore, as the world has so far only encountered a fraction of all the truly great Swedish crime writers, non-Swedish readers can look optimistically to the future for more offerings.

BIBLIOGRAPHY

Agrell, Wilhelm, 'IB-affären' [The IB affair], in *Nationalencyclopedin* [The national encyclopedia] http://www.ne.se/lang/ib-affären [accessed 3 April 2013].

Arvas, Paula, 'Contemporary Finnish Crime Fiction: Cops, Criminals and Middle Men', in *Mystery Readers Journal: Scandinavian Mysteries*, 23.3 (2007), 4–8.

Arvas, Paula, 'Next to the Final Frontier: Russians in Contemporary Finnish and Scandinavian Crime Fiction, in *Scandinavian Crime Fiction*, ed. by Andrew Nestingen and Paula Arvas (Cardiff: University of Wales Press, 2011), pp. 115–27.

Arvas, Paula, and Andrew Nestingen, 'Introduction: Contemporary Scandinavian Crime Fiction', in *Scandinavian Crime Fiction*, ed. by Andrew Nestingen and Paula Arvas (Cardiff: University of Wales Press, 2011), pp. 1–17.

'Autoren: Schweden'[Authors: Sweden], in *Schwedenkrimi* [Swedish crime fiction] http://www.schwedenkrimi.de/autoren_schweden.html [accessed 27 February 2013].

Bauman, Zygmunt, 'Identity in the Globalizing World', in *Identity, Culture and Globalization*, ed. by Eliezer Ben-Rafael and Yitzak Sternberg (Leiden: Brill, 2001), pp. 471–82.

Berglund, Karl, *Deckarboomen under lupp: Statistiska perspektiv på svensk kriminallitteratur 1977–2010* [The crime fiction boom under the magnifying glass: Statistical perspectives on Swedish crime fiction 1977–2010] (Uppsala: Avd. för litteratursociologi Uppsala universitet, 2012).

Bergman, Kerstin, 'Beyond National Allegory? Europeanization in Swedish Crime Writer Arne Dahl's *Viskleken*', forthcoming.

Bergman, Kerstin, 'Beyond Stieg Larsson: Contemporary Trends and Traditions in Swedish Crime Fiction', *Forum for World Literature Studies*, 2 (2012), 291–306.

Bergman, Kerstin, 'Crime Fiction as Popular Science: The Case of Åsa Nilsonne', in *Codex and Code: Aesthetics, Language and Politics in an Age of Digital Media*, ed. by Kerstin Bergman et.al. (Linköping: Linköping University Electronic Press, 2009), pp. 193–207 (p. 197) http://www.ep.liu.se/ecp/042/017/ecp0942017.pdf [accessed 20 September 2012].

Bergman, Kerstin, 'Deckare och andra medier' [Crime fiction and other media (than literature)], in *Kriminallitteratur: Utveckling, genrer, perspektiv* [Crime fiction: Developments, genres, perspectives], by Kerstin Bergman and Sara Kärrholm (Lund: Studentlitteratur, 2011), pp. 219–62.

Bergman, Kerstin 'Deckare och samhällskritik' [Crime fiction and social criticism], in *Kriminallitteratur: Utveckling, genrer, perspektiv* [Crime fiction: Developments, genres, perspectives], Kerstin Bergman and Sara Kärrholm (Lund: Studentlitteratur, 2011), pp. 165–83.

Bergman, Kerstin. 'Den svenska deckarhistorien' [The Swedish crime fiction history], in *Kriminallitteratur: Utveckling, genrer, perspektiv* [Crime fiction: Developments, genres, perspectives], by Kerstin Bergman and Sara Kärrholm (Lund: Studentlitteratur, 2011), pp. 33–51.

Bergman, Kerstin, 'From National Authority to Urban Underbelly: Negotiations of Power in Stockholm Crime Fiction', in *Crime Fiction in the City: Capital Crimes*, ed. by Lucy Andrew and Catherine Phelps (Cardiff: University of Wales Press, 2013), pp. 65–84.

Bergman, Kerstin, 'From "The Case of the Pressed Flowers" to the Serial Killers Torture Chamber: The Use and Function of Crime Fiction Subgenres in Stieg Larsson's *The Girl with the Dragon Tattoo*', in *Critical Insights: Crime and Detective Fiction*, ed. by Rebecca Martin (Ipswich, MA: Salem Press, 2013), pp. 38–53.

Bergman, Kerstin, 'Genre-Hybridization – A Key to Hyper-Bestsellers? The Use and Function of Different Fiction Genres in *The Da Vinci Code* and *The Millennium Trilogy*,' *Academic Quarter*, 7 (2013), pp. 106–18.

Bergman, Kerstin 'The Good, The Bad, and the Collaborators: Swedish World War II Guilt Redefined in 21st Century Crime Fiction', in *Imagining Mass Dictatorships: The Individual and the Masses in Literature and Cinema*, ed. by Michael Schoenhals and Karin Sarsenov (New York: Palgrave, 2013), pp. 183–210.

Bergman, Kerstin, 'Inför lagen och den patriarkala genren: Kvinnliga deckarförfattare i 2000-talets Sverige' [In presence of the law and the patriarchal genre: Women crime writers in 21st century Sweden], in *'Det universella och det individuella': Festskrift till Eva Hættner Aurelius* ['The universal and the individual': Festschrift in honour of Eva Hættner Aurelius], ed. by Kerstin Bergman et.al. (Göteborg/Stockholm: Makadam, 2013), pp. 39–46.

Bergman, Kerstin, 'Initiating a European Turn in Swedish Crime Fiction: Negotiation of European and National Identities in Mankell's *The Troubled Man* (2009)', *Scandinavica* 51.1 (2012), 56–78.

Bergman, Kerstin, 'Isolerad idyll och svart barndom: Marie Jungstedt (1962–)' [Isolated idyll and dark childhood: Mari Jungstedt (b. 1962)], in *Tretton svenska deckardamer* [Thirteen Swedish crime ladies] (Lund: BTJ förlag, 2009), pp. 96–111.

Bergman, Kerstin, 'Lisbeth Salander and her Swedish Crime Fiction "Sisters": Stieg Larsson's Hero in a Genre Context', in *Men Who Hate Women and Women Who Kick Their Asses: Stieg Larsson's Millennium Trilogy in Feminist Perspective*, ed. by Donna King and Carrie Lee Smith (Nashville: Vanderbilt University Press, 2012), pp. 135–144.

Bergman, Kerstin, 'Paradoxes of Understanding the Other: Mankell Explores the "African Darkness"', *Scandinavian Studies*, 82.3 (2010), 337–354.

Bergman, Kerstin, 'Polisromanen' [The police novel], in *Kriminallitteratur: Utveckling, genrer, perspektiv* [Crime fiction: Developments, genres, perspectives], Kerstin Bergman and Sara Kärrholm (Lund: Studentlitteratur, 2011), pp. 105–21.

Bergman, Kerstin, 'The Well-Adjusted Cops of the New Millennium: Neo-Romantic Tendencies in the Swedish Police Procedural', in *Scandinavian Crime Fiction*, ed. by Andrew Nestingen and Paula Arvas, (Cardiff: University of Wales Press), pp. 34–45.

Bergman, Kerstin, and Sara Kärrholm, *Kriminallitteratur: Utveckling, genrer, perspektiv* [Crime fiction: Developments, genres, perspectives] (Lund: Studentlitteratur, 2011).

Borg, Alexandra, *Brottsplats Stockholm: Urban kriminallitteratur 1851–2011* [Crime scene Stockholm: Urban crime fiction 1851–2011] (Stockholm: Stockholmia Förlag, 2012).

Bouquet, Philippe, *La bêche et la plume: L'aventure du roman prolétarien suédois* [The spade and the pen: The Adventure of the Swedish proletarian novel] (Bassac: Plein chant, 1986).

The Cambridge Companion to Crime Fiction, ed. by Martin Priestman (Cambridge: Cambridge University Press, 2003).

Carling, Bjørn, *Norsk kriminallitteratur gjennom 150 år* [Norwegian crime fiction during 150 years] (Oslo: Gyldendal, 1976).

Carlsson, Ulf, 'Stieg Trenter's 40-tal: Medelklassens hopp och ängslan'[Stieg Trenter's 1940s: The hope and fear of the middle class], in *Möten: Festskrift till Anders Palm* [Encounters: Festschrift in honour of Anders Palm], ed. by Karin Nykvist et.al. (Lund: Anacapri förlag, 2007), pp. 385–94.

'Clark Olofsson', *Nationalencyklopedin* [The national encyclopedia] http://www.ne.se/clark-olofsson [accessed 21 February 2013].

Crime and Nation: Political and Cultural Mappings of Criminality in New and Traditional Media, ed. by Immacolata Amodeo and Eva Erdmann (Trier: Wissenschaftlicher Verlag Trier, 2009).

Crime Fiction in the City: Capital Crimes, ed. by Lucy Andrew and Catherine Phelps (Cardiff: University of Wales Press, 2013).

Critical Insights: Crime and Detective Fiction, ed. by Rebecca Martin (Ipswich, MA: Salem Press, 2013).

Dahl, Arne, *Viskleken* [Chinese whispers] (Stockholm: Bonniers, 2011).

Dahl, Willy, *Dødens fortellere: Den norske kriminal- og spenningslitteraturens historie* [Storytellers of death: The history of Norwegian crime and suspense literature] (Bergen: Eide Forlag, 1993).

'Deckarkatalogen' [The crime fiction catalogue], in *Svenska deckarakademin* [The Swedish Academy of Detection], http://deckarakademin.org/hem/deckarkatalogen-3 [accessed 15 August 2013].

Demko, George J, 'Mysteries in Finland', in *Mystery Readers Journal: Scandinavian Mysteries*, 23.3 (2007), 25–27.

Dove, George N, *The Police Procedural* (Bowling Green: Bowling Green University Popular Press, 1982).

Everett, Wendy, 'Introduction: European film and the quest for identity,' in *European Identity in the Cinema*, Second Edition, ed. by Wendy Everett (Bristol/Portland, OR: Intellect, 2005), pp. 7–14.

Ferber, Abby L, 'Always Ambivalent: Why Media Is Never Just Entertainment', in *Men who Hate Women and Women who Kick Their Asses: Stieg Larsson's Millennium Trilogy in Feminist Perspective*, ed. by Donna King and Carrie Lee Smith (Nashville, TN: Vanderbilt University Press, 2012), pp. 3–14.

Following the Detectives: Real Locations in Crime Fiction, ed. by Maxim Jakubowski (London/Cape Town/Sydney/Auckland: New Holland, 2010).

Forshaw, Barry, *Death in a Cold Climate: A Guide to Scandinavian Crime Fiction* (Basingstoke: Palgrave Macmillan, 2012).

Frances, Louise, 'Queen of Crime', *The Observer*, 22 November 2009, http://www.guardian.co.uk/books/2009/nov/22/crime-thriller-majsjowall-sweden [accessed 30 August 2013].

Geherin, David, *Scene of the Crime: The Importance of Place in Crime and Mystery Fiction* (Jefferson, NC: McFarland, 2008).

Glesener, Jeanne E, 'The Crime Novel: Multiculturalism and its Impact on the Genre's Conventions', in *Crime and Nation: Political and Cultural Mappings of Criminality in New and Traditional Media*, ed. by Immacolata Amodeo and Eva Erdmann (Trier: Wissenschaftlicher Verlag Trier, 2009), pp. 15–26.

Gregersdotter, Katarina, 'The Body, Hopelessness, and Nostalgia: Representations of Rape and the Welfare State in Swedish Crime Fiction', in *Rape in Stieg Larsson's Millennium Trilogy and Beyond: Contemporary Scandinavian and Anglophone Crime Fiction*, ed. by Berit Åström, Katarina Gregersdotter and Tanya Horeck (Houndsmills: Palgrave Macmillan, 2013), pp. 81–96.

Hall, Stewart, 'Introduction: Who Needs Identity?', in *Questions of Cultural Identity*, ed. by Stewart Hall and Paul du Gay (London/Thousand Oaks/New Delhi: Sage Publications, 1996), pp. 1–17.

Hanson, Gillian Mary, *City and Shore: The Function of Setting in the British Mystery* (Jefferson/London: McFarland, 2004).

Holmberg, John-Henri, 'The Novels You Read Are Not Necessarily the Novels Stieg Larsson Wrote', in *The Tattoed Girl: The Enigma of Stieg Larsson and the Secrets Behind the Most Compelling Thrillers of Our Time*, by Dan Burstein, Arne de Keijzer, and Jon-Henri Holmberg (New York: St. Martin's Griffin, 2011), pp. 29–41.

Holmes, Leslie, and Philomena Murray, 'Introduction: Citizenship and Identity in Europe', in *Citizenship and Identity in Europe*, ed. by Leslie Holmes and Philomena Murray (Aldershot: Ashgate, 1999), pp. 1–23.

Jakobsdóttir, Katrín, 'Meaningless Icelanders: Icelandic Crime Fiction and Nationality', in *Scandinavian Crime Fiction*, ed. by Andrew Nestingen and Paula Arvas (Cardiff: University of Wales Press, 2011), pp. 46– 61.

Jakubowski, Maxim, 'Introduction: A Sense of Place', in *Following the Detectives: Real Locations in Crime Fiction*, ed. by Maxim Jakubowski (London/Cape Town/Sydney/Auckland: New Holland, 2010), pp. 12–13.

Johansson, Roland, 'Milenniums miljonsuccé' [Millennium's million success], in *Expressen*, 23 June 2011 http://www.expressen.se/noje/millenniums-miljonsucce/ [accessed 1 March 2013].

Jungstedt, Mari, *I denna stilla natt* [*Unspoken*] (Stockholm: Bonniers, 2004).

Jungstedt, Mari, *The Inner Circle*, transl. by Tiina Nunnally (New York: St. Martin's Minotaur, 2008).

Jungstedt, Mari, *Unseen*, transl. by Tiina Nunnally (London: Corgi Books, 2008).

Jungstedt, Mari, *Unspoken*, transl. by Tiina Nunnally (New York: St. Martin's Minotaur, 2007).

King, Donna, and Carrie Lee Smith, 'Introduction', in *Men who Hate Women and Women who Kick Their Asses: Stieg Larsson's Millennium Trilogy in Feminist Perspective*, ed. by Donna King and Carrie Lee Smith (Nashville, TN: Vanderbilt University Press, 2012), pp. xiii–xix.

Kirkegaard, Peter, *Blues for folkhemmet: Næranalyse af Arne Dahls Europa Blues* [Blues for the welfare state: A close reading of Arne Dahl's Europa Blues] (Aalborg: Aalborg Universitetsforlag, 2013).

Knight, Stephen, *Crime Fiction 1800–2000: Detection, Death, Diversity* (Houndsmills/New York: Palgrave Macmillan, 2004).

Kohli, Martin, 'The Battlegrounds of European Identity', *European Societies*, 2.2 (2000), 113–37.

Kärrholm, Sara, 'Is Mikael Blomkvist the Man of the Millennium? A Swedish perspective on Masculinity and Feminism in Larsson's Millennium Trilogy', in *Men who Hate Women and Women who Kick Their Asses: Stieg Larsson's Millennium Trilogy in Feminist Perspective*, ed. by Donna King and Carrie Lee Smith (Nashville, TN: Vanderbilt University Press, 2012), pp. 145–54.

Kärrholm, Sara, *Konsten att lägga pussel: Deckaren och besvärjandet av ondskan i folkhemmet* [The art of doing a jig-saw puzzle: The detecti-

ve novel and the conjuring up of evil in the Swedish Welfare State]
(Stockholm/Stehag: Symposion, 2005).

Kärrholm, Sara, 'Kvinna på gränsen till nervsammanbrott: Åsa Nilsonne
(1949–)' [Woman on the verge of a nervous breakdown: Åsa Nilsonne (b. 1949)], in *Tretton svenska deckardamer* [Thirteen Swedish crime ladies] (Lund BTJ Förlag, 2009), pp. 184–98.

Kärrholm, Sara, 'Swedish Queens of Crime: The Art of Self-Promotion
and the notion of Feminine Agency – Liza Marklund and Camilla
Läckberg', in *Scandinavian Crime Fiction*, ed. by Andrew Nestingen and Paula Arvas (Cardiff: University of Wales Press, 2011), pp.
131–47.

Lapidus, Jens, *Easy Money*, trans. Astri von Arbin Ahlander (London: Macmillan, 2012).

'Lars-Inge Svartenbrandt', in *Nationalencyklopedin* [The national encyclo-
pedia] http://www.ne.se/lars-inge-svartenbrandt [accessed 21 February 2013].

Larsson, Stieg, *The Girl With the Dragon Tattoo*, trans. By Reg Keeland
(London: MacLehose Press/Quercus, 2008).

Lidén, Svante, 'Gåtan Arne Dahl är löst: Nu träder den hemliga deckarförfattaren fram' fram' [The riddle of Arne Dahl is solved: The secret crime writer comes forward (interview with Arne Dahl/Jan Arnald)], *Aftonbladet*, 12 April 2002.

Lundin, Bo, *The Swedish Crime Story*, trans. by Anna Lena Ringarp, Ralph
A. Wilson, and Bo Lundin (Bromma: Jury, 1981).

Lutwack, Leonard, *The Role of Place in Literature* (Syracuse: Syracuse
University Press, 1984).

Malmio, Kristina, *Ett skrattretande (för)fall: Teatraliskt metaspråk, förströelselitteratur och den bildade klassen i Finland på 1910- och
1920-talen* [A laughable decline/case: Theatrical meta-language and
the educated class in Finland during the 1910s and 1920s] (Helsingfors: Helsingfors universitet/Meddelanden från avdelningen för
nordisk litteratur, 2005).

Malmio, Kristina, '"He Strongly Envied Sherlock Holmes. But He Decided
Not to Take Him to His Model": A Discursive Approach to the "Self"
in an Early Self-Reflexive Finnish Detective Novel', *Scandinavian
Studies*, 80.4 (2008), 455–76.

Mankell, Henning, *Kennedy's Brain*, transl. by Laurie Thompson (London:
Vintage, 2008).

Mankell, Henning, *The Return of the Dancing Master*, trans. by Laurie
Thompson (London: Vintage, 2003).

Mankell, Henning, *The Troubled Man*, transl. by Laurie Thompson (London: Harvill Secker, 2011).

Manns, Ulla, 'Kvinnlig rösträtt,' [Women's right to vote], *Nationalencyklopedin* [The National Encyclopedia], http://www.ne.se/lang/kvinnlig-
r%C3%B6str%C3%A4tt, [accessed 23 August 20113].

Makko, Aryo, 'Sweden, Europe, and the Cold War: A Reappraisal,' *Journal of Cold War Studies*, 2 (2012), 68–97

Marklund, Liza, *The Bomber*, trans. by Neil Smith (London: Corgi Books, 2011).

McCorristine, Shane, 'Pessimism in Henning Mankell's Kurt Wallander Series', in *Scandinavian Crime Fiction*, ed. by Andrew Nestingen and Paula Arvas (Cardiff: University of Wales Press, 2011), pp. 77–88.

'Members and Parties,' *Sveriges Riksdag* [The Swedish Parliament], http://www.riksdagen.se/en/Members-and-parties/, [accessed 23 August 2013].

Men Who Hate Women and Women Who Kick Their Asses: Stieg Larsson's Millennium Trilogy in Feminist Perspective, ed. by Donna King och Carrie Lee Smith (Nashville: Vanderbilt University Press, 2012).

Meyhoff, Karsten Wind, 'Digging into the Secrets of the Past: Rewriting History in the Modern Scandinavian Police Procedural', in *Scandinavian Crime Fiction*, ed. by Andrew Nestingen and Paula Arvas (Cardiff: University of Wales Press, 2011), pp. 62–73.

Meyhoff, Karsten Wind, *Forbrydelsens elementer: Kriminallitteraturens historie fra Poe til Ellroy* [The elements of crime: The history of crime fiction from Poe to Ellroy] (Copenhagen: Informations Forlag, 2009).

Mogensen, Harald, *Mord og mysterier: Den danske krimis historie* [Murders and mysteries; The history of Danish crime fiction] (Viby: Centrum, 1983).

Mystery Readers Journal: Scandinavian Mysteries, 23.3 (2007), 25–27.

Naumann, Ingela K, 'Child Care and Feminism in West Germany and Sweden in the 1960s and 1970s,' *Journal of European Social Policy*, 1 (2005), 47–63.

Neijmann, Daisy L, *The Icelandic Voice in Canadian Letters: The Contribution of Icelandic-Canadian Writers to Canadian Literature* (Carleton: Carleton University Press, 1997).

Nestingen, Andrew, *Crime and Fantasy in Scandinavia: Fiction, Film, and Social Change* (Seattle/London: University of Washington Press, 2008).

Nordberg, Nils, 'Stedfortredere i underverdenen: Forord' [Underworld representatives: Preface], in *De nye krimiheltene: 12 noveller* [The new crime fiction heroes: 12 short stories], ed. by Nils Nordberg (Oslo: Gyldendal, 2002), pp. 7–18.

Norðfjörð, Björn, '"A Typical Icelandic Murder?" The "Criminal" Adaptation of *Jar City*', in *Journal of Scandinavian Cinema*, 1.1 (2010), 37–49.

Persson, Magnus, 'High Crime in Contemporary Scandinavian Literature: The Case of Peter Høeg's *Miss Smilla's Feeling for Snow*', in *Scandinavian Crime Fiction*, ed. by Andrew Nestingen and Paula Arvas (Cardiff: University of Wales Press, 2011), pp. 148–58.

Peterson, Marie, 'Hålla huvudet kallt: Karin Alvtegen (1965–)' [To keep a cool head: Karin Alvtegen (b. 1965)], in *Tretton svenska deckardamer* [Thirteen Swedish crime ladies] (Lund BTJ Förlag, 2009), pp. 31–46.

Polismuseet [The police museum] http://www.polismuseet.se/Samlingar/
Polishistoria/Framvaxten-av-ett-polisvasende/ [accessed 13 February
2013].

'Bästa svenska kriminalroman' [The best Swedish crime novel of the year],
in *Svenska Deckarakademin* [The Swedish Academy of Detection],
http://deckarakademin.org/hem/priser/basta-svenska-kriminalroman
[accessed 15 August 2013].

*Rape in Stieg Larsson's Millennium Trilogy and Beyond: Contemporary
Scandinavian and Anglophone Crime Fiction*, ed. by Berit Åström,
Katarina Gregersdotter, and Tanya Horeck (Houndsmills: Palgrave
Macmillan, 2013).

Reese, Ellen, 'Straight Queers: Anne Holt's Transnational Lesbian Detective
Fiction', in *Scandinavian Crime Fiction*, ed. by Andrew Nestingen and
Paula Arvas (Cardiff: University of Wales Press, 2011), pp. 100–14.

Reddy, Maureen T, 'Women detectives', in *The Cambridge Companion to
Crime Fiction*, ed. by Martin Priestman (Cambridge: Cambridge University
Press, 2003), pp. 191–207.

Rozovsky, Peter, 'Arnaldur Indridason & Erlandur's Iceland', in *Following
the Detectives: Real Locations in Crime Fiction*, ed. by Maxim Jakubowski
(London/Cape Town/Sydney/Auckland: New Holland, 2010),
pp. 56–65.

Ruohonen, Voitto, 'English Summary', in *Paha meidän kanssamme: Matti
Yrjänä Joensuun romaanien yhteiskuntakuvasta* [The evil within us:
The image of society in the novels of Matti Yrjänä Joensuu] (Helsingki:
Kustannusosakeyhtiö Otava, 2005), pp. 557–63.

Ruohonen, Voitto, *Paha meidän kanssamme: Matti Yrjänä Joensuun romaanien
yhteiskuntakuvasta* [The evil within us: The image of society
in the novels of Matti Yrjänä Joensuu] (Helsingki: Kustannusosakeyhtiö
Otava, 2005).

Sainsbury, Diane, 'Gender and Social-Democratic Welfare States,' in *Gender
and Welfare State Regimes*, ed. Diane Sainsbury (Oxford/New
York: Oxford UP, 1999), pp. 75–115.

Salomonson, Kim, 'FNL-rörelsen' [The FNL movement], in *Nationalencyclopedin*
[The national encyclopedia] http://www.ne.se/lang/fnl-r%C3%B6relsen
[accessed 13 February 2013].

Scaggs, John, *Crime Fiction* (London/New York: Routledge, 2005).

Scandinavian Crime Fiction, ed. by Andrew Nestingen and Paula Arvas
(Cardiff: University of Wales Press, 2011).

'Scandinavian Crime Fiction: Inspector Norse', in *The Economist*, 11
March 2010, http://www.economist.com/node/15660846 [accessed
28 February 2013].

Schmidt, Lars, 'Stieg Larssons böcker sålda i 60 miljoner exemplar' [Stieg
Larsson's novels sold in 60 million copies], in *Svensk Bokhandel*
[Swedish book trade magazine], 9 June 2011 http://www.svb.se/nyheter/stieg-larssons-b-cker-s-lda-i-60-miljoner-exemplar
[accessed 28
March 2013].

Sjöholm, Carina, *Litterära resor: Turism i spåren efter böcker, filmer och författare* [Literary journeys: Tourism tracing novels, films and authors] (Gothenburg/Stockholm: Makadam, 2011).

Sjöwall, Maj, and Per Wahlöö, 'Kriminalromanens förnyelse' [The renewal of the crime novel], *Jury*, 1 (1972), 9–11.

Sjöwall, Maj, and Per Wahlöö, *Roseanna*, transl. by Lois Roth (London: Fourth Estate, 2011).

Sjöwall, Maj, and Per Wahlöö, *Terroristerna* [*The Terrorists*] (Stockholm: Norstedts, 1975).

Sjöwall, Maj, and Per Wahlöö, *The Terrorists*, transl. by Joan Tate (New York: Vintage Books, 2010).

Skei, Hans H, *Blodig alvor: Om kriminallitteraturen* [Bloody serious: On crime fiction] (Oslo: Aschehoug, 2008).

Sommar, Carl Olov, 'Stieg Trenter som stockholmsskildrare' [Stieg Trenter as a portrayer of Stockholm], in *Sankt Eriks Årsbok 1984* [Sankt Erik's yearbook 1984], ed. by Björn Hallerstedt (Stockholm: Samfundet S:t Erik, 1984), pp. 173–86.

'The Swedish Government,' *Regeringskansliet* [The Swedish Government office], http://www.regeringen.se/content/1/c6/20/76/70/349be510. pdf, [accessed 23 August 2013].

The Tattoed Girl: The Enigma of Stieg Larsson and the Secrets Behind the Most Compelling Thrillers of Our Time, by Dan Burstein, Arne de Keijzer, and Jon-Henri Holmberg (New York: St. Martin's Griffin, 2011).

Thomson, Ian, 'True Crime', *The Guardian*, 1 November 2003.

'Topplistor' [Bestseller lists], in *Svensk bokhandel* [Swedish book trade magazine], http://www.svb.se/bokfakta/svenskatopplistor, [accessed 11 January 2012].

Torén Björling, Sanna, 'Sanna Torén Björling möter Jan Arnald' [Sanna Torén Björling meets Jan Arnald (interview with Jan Arnald)], *Dagens Nyheter*, 13 June 2011.

Trenter, Ulla, 'Hur var det att skriva deckare tillsammans med Stieg Trenter?' [What it was like to write crime novels with Stieg Trenter] in *En bok om Stieg Trenter* [A book about Stieg Trenter], ed. by Bertil R Widerberg (Bromma: Jury, 1982), pp. 58–63.

Tretton svenska deckardamer [Thirteen Swedish crime ladies] (Lund: BTJ förlag, 2009).

Walton, Priscilla L, and Manina Jones, *Detective Agency: Women Rewriting the Hard-Boiled Tradition* (Berkeley, Los Angeles and London: University of California Press, 1999).

Wedding, Gunilla, 'När tonårsmamman blev deckarhjälte: Helene Tursten (1954–)' [When the mother of teenagers became a crime hero], in *Tretton svenska deckardamer* [Thirteen Swedish crime ladies] (Lund BTJ Förlag, 2009), pp. 219–237.

Weigl, Kerstin, 'Att bli känd är inget mål i sig' [To become famous is not a goal in itself (anonymous interview with 'Arne Dahl')], *Aftonbladet*, 10 November 2001.

Wendelius, Lars, *Rationalitet och kaos: Nedslag i svensk kriminalfiktion efter 1965* [Rationality and chaos: Case studies of Swedish crime fiction after 1965] (Hedemora: Gidlunds, 1999).

Westerståhl Stenport, Anna, 'Bodies Under Assault: Nation and Immigration in Henning Mankell's Faceless Killers', *Scandinavian Studies*, 79.1 (2007), 1–24.

Winston, Robert P, and Nancy C Mellerski, *The Public Eye: Ideology and the Police Procedural* (Houndsmills/London: Macmillan, 1992).

Wopenka, Johan, 'Kvinnlig Deckarhistoria: Från 1800-talets mitt till 1900-talets slut' [Women's crime fiction history: From the mid-1800s to the end of the 1900s], in Tretton svenska deckardamer [Thirteen Swedish crime ladies] (Lund: BTJ, 2009), pp. 7–30.

Wopenka, Johan, 'Länge leve Lang!' [Long live Lang!], *Jury*, 18.2 (1989), 12–15.

'Väljarbarometern mars 2013' [Voter survey March 2013], in *TNS Sifo* [The Swedish Institute for Opinion Surveys, a subsidiary of TNS Global] http://www.tns-sifo.se/media/453564/vb_mar_2013_svd.pdf [accessed 3 April 2013].

Young, Alison, *Imagining Crime: Textual Outlaws and Criminal Conversations* (London, Thousand Oaks and New Delhi: SAGE Publications, 1996).

Åström, Berit, 'Over Her Dismembered Body: The Crime Fiction of Mo Hayder and Jo Nesbø', in *Rape in Stieg Larsson's Millennium Trilogy and Beyond: Contemporary Scandinavian and Anglophone Crime Fiction*, ed. by Berit Åström, Katarina Gregersdotter, and Tanya Horeck (Houndsmills: Palgrave Macmillan, 2013), pp. 97–113.

Öhman, Anders, *Äventyrets tid: Den sociala äventyrsromanen i Sverige 1841–1859* [Time of adventure: The Swedish social-adventure novel 1841–1859] (Umeå: Universitetet i Umeå 1990).

INDEX

MIMESIS GROUP
www.mimesis-group.com

MIMESIS INTERNATIONAL
www.mimesisinternational.com
info@mimesisinternational.com

MIMESIS EDIZIONI
www.mimesisedizioni.it
mimesis@mimesisedizioni.it

ÉDITIONS MIMÉSIS
www.editionsmimesis.fr
info@editionsmimesis.fr

MIMESIS AFRICA
www.mimesisafrica.com
info@mimesisafrica.com

MIMESIS COMMUNICATION
www.mim-c.net

MIMESIS EU
www.mim-eu.com

printed by Digital Team
Fano (PU) in July 2014